PRAISE FOR ... READ:

'A dark and thrillin... ...nineties in New Orleans. W... ...ts and murder galore, this delicious and gruesome tale of the macabre will ignite a whole new generation of vampire fans.'

LAUREN JAMES

'Brimming full of nostalgia and cinematic atmosphere. I loved this heart-pounding mystery so much, I couldn't put it down. A thrilling read and a clever new twist on the vampire stories you love.'

LAURA WOOD

'Set in a world of love, loss and lies – in the heart of New Orleans – McCaw has spun the vampire myth in a way that will engross readers from the very first page.'

C. G. MOORE

'I could not put this down! Strong *Buffy* meets *Charmed* in New Orleans vibes . . . so much nineties nostalgia. I want to go for drinks at the Empire of the Dead with Mina and the gang. Vampires are officially cool again!'

CYNTHIA MURPHY

'I loved *Mina and the Undead* so much! The world is so fully realised I felt like I was there! Atmospheric and spine chilling, with characters quite literally to die for, this is a vampire book with so much humanity and heart. I absolutely devoured it!'

AVA ELDRED

'A fabulous 90s-set horror perfect for young adults but also older readers who grew up on a diet of *Buffy*, *The Lost Boys*, *Interview With The Vampire* and *Elvira*.'

ANDREINA CORDANI

'Atmospheric, thrilling, and twisty, with more '90s nostalgia than you can shake a stake at. Will keeping you guessing until the very end (and sleeping with a crucifix under your pillow).'

GEORGIA BOWERS

'A brilliantly entertaining blend of cult horror references and vampire fandom . . . I loved the New Orleans setting and the way it was interwoven with Whitby. I can't wait for the next instalment and more vampiric adventures!'

KATHARINE CORR

'I devoured this dark and delicious tale of vampires in nineties New Orleans. Fresh and original and packed with pop culture references, this is *Buffy* for YA readers.'

MARIA KUZNIAR

For Kev and Nathan

Mina and the Undead is a uclanpublishing book

First published in Great Britain in 2021 by
uclanpublishing
University of Central Lancashire
Preston, PR1 2HE, UK

978-1-9129-7947-9

3 5 7 9 10 8 6 4 2

Set in 10/16pt Kingfisher by Becky Chilcott.

A CIP catalogue record for this book is available from the British Library.

Printed and bound in Great Britain by Clays Ltd, Elcograf S.p.A.

Amy McCaw

MINA
and the Undead

uclanpublishing

Chapter 1

When I was about six, I went to school dressed as a vampire. It was Halloween, and I spent every break time stalking the Ninja Turtles and plastic-crowned princesses around the playground. Billy White told me vampires weren't real, so I bit him. The pain was real enough. His skin popped as it broke under my teeth, and I felt a mean pulse of pleasure when he screamed. I wondered if he'd get a scar on his neck like my mum. Hers was a silvery line that was hardly noticeable, but it annoyed her when we asked about it. She arrived at school, white-lipped and fuming, but I realised a lot later she was mad at my teacher for making a fuss, not me. I only recognised this as a warning sign when she'd already gone.

It was no surprise that this memory surfaced on my first night in New Orleans, as we walked past a sign that said *Fang Fest 1995*.

Excitement held back the worst of the jetlag. We passed a voodoo shop with shrunken heads in the window, bars illuminated with gaudy neon signs and elegant buildings with balconies and thin columns. There were so many things to appreciate, but the heat wasn't one of them. The air was never like this in the North of England, so thick that it felt wet on my skin. I peeled off my flannel shirt and tied it around my waist, where it hung limp in the sticky air.

"It starts in two days," Libby said, light-voiced and animated. It was so easy for her. She'd jetted off to New Orleans for university, and I'd spent almost a year carrying her absence like a stone around my neck.

Despite all of that, she threaded an arm around my waist, and I relaxed against her. My body hadn't got the message about keeping her at a distance, and maybe that was for the best. I wasn't going to let our drama ruin this experience.

Libby stopped us in front of the ugliest building on the street. It nestled between two hotels like a rotten tooth, char-black with windows sliced across by silver bars. At the top was a circular, cloudy window that reminded me of a dead eye. I felt the same delicious anticipation as reading horror in bed with my torch, darkness intruding at the edges of the light.

"So, this is where I work. It's called the Mansion of the Macabre." Libby swept her arms out grandly, pulling off the breeziness until she snatched one hand back to bite the skin around her thumbnail.

"And your job is . . .?"

She shrugged one shoulder, the corners of her mouth forming a playful smile. Our mum did name her after the bloodthirsty Countess Elizabeth Bathory. From the look of this place, maybe

Libby decided to embrace her namesake and got a job in a torture chamber.

"Hey!" a deep voice called from behind us.

In the falling dusk, I made out the guy's silhouette with his long, angular limbs. As he loped closer, I saw thick hair that curled in all directions. "Mina, this is my roommate, Jared," Libby said.

"Hey," I echoed. The new-person nerves rose up my throat, but his easy smile stopped them from choking me. He wasn't doing the back and forth most people did, noticing the wild, dark hair and even darker eyes that identified us as sisters.

"Roommate?" he asked, heavy brows raised. "How about best buddy, personal chef . . . ?"

"Jared, you know I love you," Libby said, "but we don't have time for this. Thandie will skin us alive if we're late."

"That's weirdly specific." Jared's hands were never still, first rattling in his pocket and then ruffling the back of his curly head. "I'm glad I got the chance to meet you before . . ." He trailed off like I should've been able to finish the sentence. "Are you going on the tour?" His skin was a warm shade of bronze, and he had an intriguing accent that I couldn't place. I wondered if he was nineteen, like Libby – only two years older than me.

Libby huffed. "She doesn't know about that yet!"

"Oops," Jared said, flashing a devilish grin.

I wasn't sure what a tour, the potentially deadly Thandie and this Mansion of the Macabre had in common.

"So, what kind of tours do you give?" I asked.

A scream came from inside.

Libby leaned heavily on the door to open it, and stampeding kids almost crushed us. We leaped to one side as they shoved and chatted on their way out. A skinny guy in a butler's tuxedo balanced a severed head on a tray. The rubbery tongue dangled from its mouth.

"Nice one," Libby said.

"Just giving the tourists some light refreshments, ma'am," the guy replied in a mangled British accent. He swung the head from its hair. "Nice to meet you!"

I watched him jog upstairs. "Is he supposed to be English?"

"I've tried to teach him, but he thinks we all speak like the Queen," Libby said.

Jared headed towards the stairs, pausing at the bottom. "I have to get ready, but I'll catch you later."

He set off too fast and tripped halfway up the stairs, catching himself on the wooden banister.

Perching on a chair shaped like a contorted human skeleton, Libby unlaced one glossy, black Doc Marten. While she peered into her boot, I took in the subtle ghoulish touches. The glittering chandelier was an intricate web of bear traps. I brushed my hand over the deceptively plain, grey wallpaper. It felt ridged under my fingertips, and it wasn't until I moved that I understood why. Smoky handprints with tiny palms and delicate fingerprints appeared. Children's hands. There was no natural light, and the endless twilight was fitting. "This place is amazing!"

"It has its perks. I've worked at the mansion since I moved here." It seemed like Libby was about to say more when the door opened. I knew Libby cared about the person before they were visible, from the way the taut lines of her body slackened. Libby leaned in for a quick kiss as the girl stepped into view.

She was taller than Libby, with glowing, dark brown skin and fine braids that fell past her shoulders. Their hands interlinked as the girl said, "Hey, it's Mina, right?" Her voice was low, and her accent was one I'd only heard in movies set in New Orleans. "I'm Della. Good to meet you, finally." She gave me a wide, genuine smile that put tiny dimples in her cheeks.

I liked her, an impulse that didn't always come easily. My snarky reply that I'd never even heard of her fizzled out. Our baggage wasn't Della's fault. "You too," I said.

"I should get ready too," Libby said. She passed her eyes back and forth between us. What did she think I'd do?

"Go. We're good here," Della said.

Libby raced upstairs, taking them two at a time.

"Have you been on the tour before?" I asked, taking a chance that Della was more forthcoming than my sister.

"Yeah, but I came to meet you." Her speech sounded so fluid, like 'meetchu' was all one word. "Libby told me not to tell you 'bout it, but I will, if you want."

It was tempting, but I resisted. "That's OK. I'll find out soon."

I was more curious about the two of them. Libby broke up with her long-term girlfriend before she came to New Orleans, leaving them both in pieces. Libby had moved on, and I'd missed it.

"How did you meet?"

Smiling, Della slid a finger and thumb down one braid, pinching it at the end. "At the bar where I work – Empire of the Dead. If you like how creepy the mansion is, you're gonna love it there."

I hadn't quite fit Della and Libby together yet, though their spooky workplaces helped. Della's outfit was one thing that threw me – slim-fitting, black leggings and a vest top that said 'French Quarter Mixed Martial Arts Academy'. Back home, Libby's idea of exercise was running for the school bus when she was late. That'd happened often enough to keep her in shape.

"Have you been working out?" I asked.

"I do MMA. I go a few times a week, if you ever wanna come with."

"Thanks – that'd be great. Does Libby go with you?" I liked the idea of hitting her in a controlled environment.

"Not yet. I took Jared once, but he said 'sorry' every time he hit me. I told him to stick with weightliftin'."

Stomping footsteps announced Libby before she appeared at the top of the stairs. She'd always walked like the floor made her mad. She wore a fitted tuxedo jacket for a dress, and her hair was frizzed out around her face. Grey make-up lined her cheekbones and eye sockets, casting a sickly hue over her complexion.

"The show's about to start. Are you ready?" Libby skimmed both hands through her messy curls and over her dress.

"I can't wait!" I said as she crossed the hall.

"Pretend you don't know me, and have fun!" She flung the front door open.

Della and I shifted to one side of the hallway as a mismatched group of people entered. Libby collected tickets, and Della watched the group with natural confidence.

Two men in their fifties held hands and whispered while a group of young girls chattered nervously and glanced around them. A few college guys laughed too loud and jostled each other. The last guy to enter stood apart like us. He was about six inches taller than everyone else, with a jawline and resting broody face that Jared Leto would envy.

A chainsaw squealed in the distance and snuffed out the

conversations. Someone shrieked, and my heart threatened to burst out of my chest, *Alien*-style.

"Good evening, everyone." Libby's greeting cut through the nervous whispers as she skipped up a few steps to address us. "Welcome to the Mansion of the Macabre. Your horror movie tour will start momentarily. Please keep your hands to yourself, as the actors will do the same. Stay close at all times, and don't progress without me."

Upstairs, Libby led us into a cramped, dated bathroom with beige walls, a grubby white sink and a bath shrouded with a stained shower curtain. The lights flickered, and the stench of clogged drains triggered my gag reflex.

We crowded around the sink at Libby's instruction, our reflection distorted by the speckled mirror. Was this a *Candyman*-themed room? Did Libby have the guts to summon him by saying his name in front of the mirror five times?

Distant children's laughter drifted up from the plughole. Soon, their giggles became high-pitched and garbled, like a chewed-up cassette. A chill trickled over my skin. I knew this book and movie. We were dealing with a much worse monster than the Candyman.

Thick blood threaded with black clots rose from the plughole until the sink was full. A bubble hiccupped in the middle. I knew there were no children down there but I got a clear picture of tiny faces, stuck like that for ever because he killed them.

It all worked as a diversion.

A clown sprang up behind us with an exuberant chuckle. We burst outwards like shrapnel, bolting for the door. Panting, I made it and found Della had beaten me there.

The clown leapt in front of our exit, revealing a mouth crammed with spiky teeth as fine as blades. His eyes were pure white, flat and vacant. Sludgy paint the colour of old bones disguised his skin.

A cloud of balloons drifted over us and he plucked one of the strings, giving a jaunty wave with his knife. He offered us the balloon, which was the same deep crimson as the blood in the sink.

We shrank back. Though this was all pretend, my instinct to run fired up.

Libby stepped between us and the clown. Drawing a slingshot from her pocket, she palmed a silver slug and pulled back the elastic. The clown blinked hard as she aimed right for his head. Hissing, he shambled out of the way, with jerky movements like a video being rewound.

Yanking the door open, Libby ushered us through and slammed it shut. There was no easing us into the horror in this place, and it was exhilarating.

The mansion provided one thrill after another. Freddie Krueger chased us through a foggy dreamscape, knife-hands slashing. We had run-ins with Jason, Pinhead and a cross-dressing Norman Bates. An animatronic Chucky doll jabbed our ankles with a plastic dagger.

Libby slammed the door on Chucky, pretending to gather her composure. "Sorry everyone, I don't know what happened in there. You may be pleased to know this is our last room."

The crowd hemmed me in, so I rose to my tiptoes. Artificial candles glowed against the gold wallpaper, which had a pattern like mouths opened in endless screams. We inched forwards, and my feet sank into the carpet.

"This is our most popular exhibit," Libby began, "the *Interview with the Vampire* room." My favourite book – the perfect finale.

"Are you here to interview me?" Jared hadn't made an appearance yet, so that commanding voice had to be his. "Usually, reporters go for my insufferable companion, Louis."

The crowd shifted, revealing Jared lounging on an opulent four-poster bed, with carved bedposts the shape of lions' heads. His head was propped up on one hand and his curly hair was slicked down into a side parting. Smudgy black lined his eyes, and white powder obscured his bronze skin. His mouth was red and slick, with fangs sinking into his lower lip.

"The tour is over, Lestat," Libby said, striding towards the exit.

"He thrives on this," Della murmured in my ear. All of a sudden, it was heating up in there.

Jared slid off the bed and leaned against the door. This stance showed the full extent of his costume: leather trousers that clung to interesting places and a frilly, white shirt that flopped open to reveal the ridged lines of his powdered chest.

He had Lestat's confidence down, appraising our group as if he was sorting us into food and playthings. I was happy to be both.

Libby played her part well, positioning herself in front of us with her hands on her hips. Some girls shifted so she wasn't blocking their view. Monsters with beautiful faces were infinitely intriguing.

"Allow me to play with one and the rest may leave." Jared licked his wet lips. "I'll take . . . that one." He extended his open hand towards me.

The crowd parted to a chorus of mumbles, split between sighs of relief and grumbles of disappointment. Jared's fingers curled up in preparation for mine. He wasn't supposed to touch the customers, but I had no complaints.

He took my hand and pulled so hard that I bumped into him. Even though I wasn't a damsel willing to be dragged around, I had no desire to fight this. With a hand around my wrist, he turned me slowly to face the envious girls at the front of the group. Jared's fingers grazed my palm when he released me, and the tingles spread much further than the surface of my skin.

Waiting with Jared behind me was unbearable. Though he didn't touch me, I sensed his warmth, not sure what he was going to do next. It was all part of the act but every one of my muscles tensed, waiting for his touch.

He flipped my hair back and I closed my eyes, torn between embarrassment and wanting. One bold fingertip skimmed the hollow of my throat and I was done. He was playing a part, but I wanted him for real.

Soft breath brushed my neck as his mouth came down.

Chapter 2

*S*ticky lips skimmed my throat with the feather-light touch of his tongue. Water rained down and red strobes flashed, simulating my spouting blood. It sent squeals through the crowd as the lights cut out. The door closed behind the tour group, and I was left alone in the dark with Jared.

When the lights came on, we were a lot closer than I expected. The hazel-green kaleidoscope of his eyes drew me in. Something hung between us, not yet broken, and Lestat's mischievousness lingered.

"You can thank Thandie," Jared said, removing his plastic fangs. Nothing killed the mood like a string of saliva. "She told me to pull you out."

Touching my neck, my fingers came away syrupy and wet. They smelled like cherries, and I resisted the urge to lick them. "Lucky me."

"We should get down there. She wants to see you."

Chatter greeted us from the bottom of the stairs, where Libby was waving off the last of the tour group. Jared shrank back, and I joined him.

"It kind of ruins the mystique if they see me out here," Jared said. "I'm supposed to be all mysterious." He tried to deepen his voice but went too far, ending in a coughing fit.

"It's best we stay up here then," I said.

Jared chuckled, clearing his throat. "You're right. The outfit can only do so much."

The door slammed shut and Jared set off downstairs, so I escaped admitting what his outfit did for me.

"Thandie first, then you can tell me how great I was," Libby said, dipping into a lazy curtsey. "I need to get back. Good luck!"

That was the extent of her supportive sistering. She was halfway up the stairs before we knocked on Thandie's office door.

Thandie sat behind a desk covered with a trove of treasures: a golden idol worthy of Indiana Jones, a wooden mask that had been hacked into the shape of a face and more oddities than I could appreciate.

She wore a midnight-blue, beaded corset that pinched in her already slender waist. A black afro of spiral curls framed her flawless face and brushed her collarbone. Her scrutiny peeled layers off me. "What did you think of my tour?" Her voice was gravel-rough, with an accent similar to Della's.

My throat was stripped by air stale with old cigarette smoke and burned-out incense. "I've never done anything like it – it's like being immersed in a horror movie. The sets are amazing, and the actors really sold it." I was conscious of Jared beside me and hoped she wouldn't ask for specifics.

"How'd she do?" Thandie asked him.

"Great. She didn't flinch when I pulled her out and played along like a pro."

It was some consolation that he thought I was acting.

Thandie's gaze held me in place like a moth with pins driven through the wings. She drummed glossy, black nails on the desk. "Elizabeth asked me to give you a job here but as I said to her, I don't take applications. I'll give you one tour to prove you can scare people. Come back tomorrow night."

"Thanks, I'd love that," I said, stunned. I'd only just learned that places like this existed, and there was a chance I could get to work here. Even better, Libby tried to arrange it.

Back in the hallway, Jared said, "You didn't cry. That's a good first impression."

After meeting Thandie, I didn't know if he was joking.

His hair had sprung free into wet-looking curls, and his eyeliner was streaked. Lestat's slick charm had only lasted so long, which made it easier to hold a conversation with him.

"I have to fix this – there's another tour in ten minutes." He gestured at his face, frowning at a red mark on one sleeve. "Will you be OK down here?"

As great as the tour was, I wasn't ready to go on it again. "I'll be fine."

"Later then."

As Jared ambled upstairs, I retrieved the battered copy of *Interview with the Vampire* from my backpack. Jared crossed paths with Della on the landing, and she jogged down the stairs on light feet. "Well? Did the mansion win you over?"

"Yeah, it got me," I said.

"Jared keeps tellin' me to read that. Any good?"

That explained his desire to dress up as Lestat. "It's amazing! I couldn't resist rereading it while I'm here."

"I've lived here my whole life – I should check it out. I have to get to work, but I'll see you soon." She swung the heavy door open a lot easier than Libby did earlier and waved before it closed.

Finally alone, I sat on the skeleton chair. Shifting around made it no comfier. I wondered whether it was real bone that had been forced into shape.

The spine of my book was so cracked that it fell open at a memorable scene – the terrible hardship when Louis and Lestat had to share a coffin. I flipped to the chapter where Louis's slaves suspected he'd become a vampire.

I'd only read a few pages when Libby bolted back down. "I'm so late! When I'm done, tell me exactly what you thought."

The next tour group filled the space around me, but the book drowned them out.

I got so engrossed that I only noticed how stiff I was when Libby and Jared returned three tours later. They were back in ordinary clothes, though Libby still had the make-up on and her hair in a frizz.

I lurched to my feet and discreetly slid the battered book into my bag. I almost got away with it when Jared said, "I take it you've read that before." He'd attempted to remove the make-up, but he missed some black smudges.

"Yeah." I was conscious of how close Jared was to unearthing his starring role in my Lestat fantasy. "It's one of my favourites."

"Mine too," he said. "I only discovered it when I came here for college. Could be the books never made it big in Honolulu."

That was the accent I recognised. He was from Hawaii.

Libby wrenched the front door open, and we headed out into the balmy night. "So, what did you think of the tour?"

"I loved it," I said, "and you made an amazing tour guide."

"Why, thank you." She nudged her shoulder against mine. The sisterly contact felt good – natural even.

"I hear Lestat gave a standout performance." Jared came up on the other side of me as we headed onto the street.

"Stop fishing," Libby said, saving me before the humiliating truth popped out. "I'm glad you liked it because I was kind of hoping you'd want to work here this summer. With me, I mean." This was the real Libby, when her sincerity showed. "I meant to give you a heads-up earlier. What did Thandie say?"

"She asked me to try out tomorrow." I let myself picture the summer in this strange and intriguing place, working at the mansion and wandering the city with Libby.

I'd wanted these things for us before. I shouldn't get fixated on them, and I found the perfect change of subject. Jared's T-shirt had an impressionistic print of Brandon Lee from *The Crow* on it, with the recognisable painted face and ragged, black hair. "I like your T-shirt," I said, not sure why I'd gone shy. I wasn't great at taking compliments, but I could usually dish them out.

"It's a good movie," he said. "Lucas painted it. You'll meet him when we get back."

"If he's there," Libby added. "He's a bit of a social butterfly, our Lucas."

Libby had made a great life here without me in it.

My negativity melted away when we stepped onto Bourbon Street. The city had well and truly woken up. It was so incredible to think that six months ago I was watching *Interview with the Vampire* in the cinema at home. Finally, I was here.

Neon lights glared against the brewing darkness and people were everywhere. Tourists stumbled in groups, arms around each other's backs and long tubes of fluorescent drinks sloshing over their hands. There were also people begging, pleading with their hands outstretched. Different music blended with the babble of chatter. A raw, soulful song drifted through an open bar front and a saxophone blurted out a flurry of jazz.

Libby linked arms with me, and her skin was sticky against mine. Metal balconies were strung with fairy lights, and potted plants trailed colour over an endless string of bars and shops. A woman passed with a jumble of beads around her neck. She motioned towards the colourful strands, and Libby dragged me onwards. "Remember, some people are only here to con you."

Whitby was a quiet coastal town and the most action we got was lively tourists and greedy seagulls. Here, danger lingered at the fringes of the street. Two men watched passersby with scheming eyes, and a huddle of children separated and slipped among the tourists. I spun my backpack to the front, wrapping my arms around it. This street was a bright jewel that could slice your palm if you gripped too tightly.

Through the spicy food and spilled drinks, I caught a less pleasant scent. "What's that smell?"

"Do you really want to know?" Libby asked. "I think it's a heady mixture of sewers and piss."

"Glad I asked."

A *Fang Fest 1995* sign captured my attention. It was strung across the street from two balconies and more signs were tied to street lights. Eagerness mixed in with anxiety, though I wasn't sure what the festival would entail. Some people on the street gave me a clue, with their black leather, satin in berry hues and splashes of fake blood. At least, I assumed it was fake.

Gradually, the vibrant colours and noises faded. When we reached the quieter streets near Libby's, the darkness gave my imagination plenty of material. I caught shadowy movements down alleys and squat shapes on balconies, imagining evil things, definitely not cats and plants. My mum was all too quick to believe in the supernatural and it ended badly. I should have known better.

An ambulance tore past us, leaving streaks of blue on my retinas and ringing in my ears. "First one I've heard tonight," Libby said.

"Does that happen a lot?" I asked.

"You'll get used to it," Jared said. "424 people were murdered in New Orleans last year." More than one person a day.

"Nice fact," Libby said. "Do you want to add that most of them were seventeen-year-old English girls?"

I didn't need Libby to shield me. The cluster of flashing blue lights down the road filled me with disquiet, along with quite a bit of curiosity. Jared steered us closer to them.

"Can't we just go home and eat popcorn?" Libby complained.

"This place is less than a mile from our house," Jared said. "Don't you wanna find out what happened?"

We reached a huddle of onlookers behind a yellow strand of tape. Police officers were spaced out along it, and there was no getting past them.

Further down, an ambulance and several police cars circled an imposing white building with a high wall around it.

We joined the waiting crowd, brought together by our need to discover what was beyond the plastic tape.

Everyone was staring at the large building, with its orderly rows of windows and cross on the roof. Paramedics were moving around with quick efficiency by the gates. They lifted a stretcher into the ambulance, though I couldn't see the condition of the person. I hoped the paramedics got to them fast enough. "What is that place?" I asked.

"It's called the Ursuline Convent," Jared said. "Hey, do you know what happened?"

He directed the question at a short guy staring at the scene, who glowered at Jared. "A girl got mugged."

"Let's go," Libby said. "I'm not standing around to stare at that."

Reluctantly, Jared followed Libby, considering me with a speculative gleam in his eyes. "You're into vampire stories, right? I know a good one about the convent, if you're interested."

"Always," I said.

Chapter 3

Libby groaned. "You and your stories."

Jared ignored her. "Do you know the one about how vampires came to New Orleans?"

"I come from Whitby – we only learn about Dracula. But I've always got time for more."

"I suppose it's been a while since you've told this one. Let's hear it," Libby said.

"Like you could stop me." Jared veered behind Libby to walk in the middle. His arm brushed against mine and set off spreading heat that I couldn't blame on the muggy air.

"So, in the 18th century, the Ursuline Convent was a sanctuary for girls sent from France to populate New Orleans. A group of girls were sent with casket-shaped boxes. One story is that they were empty coffins, in case they died on the journey." He gave an apologetic grin, even though I was all about the gory bits. "Some people say they were weird suitcases. Either way, the nuns locked the caskets on the third floor of the convent and closed the shutters. You saw those windows set into the roof? That's the attic where the caskets were kept."

I pictured the small, shuttered windows shielding a gloomy attic from daylight, with a row of coffin-shaped boxes along one wall. "If they were ordinary suitcases, why did the nuns lock them away?"

"Good question," Jared said, pausing to look both ways as we crossed a road.

"Suck-up," Libby muttered, though it could've been aimed at either of us.

Jared continued as if she never spoke. "At the time, there were reports of the windows bursting open around midnight. Some people saw ghostly figures flying out of the building. The nuns had the windows sealed with screws blessed by the Pope, but it did no good. Something left the convent under the cover of darkness every night."

"So, were the sweet little convent girls vampires?" I asked.

"That's one version of the story," Jared said. "My favourite is that the innocent casket girls unknowingly brought vampires over from Europe. The coffins kept them safe from sunlight on the journey.

When they arrived in New Orleans, the creatures went out on the town and then returned to the safety of their coffins in the convent attic. The story went around for years, and two paranormal investigators came sniffing around in the seventies. They had this great idea to camp outside the convent walls."

"This part gives me the creeps," Libby said. Only this part? I was enjoying every gruesome detail.

"I presume they didn't go home disappointed," I said.

"Sadly not," Jared said, his tone turning sombre. "The nuns found them the next morning. Both bodies were shrivelled husks – no blood left in them, or on the ground. The thing is, they camped right outside the gate we saw."

"Where the girl was mugged," I said, catching up.

Libby waved a dismissive hand before he even finished. "People are killed in a lot of places. It's called a coincidence."

"Sensitive much?" Jared said, eyebrows raised. "The girl's not necessarily dead. Come on, Libs – you have to admit, it's weird."

"It is weird," I said, talking and thinking fast, "and if it's a coincidence, it's a pretty big one." A realisation stopped me there. I'd grasped for the goriest explanation, exactly like Mum would've done. I'd always worried that her future was waiting inside me, like a dormant disease. She'd written it out when she named me after the girl in *Dracula*, the heroine who barely got away.

Libby's house drew me out of my troubled thoughts. Delicate, almost lacy roof supports cast shadows over the arched window. Though there were no streetlamps around here, each house had a light on the wall by the front door.

Inside, I followed Libby into the kitchen, while Jared wandered off to his room. I liked the layout of the house: an empty central hallway with bedrooms and a kitchen that branched off from it. Libby told me earlier that it was called a shotgun house, because standing in the entrance was like looking down the long, thin barrel of a shotgun.

"I take it you're in for movie night, like old times," Libby said, ripping open a bag of popcorn kernels. She tipped them into a bowl with a clatter, dropped a plate on top and jammed it into the microwave. Nothing had changed with how Libby got things done. Every move was loud and decisive.

"Sure," I said. It'd been an eventful first night. Two hours in front of a screen sounded good. "What are we watching?"

"I rented *The Burbs*," Libby said.

"Sweet." Jared appeared and joined in with the conversation. He put a pan on the hob and sliced a slab of butter into it. "Tom Hanks and serial killers."

"They're not necessarily serial killers," Libby said, rummaging through a cupboard. "That's sort of the point of the movie."

She drew her head out of the cupboard with a bag of sugar in one hand and a salt shaker in the other. "Those sweatpants? We have company!"

Jared was still wearing the Brandon Lee T-shirt, only now he'd paired it with well-worn grey jogging bottoms. I was equally offended that Libby called me company and was picking up Americanisms. Did she want to erase our past completely, with me in it?

"*These sweatpants* are part of movie night tradition. I didn't want Mina to miss out."

"How about we skip your other tradition of spoiling movie plots?" Libby asked, retrieving the popcorn from the microwave and slopping Jared's melted butter over it.

He sprinkled in sugar and salt, never breaking the flow of conversation. "You're just jealous that I always guess right."

I followed their trail of bickering into Libby's room, finding no spot in their easy back and forth for me.

We settled onto Libby's bed, and I took in the familiar posters of Bikini Kill, No Doubt and other bands, alongside torn images of beautiful women like Kelly from *Saved by the Bell*. I smiled at the sight of her old troll collection crowded on a shelf, with every hair colour from lime green to deep purple.

The TV was at the end of her bed, and Jared crawled to put the video in while Libby and I got comfortable on the pillows. I jammed myself into the corner because two hours next to Jared wouldn't have helped me follow the movie. Libby balanced the bowl on her lap and Jared shuffled back beside her, grabbing a handful of popcorn and stuffing it in his mouth. "It's called sharing," Libby pointed out as she fast-forwarded through the trailers.

Jared grinned with his cheeks full like a chipmunk. He swallowed the popcorn with a loud gulp. "Wait, you've gone too far! Rewind, rewind!" He peeked at the screen through parted fingers.

Libby rewound the video, muttering about what Jared could do with the remote control.

Discordant music played as the camera zoomed in on a suburban street at night, landing on a dilapidated house. "Looks like the mansion," Jared said.

"Don't let Thandie hear you say that," Libby warned.

Tom Hanks went out in his dressing gown to stare at bright lights flashing through his neighbours' basement windows. Metallic noises clanked and buzzed down there. I reached for the popcorn and shoved in a buttery mouthful.

"What's going on?" Libby asked.

"I think we're supposed to watch it and find out, but my guess is . . ." Jared said.

"Let's keep the guesses to ourselves," Libby said. "Ooh, Princess Leia's on. I like this movie." I reached into the popcorn bowl and my fingers brushed against Jared's. Retrieving them hastily, I only came away with a few kernels of popcorn. From the way he was staring unblinking at the screen, the whole thing must have passed him by.

"OK, so if I'm not telling you my theory, what do you guys think?" Jared asked, as Tom Hanks smoked on his friend's porch and debated what his neighbours had buried in the garden. "Serial killers or bad neighbours?"

"Don't serial killers make pretty bad neighbours?" Libby asked. "Anyway, they're probably burying trash. Tom Hanks needs to get a hobby and stop spying on people."

"What do you think, Mina?" Jared asked over Libby's head.

"His neighbours buried a person-sized bag in their garden, and Tom Hanks's friend is talking about a murdered family. They have to be serial killers," I said.

"Exactly," Jared said, reaching into the popcorn bowl again.

"What did I say about theories?" Libby asked. She'd shared her prediction but couldn't take it when we did the same.

While Tom Hanks watched TV on our TV, I made a quick bathroom stop. "You don't have to pause it," I said when Libby reached for the remote. "I'll be quick."

A couple of minutes later, I headed out of the bathroom into the unlit hallway. The boom of thunder and menacing music came from Libby's room as the front door rattled.

With the jarring music playing, I was on edge. Then the movie cut off and the silence was worse. Clattering came from outside, followed by the rattle of a key turning in the lock.

The door swung open and a slight figure staggered inside. He had golden hair that flopped into huge, expressive eyes like

Leonardo DiCaprio in *The Basketball Diaries*. He was also most definitely on something. "Hi," he said, "I'm Lucas. Did I wake you, little Libby?" If the mumbling wasn't a giveaway, the fog of alcohol and smoke did the trick.

"I'm Mina." Either Libby forgot to tell him my name, or he managed it all by himself. Either way, little Libby? I was bigger than her in every direction. "You're fine, we're watching a movie."

"You're missing it!" Libby called. "Get in here, you two."

Lucas made a detour to the kitchen to grab a chair, and there was a lot of banging as I climbed back onto the bed. Libby had paused the movie. "Is he wasted?" Jared asked, quiet and intense.

"I think so," I murmured.

"Makes a change," Jared said sarcastically, and the venom surprised me.

Lucas stumbled into the room and put the chair down by the bed.

Jared faced Lucas, tension snapping across his shoulders. Lucas slouched low in his chair in response to whatever Jared's face did.

"Let's go," Libby said and clicked play.

Even though I was enjoying the movie, I was also invested in what was going on in the room.

Libby was absorbed in the movie as she mechanically fed popcorn into her mouth. Jared kept glancing at Lucas, until the movie sucked him back in. "*The Exorcist, The Texas Chainsaw Massacre,*" he listed as we watched Tom Hanks channel surfing. "We should watch those soon."

"Technically, we live through them at the mansion," Libby said, scrabbling around in the bowl. "Hey, someone ate all the popcorn."

Lucas stayed out of their rapport. I couldn't see him well from my corner, though I caught the smoke and beer odours coming off him.

I leant down, pretending to pull up my sock. Lucas's eyes faced the vague direction of the TV, but they were tired and unfocused.

I was sleepy when the movie finished. With the time difference and jetlag, I had no idea what time zone I was running on.

"So, Mina and I called that one," Jared said, offering a hand for me to high five. "Like we said – serial killers."

"Yes, you're both geniuses," Libby said.

"You said it," Jared replied.

We drifted off separately, and I heard Lucas crashing around in his room across the hallway.

My room at Libby's was welcoming, with a sanded, wooden floor and teal patchwork quilt that she picked out for me. It was my favourite colour. I was glad their other roommate, Tessa, went home for the summer. I'd always liked having my own space.

I got ready and then climbed into my new bed for the first time, satisfied that the mattress had the right amount of bounce. I pressed play on my Walkman and Salt-N-Pepa blasted into my ears. Whatever 'shooping' was, they made it sound fun.

There was a knock on the door, and I slipped my headphones off. "Come in," I called.

Libby tiptoed in and stood in the middle of the floor, tugging on the hemline of her Rolling Stones T-shirt. "So, tonight was a blast..."

"Yeah. I had a great time." We were doing small talk, when we hadn't seen each other for nearly a year. My anger swelled all over again. Back then, she'd accepted her place at the University of York and I was supposed to visit her some weekends, sneaking into student parties and watching videos all night. Our mum had just left us, and the next thing I knew, Libby got a student visa and left me for university on another continent. This was our chance to talk about it, and we may as well have been discussing the weather.

"Well . . . good night." She turned to leave.

I made a last attempt to connect. "Aren't we going to talk?"

Libby stiffened. Her smile was bright and false when she faced me again. "What about?"

Either she was unaware we had a problem or was in denial. "Never mind."

"OK, 'night," she said again and hastily closed the door.

I tugged off the headphones and got settled, glad in a way that she was struggling. It gave us one thing in common, and we had the whole summer to work through it.

I tried reading but my mind kept drifting to the New Orleans out there, not the one crafted by Anne Rice. Less than a mile away, the police were probably trying to find out who attacked that poor girl.

I jerked awake as if I was falling. For a few seconds, the muggy air and unfamiliar woody fragrance disoriented me. Comfort smoothed over the anxiety as I recognised where I was.

It was deadly quiet until a thump reverberated through the house. That was followed by a groan. I swung my legs out of bed and set my feet on the smooth, hardwood floor. There it was again – another whimper of distress. Had Libby locked the front door? She'd sometimes forgotten at home, but it wasn't so important when the local murder rate was practically zero.

I crept across my floor, listening. Libby or one of the others could have been wandering the house. So why was my heart hammering out a warning?

"Hello?" I whispered.

I wasn't planning to spend the summer hiding from every little thing, so I cautiously pushed my door open.

The hallway was filled with an odd, chemical scent, and there was a patch of faint light. That time I definitely heard it – a struggling breath. It came from Lucas's room.

I could've woken Libby or done plenty of logical things. I surged towards the sound. The door was slightly open, and Lucas was sprawled across the bed. His breathing was shallow and his features contorted. I laid a light hand on the door. It opened fully with a jarring creak. In the lamplight, I saw a bloody stain where Lucas's fingers clasped his white vest.

Chapter 4

Too shocked to scream, I gasped loud enough to rouse Lucas. His eyes shot open, and he raised his bloody hands to stare at them.

"Are you OK?"

I was about to call for help when I noticed a few things. There was a row of empty beer bottles on his bedside table. A canvas was set up, with tubes of oil paint scattered on the floor around it. The pallet at the bottom of the canvas was a mess of reds and oranges.

"Why am I . . .?" His speech was garbled. He wiped his hands on his shirt, leaving more stains. He tried to push himself up onto his elbows, clutching his head. "I . . . painted myself."

"Can I get you some water?" I asked, my heart still keeping a frantic beat.

He burped and then collapsed back on his bed.

I retreated to my room, embarrassed but glad I hadn't woken the whole house.

The first thing I remembered the next morning was my encounter with Lucas. My only chance was that he was drunk enough to forget it.

I plodded into the kitchen in desperate need of food. Jared was stirring a mixture that smelled buttery and amazing in a silver wok, peering into it through smudged plastic glasses. He had morning hair and wore grey pyjamas that dragged on the tiles. "Hey," he said. "You want eggs? I'm guessing you don't want a protein shake." He shook a plastic bottle of brown, lumpy liquid.

"Good guess. Eggs would be great." His sleeveless top drew attention to leanly muscled arms. The shakes were working.

Sliding into my seat, it occurred to me that I was also wearing pyjamas. Why weren't these things more supportive?

The Times-Picayune newspaper was on the table. "Do you mind?" I asked.

"Go ahead."

I opened the paper and used it as a shield to check my pyjama top was doing its job. My satisfaction faded when I found out what happened at the convent. The girl had died there. The article said the cause of death was blood loss from a neck wound, though there wasn't much around her. It gave the brutal facts but not her name. Libby's joke from last night about dead teenage girls took on a sinister shade.

The chime of porcelain on the tiled table jolted me out of my thoughts. I put the paper aside, revealing a plate of thick, brown toast piled with scrambled eggs. "Thanks, it looks great," I said.

Jared grabbed a bottle of Texas Pete hot sauce and splashed it over his eggs, leaving a pattern a lot like blood spatter. He dug into his eggs with enthusiasm while I cut my toast into small pieces. The article filled in what we couldn't see outside the convent: a scene filtered through the grey tones of night against the red slick of blood. A girl lying there all alone on the cold concrete.

"Did you read this?" I asked.

"Yeah, it's messed up," Jared said, taking a huge bite from his toast.

"Come on, your cooking's not that bad." Libby came in and went straight for the kettle. She'd always been annoyingly upbeat in the mornings.

"We're talking about the girl who was attacked. She died last night," I said, with more attitude than I intended.

"That sucks," Libby declared. "Anyone want a drink?"

How did she push it aside so easily? A girl died. She deserved at least a pause in the conversation.

"Oh, I meant to ask you . . ." Libby began, and I was optimistic that she'd dug down for some compassion. "Did you borrow my hairbrush? I can't find it anywhere." Or maybe not.

"Do I look like I used your hairbrush?" I asked, fully aware of my tangled morning hair.

The phone rang in the hallway. Libby retreated to answer it, forgetting her lost possession. "Hello? Hi, Sandra." She always drew out our aunt's name like a satisfying swearword. "Yeah, she's fine. I'll get her."

Libby held out the phone as I reached the hallway, the spiral cable stretching taut. She rolled her eyes. "Hello?" I said.

"Mina?" Sandra sounded breathless and far away.

"Hi. How's France?"

"Cold! And beautiful! Is everything good with Libby? Are you all settled in?"

My reply worked for both questions. "Yep."

There was a high-pitched beep in the background. "Damn, I'm out of centimes. Is there anything I can do?"

What could she possibly help with from thousands of miles away? "We're fine here. Enjoy your summer."

"OK! Bye, Mi—"

The second I accepted Libby's invitation, Aunt Sandra booked a flight to Paris and a string of other amazing locations. Her job as an English lecturer meant she got long holidays, but she wasn't able to make the most of them with her 'sister's kids hanging around'. My mum used to say I got my love of language from her, but that's where Aunt Sandra's emotions ended. I had a feeling her care for me would expire when I turned eighteen in September. That gave me two months to work out what to do with my life.

"So Sandra's as talkative as ever," Libby said from the kitchen. "Let's finish breakfast."

Libby nibbled a stale croissant while I finished eating my cold eggs and reading the newspaper. Jared and Libby chatted occasionally, and the background noise was soothing.

I read articles about the recent flooding and the upcoming vampire festival. I'd looked forward to it for weeks, and there was only a day of waiting left.

Near the back of the paper, there was a tiny article about another murder. A girl called Betty Watson had been killed with an axe a few days ago. Her parents found her dead in their kitchen, and the police had no leads. It was hard to reconcile the sunlit kitchen and vibrancy of Bourbon Street the night before with two murdered girls. Libby and Jared seemed unfazed. I never wanted death to feel ordinary.

Lucas met us outside, wearing a loose, white shirt with the sleeves rolled up and sunglasses that didn't cover his puffy eyes. A chunky camera hung around his neck. He took a last long drag on his cigarette, making a deep line between his eyebrows, and stubbed it out under one trainer.

Lucas's cheeks flushed. His eyes met mine and immediately dipped again. "Sorry about last night. I can't remember much."

"You're fine," I said. If he recalled the paint mishap, I was glad he kept it from the others. "You didn't do anything."

He wilted under Jared's glare, and they moved off ahead, arguing quietly.

Libby apparently failed to notice. "So, I was thinking we could go to the bar to say hi to Della."

I could've pointed out that she saw Della yesterday and it was my very first morning here. It was too hot to argue, and we were supposed to be getting on. "I was thinking we could go to St. Louis Cemetery."

Libby's mouth made a hard, angry little bud. She wasn't used to me standing my ground.

"Did someone say cemetery?" Jared asked as he and Lucas dropped back. "How about Libby goes to see Della and I'll come with you? We can all hang out after."

"Great," Libby said brightly. She would, since she got her own way. I realised there was nothing to complain about when I replayed what Jared said. He wanted to go to the cemetery alone with me.

"Can I tag along?" Lucas asked so sweetly that I hardly minded the intrusion. Technically, there was nothing to intrude on. It was definitely the dusty, old graves and bones that had my heart racing.

In St. Louis Cemetery No. 1, orderly lines of tombs fanned out around us. Some were surrounded by weathered, metal fencing, and many were painted bone white or left as bare brick. The hot, dusty air sat heavy on my lungs. In the hush, I imagined us suspended between the living and the dead.

Lucas drifted off, examining tombs and plaques through the lens of his camera. With his fair hair and loose, white shirt, he was like a ghost among the crypts.

A brick tomb drew my attention. There were crosses scratched all over it and objects scattered round the base. I moved closer and saw beads, candles, dead flowers and tiny bones. My fingers twitched to touch them, but intuition told me to leave them alone.

Lucas crouched down and snapped a photo. I hadn't heard him approach us, and he was gone before anyone spoke.

Jared wasn't one to leave a silence hanging. "Some people think Marie Laveau, the voodoo priestess, is buried here. They leave offerings in exchange for wishes."

"I wouldn't scratch up someone's grave, even if I got a wish," I said. In some places, the brick had crumbled around the crosses.

"Right," he said, his eyebrows lifting like it was news that I had a conscience. His expressive face revealed everything he felt, and I liked how uncomplicated that was.

I meant what I said, though I understood desperation. It'd been

34

over a year since Mum left, and I would've done almost anything to get her back or even hear from her.

After that, we were quiet for a bit, my mind and body turning sluggish and dreamy in the sunshine. Louis's empty tomb was in this cemetery in *Interview with the Vampire*, and his departed family members were buried here. I saw Brad Pitt as my Louis whenever I read the book now, stalking amongst the tombs like a wraith with his soulful eyes full of grief.

"So, do you know why tombs are above ground in New Orleans?" Jared asked.

"No, why?"

"After a storm, bodies had a nasty habit of floating to the surface. Plus, with the heat built up inside these tombs, bodies decompose fast. There's a rule that tombs have to stay sealed for a year and a day, but then they can be opened to add the remains of other family members."

"Wow." I took a beat to digest that. It made a bleak kind of sense. "Thanks for coming along and giving me the tour."

"Not a problem," he said, pausing in front of a tomb to read the inscription etched into the stone. "I love this stuff. But you do too, right?"

"Definitely," I agreed.

Being here with Jared was only soured because Libby let me come without her. I should have been used to it. I thought when Mum disappeared it would make us closer. Instead, Libby left for university where I couldn't afford to visit.

"Everything OK?" Jared asked.

"I was thinking about our mum," I said, surprised by how easily it came out. "Did Libby tell you she left last year?"

"That's pretty much all she told me," Jared said, his eyebrows scrunching down low as he studied me.

"She doesn't really do opening up," I said, so bitter that I shocked myself. Jared was Libby's friend and I should've been more careful about trusting him. For some reason, perhaps his patience or how he wasn't bombarding me with questions, I wanted to share this with him. "It shouldn't have been such a shock . . . when Mum left, I mean. She was gone a lot of the time, sometimes for days, and finally she just . . . didn't come back." The constant ache for her intensified into a jagged, ruthless pain, a rusty shard of metal that had dug in deep. I couldn't tell him my suspicions about why she left – that her research became more important than us. That my life was a pattern of people leaving: first Dad, then Mum, Libby and even Aunt Sandra.

I'd left the silence for so long it had become a living thing, too watchful to disturb.

"Sorry you had to go through that," Jared said. I'd heard it all before, but with him, there was genuine empathy.

"Yeah, me too," I said, casting my gaze around for anything else to talk about.

There was a stone tomb beside us where the front panel had crumbled in one corner. I stood on my tiptoes to peer inside.

Jared caught my arm. "You don't want to do that. You're going to have to trust me."

Reluctantly, I tore my attention away from the hole. His hand was still on my upper arm. Even though we were both slick with sweat and I'd exposed my family secrets, it was almost a perfect moment. The sun struck him just right, making his eyes flare dollar-bill green. He smiled with his whole face: crinkled eyes and deep grooves by his mouth.

"You guys ready to go?" I'd forgotten all about Lucas, and he appeared with an astonishing lack of timing.

"Are we done?" Jared asked. His hand fell away, along with the feeling.

The air was stifling and my scalp prickled. I'd been so wrapped up in our conversation that it'd been way too long since I drank anything or put on sun cream. "Sure," I said. "We should go and find Libby."

Right near the exit, Lucas paused in front of a grey, brick tomb. So much for leaving. He raised the camera and pointed it at the tomb, stepping back before he took the picture.

There was a cracked cross on top of the brick structure, over a faint inscription. "Who's Carter?" I asked. There were two sets of dates underneath: 1899–1932 and 1903–1932.

"You never heard this one?" Jared teased. "It's another famous vampire story."

"You know you want to tell me," I said.

"Yeah, you're right," he said, laying a hand on the tomb. "These two were brothers: John and Wayne Carter. New Orleans, born and raised. They used to work on the docks hauling fish in the Great Depression during the early 1930s, until they got a taste for something different."

Jared's voice was soothing and animated, pitching me into the story. I could almost smell the salt and rotten fish stench of the docks. Lucas watched silently as we waited for Jared to continue.

"Some people say they found a willing vampire to turn them. Others claim John was turned and he enslaved his brother to a half-life of drinking blood. Either way, they had an unconventional method of getting their fix."

"Yeah?" I asked, failing to come off as cool and disinterested.

"They kidnapped people and tied them up, drugging them. They fed from whichever victim they wanted and kept adding to their collection. Some died, and the brothers replaced them. This could've gone on indefinitely; people have always vanished here, and the swamps are right there to get rid of them. One night, a girl covered in blood burst out onto the street. She told the story of escaping two murderous brothers to the police and a team surrounded their place. It took eight of them to take the brothers down, and three officers were killed. It was only when the surviving officers dragged them out onto the street that the brothers weakened. The police didn't know they had vampires on their hands, so exposing them to sunlight was a lucky accident. They were hung the next day and entombed right here."

"So they got what they deserved," I said.

"Not quite," Lucas added quietly.

"Why don't you tell the rest?" Jared leaned against the tomb.

Lucas licked his teeth. "Tombs in New Orleans are reused . . . when other family members die. The remains are pushed to the back of the tomb and they fall down a kind of . . . channel."

Lucas was gathering confidence, though he lacked Jared's compelling storytelling style. "They opened the Carter brothers' tomb when the next family member died. The brothers' bodies were gone."

"They decomposed?" I asked. Jared did say the heat made bodies decay faster.

Lucas hesitated, looking to Jared. He took over the story. "Well . . .

38

every once in a while, people say they've seen the brothers wandering the streets of New Orleans, hunting down their next kill."

Jared piled on the drama for the big finish, and I laughed. "Now that was a good legend."

"We've got hundreds of them," Jared said. "Mostly, legends are all they are. I can't find any official records about the brothers."

"Doesn't the tomb prove it?" I asked.

"Or they're just some poor family called Carter who got pulled into the myth. That happens a lot here – facts get mixed in with fiction."

We headed out of the cemetery, while I was thinking about the myth and the faint scar on Mum's neck. The distinctive marks of teeth. Her story had the same blurred lines as the myths about New Orleans.

"How do you know all of this?" I asked Jared.

"I've read a lot about New Orleans. I can lend you books, if you want. Actually, I can do one better than that."

Lucas turned his head away to cough. "I have to get my film developed. I'll catch up with you guys at Jackson Square."

"See you soon," I said.

Lucas gave an awkward nod and walked away.

"How did you meet?" I asked, watching him. Lucas was part of the group, but he didn't quite fit like the others.

"Same place I met Libby – the mansion. Only about a year earlier."

"He was on the tour?"

"Nah, he helped with the redesign. The creepy wallpaper in the hallway, with the handprints? That's his. He painted some of the props too."

Working behind the scenes suited him. "What's his story?" That came out blunter than I intended.

"He's a good friend, but he's had it rough. His parents aren't artists. They don't really see eye to eye with Lucas, about a lot of things. It takes time to get to know him, but he's worth the effort."

"I get that," I said. "So, where are you taking me?"

"You'll see," Jared said. "It's at the mansion."

Chapter 5

On the walk, Jared played tour guide. He pointed out plants called hanging ferns and tropical hibiscus, which framed brightly painted shops that sold Gothic clothes and souvenirs. "At night, you wanna stick to the French Quarter. If you stray from the well-lit path, you'd better turn back."

I wasn't planning to wander New Orleans by myself, especially at night, but I wouldn't say no to going with Jared again.

We crossed a busy road wider than any we had in Whitby, then entered a community with red brick paths and carefully tended houses. The colours were pastel or vibrant shades like on Libby's street and a lot were in the same shotgun style as hers. Occasional slender trees created patches of shade, and we paused beneath one. The nearest balcony had a spray of vines and shiny, purple beads dangling from it. I could see myself living here amidst the myths and the sunshine.

Even I recognised Bourbon Street as we drew near. A flag and sun umbrella marked the balcony on the corner, and a stream of tourists crossed the road ahead of us.

Jared pointed out a window displaying cardboard Lestat and Louis masks on thin pieces of elastic. "Do you think Thandie would go for these? It'd save on make-up."

We ventured a short way down Bourbon Street then turned off towards the side street that was home to the mansion. Jared knocked on the door and then dug out a key. "Do all of Thandie's staff have keys?" I asked, as we stepped into the cool hallway. Faint yellow light came from bulbs woven through the bear traps overhead, and it felt oddly deserted.

"Only her favourites," he murmured, before calling out, "Thandie?" Jared tapped on her office door with his knuckles.

She was sitting behind the desk, pen poised. "You're early for your shift." She set the pen down. "What can I do for you?"

Jared wasn't put off by Thandie's abruptness. "I was telling Mina the story of the Carter brothers. Would you mind lending her a copy of the diary?"

Thandie's lips thinned, and her arms tightened across her body. "Trying to impress girls with myths about serial killers? Aren't you better than that?"

Jared shifted around next to me, but I couldn't face him. Thandie reached down by her desk and opened a drawer. "Here," she said, holding out a photocopied booklet with a staple in one corner. "Will that be all?"

Jared checked his watch as I accepted the booklet, forming

theories. "I was gonna show you the museum, but we're late."

"So you'll see yourselves out then." Thandie picked up her pen and we left.

I waited until we got outside, brandishing the pages. "Do I have one of the Carter brother's diaries?"

"Don't get too excited," he warned, even though he was beaming wide enough to split his face in half. "Thandie bought the original for the museum a few years ago from a collector. He claimed it'd been in their family since the brothers were executed in 1932. His grandpa worked at the jail, but there's no proof Wayne Carter really wrote it, or if the brothers existed at all. Fake artefacts show up all the time. Some analysts even think Jack the Ripper's letters were fake."

"Wait, seriously?" I asked. If so, that was my favourite serial killer story blown to bits.

Jared shrugged and I circled back to the murderers in question. "I'm guessing you read the diary. Do you think it's real?" I asked, unzipping my bag and putting the booklet away.

"Probably not," Jared said. "But it's a good story."

We met Libby outside St. Louis Cathedral, a gorgeous Gothic structure that was painted white, with three spiky, black spires and slender columns.

Libby held out a paper bag for each of us, and I inhaled the sugary goodness. "What's this?"

"A local pastry called a beignet," Libby said. "Wait until you taste it."

"Can we always greet each other with pastries?" I asked, taking a bite of the fried delicacy.

"Sure, where's mine?" Libby asked, smirking as we set off at a slow pace. Somehow, Jared's beignet was gone, and his lips were glazed with powdered sugar. I refused to let myself open that door.

Instead, I said, "I assume you ate it."

Libby held up the last bag. "If Lucas doesn't get here soon, I might eat his."

"No, you won't," Lucas said, arriving to rescue his bag just in time.

"Did you see Della?" I took another fluffy bite, chewing slowly.

"Yeah, I didn't stay long though," Libby said. "Her creepy boss was there."

"You think he's creepy," Lucas corrected mildly. "He seems fine to me."

Libby leaned her cheek against Lucas's arm. "You like everybody."

Finishing my beignet, I soaked in the surroundings. People lounged on benches and milled around in the sunshine, with the cathedral on one side and the greenery of Jackson Square on the other.

Further around the square, we passed a row of red-brick buildings with two floors of metal balconies that were decorated with swirling patterns.

Towering oaks cast us in welcome shade. Artists had set up their wares along the spiky, metal fence, so we ambled by paintings and stands of beaded earrings glittering in the sunlight. Some stalls sold Gothic souvenirs: spiked wristbands, dainty bird skull earrings and even silk corsets.

"Lucas shows his stuff along here," Jared said. "He's good too." He was all proud and oblivious of the flush along Lucas's cheeks.

Jared drifted ahead to Libby, where she was examining a display of scrunchies and rubber bangles.

"What kind of art do you do?" I asked Lucas, remembering what Jared had said about him being worth the effort.

"I paint, mostly," he said quietly, examining an enormous image of a waterfall. "What do you think of this?" He leaned in closer to the painting.

I had no experience of talking about art, but I gave it a go. "I like the shades of turquoise and the glossy effect."

He nodded intently, like what I said was worth hearing, which made his blond hair flop into his eyes. He really was cute, with his big, blue eyes set against all that artistic intensity. His fingers twitched into a V by his side like he wanted to smoke. I was glad he didn't. "It's a clear lacquer that brings out the colour in the paint and makes it last longer." He barely made eye contact with me. His shyness was endearing. "That's what I love about art – it can last for ever."

"I've never thought about it like that."

"Hey . . . Sorry if I freaked you out last night," Lucas said, and I recalled the split second when I thought he was bleeding. "For some reason, I mixed the paint with my hands . . . I was drunk," he finished, sheepish.

"I guessed," I said.

Lucas smiled, his head dropping to one side. His attention landed on the next stall, and I squinted to read the sign. "Wanna get your fortune told?" he asked.

"Why not? Are you coming with me?"

"No thanks," Lucas said quietly, his floppy hair falling down again. "I'm fine not knowing."

A white tent hid the fortune teller, so I had to approach the peeled-back strip of canvas at the front. The guy behind the table was dressed in black, with long sleeves and trousers. He was younger than I expected, with light brown skin and hair dyed black. His face was intelligent and fine-boned, with a politely blank expression.

On the table was a square of velvet scattered with bones. I knew it was all fake – I wasn't that gullible. The sight of the bones did kindle my curiosity.

"Would you like me to read your fortune?" His guttural accent sounded real, though I was no expert. It had a touch of Gary Oldman's Dracula, somewhere Eastern European that I couldn't pin down.

Even though I was tempted, there was a big sign by his table that said ten dollars. I had no job yet, and my savings needed to last. "Um, sorry. I don't have the money."

Fleeting desperation touched his features. "What if I can be quick and free?"

That was what every girl wanted to hear. It couldn't have been any way to do business, but it got me to sit. "I can stay for a few minutes."

The bones were about the size of fingers and scraps of leathery skin clung to the rough, beige surface. I wondered what animal they came from and if it was dead when it met the psychic. My palms were damp as I pressed them into my thighs.

Scooping the bones up, he sprinkled them across the velvet. He considered the pattern with unblinking focus while I tried to work him out. What made someone go into this line of work?

"There is a beautiful boy," he said, not taking his eyes from the

46

bones. "You are attracted to him, though it would be easier not to be."

He must have seen me with Lucas and presumed I was into someone who looked like that. He'd got the wrong boy. My traitorous thoughts strayed to the one wandering the stalls with my sister.

"Not all is love and happiness," he said, plucking a bone between two fingers.

I contemplated how the bone might have felt: spongy soft, or chalky and dry. "Really?"

"There is tragedy in the attic: cruel games, with bloody secrets and lies that will change the course of lives."

That was likely his go-to prophecy for scaring the crap out of people. "Thanks a lot," I said. Everyone had a past and some trait in me must have told him to go dark.

The psychic produced a white card as I stood. "If you need me, Mina. The stall is new – you can usually find me at this address."

My name sounded strange in his accent. Lucas must have said it within his earshot. The card had his address on it, but I knew the name 'Armand' was fake. So he got his accent from *Dracula* and name from *Interview with the Vampire*. Who was I to judge? I stuffed the card in my backpack and went to find Libby.

She was examining a stall selling sparkly butterfly hair clips. I thought her tastes must have changed a lot until I saw her holding a pair decorated with bats.

"So, do you have any lottery wins in your future?" she asked, paying for the clips and stuffing them into her handbag.

"No, just chaos and destruction."

"Just an average day in our house then."

As soon as we returned to Libby's, we headed to our own rooms and I picked up the diary.

The photocopied pages were grey and crumpled at the edges, as though someone had read and reread them many times – most likely Jared. If this was a hoax, it was an elaborate one, with pages of careful, flowing handwriting. I curled up on the bed to read.

May 22nd 1932

I love my brother very much, but at times he frightens me. He paces the apartment now, talking fanatically to himself.

Earlier tonight, we stumbled out of a speakeasy onto Pirate's Alley when the sun had long since set. My whole body was relaxed by drink. The infamous pirate Jean Lafitte had stalked these streets over a century ago. I wish I had known we would stumble upon a different beast.

At that late hour, the deserted alley was unlit and oppressive, with metal balconies closing in from overhead and fingers of thick mist which swirled at our feet. The conversations of revelers and glorious chaos of jazz were far away.

A feminine cry broke through the quiet night, so John and I rushed to save her. We drew up when we realized our mistake. She was not the victim.

A silhouette moaned against an alley wall, where a young woman's face was buried in the throat of an older man. Her fair hair was silver in the moonlight. She ripped her mouth free with a spurt of blood, teeth saturated with gore. I shouted for her to let him go, fright betraying me with the lightest tremor.

The girl's laugh was low and unhinged. She dropped the man on the ground, and he lay there moaning, hands clasped to the remains of his throat. Blood spilled over his fingers. He took a strangled breath and did not move again.

The woman bared her bloody teeth. Her modest dress fell below the knees and was topped with a frilly collar. Lacy, once-white fabric was stained red. Sickly blood mingled with our fish stench and the citrus cologne John uses to disguise it.

We ran like the Devil was behind us. Breath came in an uneasy rush and my beliefs crashed against one another, reshaping into unsettling new ones.

"What was she?" I asked, fearing how John would reply.

"A vampire, brother."

*Whilst I've written this entry, John's endless footfalls
have reassured me his plan is yet to take shape. This
obsession could be his most dangerous yet. I know
my brother well and observed his fascination with the
woman . . . the vampire. I wish this were all some
hallucination, conjured by moonshine and exhaustion.
I fear this is the start of a dangerous new chapter in
John's life, and my own by extension.*

The entry finished there. Had I just read a true account of a
vampire attack? Even though I knew there were authors who
could spin whole worlds out of words, the story was so compelling.
These pages transported me to a grim alley decades ago and the
first seeds of a psychopath's plan to become a vampire.

"Mina!" Libby sounded ratty so I reluctantly left the diary
behind. I had to be on time for my first shift, unless I wanted it to
be my last.

The day had been too busy to worry about the mansion. Now
the night had arrived, so did my nerves.

Chapter 6

At the top of the mansion staircase, the door ahead marked the beginning of the tour. It was the first on a long landing of closed doors. We walked to an open doorway that let out the racket of competing voices. Libby entered the noisy room, but I paused to collect myself. I'd never found a job I wanted this much, and with my sister. All I had to do was prove I deserved to be there. Libby had given me the drill. For now, I had a simple role and only one tour group. Someone else was going to take over my part afterwards. Surely I could handle that without messing it up.

To one side of the room, there were guys getting changed: lean bodies, underwear with names around the bands and hairy legs. I'd seen it all before, but one boy at a time was enough for me.

Libby whisked me onto the girls' side, where the air

was sticky with hairspray and thick with perfume. A wooden divide separated us from the boys, though it didn't keep my imagination at bay. The girls introduced themselves, but it was a lot to take in.

"I wanted to introduce you to Heather, but she isn't here yet," Libby said, standing on her tiptoes to survey the room. "She's such a flake."

"Heather?" I asked.

"The girl who's taking over the meat locker after you. She'll need the dress when you're done with it."

Someone put a cassette into the stereo and 'Basket Case' by Green Day blared out, reflecting my state of mind. People sang and chatted as Libby handed me a yellow scrap of fabric.

Slipping into my dress, the slash across my stomach was a dead giveaway – I was a victim. At least the attacker got the outfit rather than my guts.

Libby was in her tuxedo dress by the time I faced her. "Where are my shoes?" I asked.

"You don't get any," she said.

So my girl fled from a killer armed with only a summer dress.

Libby smeared mousse through my hair to tame the curls. We got to the door as Jared appeared in his Lestat getup. I should have been used to the sight of him in that outfit, but my brain supplied a flashback of him hovering behind me and his lips grazing my neck.

"Can you do my make-up?" he asked Libby, noticing me. "Nice outfit."

"Bite me," I said.

He chuckled. "Not tonight."

"Come here," Libby said. Jared held out a bowl of red, cherry-scented paste.

Libby dipped a make-up brush into the fake blood, and I felt a twinge of jealousy. Even though there was no chance of Libby liking him, it could've gone the other way. It was always girls for her, from Lisa Bonet in *The Cosby Show* to people at school. That didn't stop boys from wanting her, sometimes the ones I liked.

"You're done," Libby said. "Don't lick it."

He produced an eye pencil from his pocket, and she lined and smudged like an expert. I shouldn't have stared when his eyes were shut, but I couldn't help it. His bone structure was so distinctive, all strong lines along his brow and cheekbones. I also liked the small details: the tiny kink at the top of his nose and the white shadow of a scar on his upper lip.

Once Libby finished, Jared had a question for me. "Did you read the diary yet?"

It was strange to have a normal conversation while he was dressed like that. The surface was all seduction, with his usual sweetness underneath. "Just the first entry."

"And . . .?" he asked, giving a smirk that was more Lestat's than his own.

"It's very intriguing," I said, not wanting to show my hand until I'd read more.

"Diary?" Libby cut in.

"Wayne Carter's," Jared said.

Libby groaned. "Don't get him started on that again!"

Anything close to studying bored Libby, while it only made me like Jared more.

Luckily, Libby took me to the perfect place to cool off – the meat locker from *The Texas Chainsaw Massacre*. On the way, she laid out what I needed to do and not do. Most importantly, if I touched somebody, it was over. Thandie's rules were absolute, though Jared wasn't playing by them yesterday.

"Good luck," Libby said from the doorway. "You'll be great."

"Thanks," I said.

The metal door closed behind her. Cold air pumped in from somewhere and goosebumps prickled on my arms. I studied the plastic hunks of meat and body bags on meat hooks. White wax mimicked fat on the meat and a sickly, rotten stench came in with the cold. With all of these touches, I saw how this place could get under my skin. I even felt a creeping paranoia that I wasn't alone.

That was when I was hit in the back.

"My bad! You OK?" a guy gasped, holding the heavy door that did the damage.

"I'm fine," I said, even though my right shoulder ached. It was my fault. I was the genius who stood by a closed door.

"I'm Jason," he said, seeming relieved that he hadn't killed me yet. That part came later.

He was tall and lanky, with curly, black hair and a dimpled smile. He held a mask and a realistic chainsaw.

"Shouldn't you be in the *Friday the 13th* room?" I asked, thinking of the hockey mask wearing killer who shared his name.

"Thandie wouldn't go for it." He tugged the mask over his head. The rubbery flesh took my breath away. It looked like shrivelled pieces of human skin, held together with thick, black stitches. With the mop of brown hair attached to it and his bloodstained shirt, the effect was chilling. "I'd better get into position." He hid behind a massive hunk of meat in the corner. It dangled from a hook, turning slowly.

When the lights went down, the props were even more believable. I slipped easily into character, excited to prove myself.

The door opened with a piercing creak. Della bobbed up behind the group with a quick thumbs-up and I held back a grin. This time, she came to support me.

As instructed, I ignored Libby and targeted a girl at the front of the group. Her hair was blow-dried into a Rachel and she had Jennifer Aniston's poise to go with it. "Please, help me," I gasped. "Did you see him?"

"Him who?" she asked, flipping her hair. She put on a good front, but her gaze flitted between the fake meat and plastic-wrapped bodies suspended from very real meat hooks.

With a gurgling howl, Jason leaped out and my ear-busting scream rivalled the roar of his chainsaw.

Chaos tore the group apart. Libby had told me to lead them towards the exit while she herded from the sides, but it was a challenge. We had to push between the body bags and hunks of meat. The rotten meat stench was so thick that my skin felt scaled with it.

I forced my bare shoulder between two body bags, static rippling over my skin. All around me were slack faces and dead eyes captured behind the clear plastic. The shrieking hoard pushed from behind me. Their exhilaration fed mine.

When the gauntlet was over, I sagged to one side as the crowd rushed past, squealing and elated. Della slowed down to whisper, "Good job, girl."

Libby jogged past, sparing me a wink before she let the screaming group into the next room.

As soon as the door shut, Jason sprang up. Adrenaline flared and my hands made fists. God, that mask was realistic. I once read about a murderer called Ed Gein, an inspiration for *The Silence of the Lambs*. He stitched fragments of human skin together to make gloves, a lampshade and even a dress for his mother.

Jason whipped the mask off and his skin glistened with sweat. He was so smiley that my fingers unclenched. "You did good – I'll be sure to tell Thandie. I gotta help out with the Chuckie tech, do you need to get to another room?"

"No, that's it for me." I had a strong desire to put on shoes and shorts. "I need to find Heather."

Taking the stairs two at a time, I fantasised about getting paid to do this if Thandie approved of my performance.

The landing was quiet, with everyone else playing their roles on the tour. I heard shrieks and relieved laughter from somewhere on this floor. Heather wasn't in the hallway, so I tried the changing rooms. Both sides were empty.

I was planning to change out of the dress when I heard quiet footsteps. By the time I got into the hallway, no one was there. From this angle, I was facing up a steep flight of stairs with an open door at the top.

It was hard to pinpoint what made me go up there. I had to find Heather, and she could've been upstairs. I also relished the prospect of exploring the mansion.

There was a spot of blood on the second stair, a glossy jewel that was still wet and crimson on the grey carpet. If I'd been anywhere else, I would've guessed someone had a nosebleed or sliced their hand on a prop. Since this was the mansion, Thandie was probably working on a new room.

I didn't really expect to find Heather up there, but it gave me a good excuse to snoop around. Further up the stairs, there was more blood – a splash this time.

I brushed off the touch of doubt and went on. That was when I saw the pool of blood at the top of the stairs.

Chapter 7

It could've been one of Thandie's sets: just a mannequin surrounded by blood and soaked in it from head to toe.

The sickly, metallic stench gave it away, scouring the back of my throat. There was a clean, citrus scent too, but it wasn't enough to hide the decay. A girl was dead.

More details struck me in fragments sharp as broken glass. She was on a chair, with chains wrapped around her body that cut snaking paths through the blood. Her lips were parted, and a gash split her throat. The blood disguised who she was, if I knew her at all.

Logic rushed back in and I yelled, "Help!" It came out loud enough to hurt my throat. I heard people running up the stairs as I noticed how close my toes were to the blood. It was so thick, with clumpy clots in it.

I turned to face Jared and a couple of the other boys, but they stared past me. Jared's eyes widened as they took in the whole bloody tableau.

After the silence came a surge of questions. "Is she alive? Did somebody phone a fucking ambulance?"

"Is that *Heather*?" Jason asked. She was the girl who was supposed to cover the meat locker after me. So I did find her – just too late.

Shock must have protected me, otherwise I would've crumpled in a crying heap. Libby and Della joined the group, and my sister wrapped me in a hug. All I could feel was the pressure on my ribs and air squashed from my lungs. I was as empty as Heather.

Thandie ushered the witnesses into the kitchen. The tour had ended, so the customers had left without seeing anything. Lucky them.

The unlucky few of us sat around a glossy marble table, in a room so clean and white that I couldn't see much cooking going on. The only vivid colour was a vase of magenta flowers in the window, with petals the shape of fingerprints.

The six of us sat there, stunned into silence, while Thandie waited to one side. She was rigid with fury. Libby grabbed my hand, and her skin was damp. Her eyes never left me, as if she could protect me from what had already happened.

Della was on her other side. Her face showed no sign of anxiety, but her hands wrung her skirt under the table. I felt like that skirt. The night had bent me out of shape, and I could never go back to who I was before. I wished I had folds of fabric to clutch like Della. I tugged on the skirt of my skimpy costume, holding my feet off the cold marble tiles.

Jason and Connor weren't coping well. Jason had his head in his hands and Connor shook, swiping his fingertips over his damp cheeks. His tuxedo was rumpled, with orange make-up on the collar.

Jared's Lestat outfit looked as out of place as mine felt, and his eyes were unfocused. He knew Heather, so he had to feel worse than I did. Earlier today, Heather was like us, thinking and breathing and living. Now, her dead body was upstairs.

"I'm sorry," Libby whispered, hanging on to my hand. "I shouldn't have asked you to come here."

"How were you supposed to know this would happen?" I answered automatically, though my attention was elsewhere. Any of us could have ended up dead instead of Heather. It could've been Libby, or me.

We must have all been thinking about her. Jason said, "I can't believe she's gone."

The silence stretched on until Connor broke it. "Do you think we can get our clothes?" he asked, gesturing at his tuxedo. He was crying and I understood the urge to move, to reach out for normal, familiar things after what we'd seen.

"Absolutely not," Thandie said. "We can't have you wandering the house before the police arrive."

A killer had walked through this house, possibly while we were in it. We could've trampled evidence that might've led them to Heather's murderer.

I was almost relieved when two suited detectives walked in. I needed to get out of my head.

The first one was young, blond and white, with a square jaw like a Hollywood quarterback. His hair was parted on one side so it fell in his eyes, which were very well-meaning and blue. He was so tall that he had to duck slightly to get into Thandie's kitchen. The older detective was a black woman with her hair scraped back, exposing defined cheekbones and large, almost black eyes that appraised each of us. She was a lot shorter than the other detective but carried herself with more self-confidence and authority. One hand rested on her hip, pushing back the front of her jacket to expose the detective's badge on her belt.

"My name is Detective Boudreaux, and this is Detective Cafferty." Her voice was pleasant and precise. She talked slowly, as if she measured every word to ensure not a single one was wasted. "I'm not planning to keep y'all here long. I know this must be very difficult. Ordinarily, we'd separate witnesses in a case like this . . ." She deferred to Thandie with a patient pause. Everything about the detective was control and poise.

"That won't be possible," Thandie said. "There's nowhere to go, unless you'd like to leave a scared teenager alone in a scene from a horror movie."

Boudreaux nodded, unperturbed. "Fine. I'll interview one witness at a time, and Detective Cafferty will stay with the rest."

Cafferty gave a disgruntled scowl but recovered quickly, offering a terse nod.

"When did the members of the public leave?" Boudreaux asked Thandie.

"They'd left when Mina . . . screamed," Thandie said. "I take contact details when they book tickets – I can find them for you."

"That would be very helpful." Boudreaux turned eyes on me that were compassionate but alert. "Mina?" I nodded. "You found the body? I'm sorry about that."

Her sympathy seemed genuine, and it threatened to break through the weak shell that held me together.

"She's a minor," Thandie said. "I believe that means she can't be interviewed alone."

"I'll go with her." Libby got to her feet. "She's my sister."

"You can use my office." Thandie sounded thrilled.

Boudreaux sat on the visitors' side of Thandie's desk with us, her back dead straight but eyes full of understanding. Libby took my hand again, and my fingers slid between hers.

"When you're ready, Mina, can you tell me what happened when you found the body?" Boudreaux had her pen out but concentrated on me. I noticed a simple gold band on her ring finger. Did she have a family who supported her after days like this, maybe even a daughter Heather's age?

I went back to her question. "I finished my part in the tour, so I went up to get my clothes." The scene replayed in my mind. It was like watching a horror movie and waiting for the bloodshed, though so much worse because I lived through it.

"I came out of the changing room and noticed blood on the stairs." My throat thickened. "I only saw a drop at first and I didn't know . . . I thought it was from another set in the mansion."

"What happened next?" Boudreaux asked, still not writing. She had a reassuring way about her, but nothing could make this any easier.

"There was more blood near the top of the stairs. I knew what happened when I . . . saw her." Libby gave my hand a series of pulses in wordless support.

Boudreaux made a few quick notes and I waited, dreading the next question.

Boudreaux stopped writing. "What did you see in the attic?"

Blinking hard, I found the words. "I saw the girl . . . Heather sitting on a chair. There was blood . . . everywhere . . . all over her and the floor."

"Did you go into the room?" Boudreaux asked, and the mood intensified.

"No," I said. "Someone had . . . Her throat was . . . cut. There was a lot of blood. I could see she wasn't alive." I tried to breathe in and my lungs felt too small, like a pair of deflated balloons. Heather deserved justice, and I couldn't do anything to help.

"When did the others arrive on the scene?" Boudreaux asked, quick and efficient now.

"When I yelled," I said. I wanted to crawl into bed at Libby's and close my eyes on this day.

"What did you yell?" Boudreaux was still kind, but there was steel behind it.

It was the strangest thing; I couldn't remember. I pictured the room again, and it was too much. "Help," I said quietly, not sure whether it was true.

"Last question," Boudreaux said. "You're doin' well. Did you know Heather?"

"No," I said. I only saw her when she was dead.

"Thank you, Mina," Boudreaux said, too busy writing to notice my tears. "Can you go on back to the kitchen while I speak with your sister?"

"Can't I stay with her?" I asked.

Boudreaux finally looked at me, without commenting on the tears. "It doesn't work that way, I'm afraid. She's an adult."

And I was a child to her. Too wound up to respond to Boudreaux,

I said, "Good luck, Libs."

I didn't go into the kitchen like Boudreaux told me. I sat on the skeleton chair to wait for Libby. Above me, the house bustled with activity. Every so often, a person all in white or a uniformed police officer jogged down the stairs and out of the front door, or came in from outside and up the stairs. No one paid me much attention.

Boudreaux returned with Libby a few minutes later. If she was aware I ignored her instructions, she decided not to mention it.

"Detective Boudreaux said we can collect our clothes," Libby said.

"An officer will see y'all up there," Boudreaux confirmed and went to the kitchen to claim her next interviewee.

Libby headed upstairs, so sure I'd follow. I did, wondering if she noticed the blotches where tears had dried on my cheeks or cared how this had affected me.

A uniformed female officer greeted us as we went into the changing room. Libby closed the door and we changed fast, hanging our dresses on the rail.

I had no intention of looking up at the attic again, but when we left the changing room, the stairs were right there in my eyeline. The blood wasn't visible from here, but even the stairs stirred up a vivid flashback. People moved around at the top of them, and all I thought about was Heather.

"Are you two OK?" Jared's question made me jump, but at least it drew my thoughts out of the attic.

"Fine and dandy," Libby said for both of us.

Jared frowned, glancing at me. "I'll see you downstairs then."

Boudreaux was flying through the interviews. She was in the hallway walking Della back when we got downstairs.

That was when the interviews had an unscheduled break. A

guy dressed in white overalls hurried down the stairs behind us. "Detectives!" he wheezed. I'd watched enough movies to guess he was some kind of crime-scene investigator. "Y'all need to see this."

"Go on back to the kitchen," Detective Boudreaux ordered.

We waited quietly, and soon Jared joined us. The others whispered about when they could get out of here or grab their stuff. I listened to the hushed conversation in the hallway. I caught only mumbled phrases, and it made me edgy. Thandie leaned against a counter, pinching the bridge of her nose.

"How're you doin'?" Della murmured, sympathetic eyes on me. She'd been quietly composed up to that point, but her tiredness was showing.

"I'm coping." I'd had a lot of practice at stock responses, the ones that reassured other people. I had my mum and dad to thank for that.

Boudreaux and Cafferty strode back into the room. She had a clear, plastic bag in her hand. It contained a bloody hairball.

Detective Boudreaux sounded exhausted as she said, "Mina and Elizabeth – we need a few strands of your hair."

Libby looped her fingers around a thin strand of hair and yanked, but I asked, "What's this about? Why us?" Detective Cafferty held out an open evidence bag and Libby released her hair. The strands fluttered into the bag, and Cafferty sealed it.

"This was found in the victim's hand," Boudreaux answered, holding up the bag.

Under all that blood, Heather's hair was light blond. The hair in the plastic bag was curly and dark – like ours.

Chapter 8

Detective Boudreaux extended another bag towards me. "Yours too, please."

It was only hair, what was the big deal? Still, my hand shook as I twined a strand around my finger and pulled it out.

"Excuse me ma'am, but doesn't hair transfer real easy?" Della asked. "There are a lot of ways it could've gotten up there."

"The victim's hand was closed around it," Boudreaux said as I released my hair into the bag. I wanted to point out that the victim was called Heather, but she went on. "She must have grabbed the hair when she was alive." Boudreaux pinched her gloved fingers along the top of the bag, sealing my future inside with the hair.

"Do any other members of staff have long, curly brown hair?" Boudreaux asked Thandie.

"No," Thandie said sourly.

"In that case, you're all free to go. Thank you for your help – we may be in touch again. We'll be in the attic."

Cafferty scanned the room, and our gazes caught. There was a familiar quality about him. I almost had it when Boudreaux added, "Thank you for y'all's cooperation."

They left the room. All I could think of was Heather, there in the attic but absent at the same time. That brought back what the psychic said, and I hurried after the detectives. If there was even a small chance Armand was genuine, I had to speak up.

I caught up as Boudreaux was mounting the stairs. "I remembered something."

She retreated reluctantly.

"I talked to a fortune teller earlier. He told me a tragedy would take place in an attic." The second I said it, I wished I'd stayed in the kitchen.

Boudreaux was a professional, and her face remained mostly composed. A small sigh escaped. "Thank you," she said. "We'll look into that." That was unlikely, without his name or contact information.

The second we were out in the starless night, Libby laid into me. "Why did you stop them for that?"

"For what, the truth?" I asked.

"We should stay out of it. They're not going to follow up on a phony psychic. Why give them more excuses to look into us?"

"I was trying to help, but we can do it your way." I was only the annoying little sister. What did I know?

There was no chance of sleep when the four of us got back. Libby and Della went into Libby's room and closed the door. As always, if Libby wasn't in the mood to talk, that was the end of it.

Lucas surfaced from his room, bringing the chemical scent of oil paint. His fingers were stained with paint the deep purple of bruises, and there were matching circles under his eyes. "What happened?" he asked.

Jared rubbed his eyes with one hand, and they were bloodshot when he released them. "A girl who works at the mansion was found dead."

Libby shouted from her bedroom, but I followed the boys into the kitchen. Jared told Lucas the whole story, and I let him talk.

Lucas blinked hard and stuck a hand in his pocket, withdrawing a cigarette packet. He passed it from hand to hand without removing one. "I can't believe they took your hair."

"The police know what they're doing," Jared said. "They have to follow every lead, but this is obviously a dead end."

"Sure," Lucas agreed. "Everything happens for a reason."

Experience told me otherwise. The last time I was involved with the police was when Mum went missing. They didn't find her and concluded she went off without us.

Libby hurried into the kitchen with a clatter of heels on the wooden floor and a wide, black velvet choker around her neck. "You're not dressed," she said, looking my day-old clothes up and down.

"For what?" There was no dress code for talking about what we'd been through.

"Della's covering the bar for a couple of hours, so I'm going with her." There was a long, telling pause. "Why don't you come?"

"I was hoping we could stay here and talk about what happened."

Libby's eyes flitted to Lucas and then Jared. What a catastrophe if they caught us discussing our feelings. "Can't we go for a drink and forget about it?"

"I don't want to forget about it!" I raised my voice, and Lucas flinched. He and Jared could've escaped, but they were frozen in place. "I found a dead body! Don't you see how hard it was for me? I just wanted to talk to you about it!" I was so furious that my face ached.

Libby's arms snapped into the defensive, folded position. "You never even met Heather," she said, so dismissive and patronising that I wanted to scream. "I hardly said two words to her. It's sad that she died, but we can't wreck our lives over it."

"Fine," I said, burying my fury. If she was going to treat me like a child, I wouldn't give her the satisfaction of acting like one. "You go. Have a great time."

Della came into the kitchen, standing beside Libby. "I'm just working. Sounds like you might be needed here."

"No, we're done."

Libby's heels hit the hallway floor like bullets, but Della paused to say, "I'll talk to her."

Jared waited until they were gone. "Wow. I used to fight with my sisters, but that was somethin' else."

"I'm glad you're impressed," I mumbled.

"That was nothing," Lucas said, with a wry twist that was more grimace than smile. "By the time me and my dad finish, we're hoarse from screaming."

"Sorry, that's rough," I said.

Lucas lost eye contact, blinking hard. He stood up. "I have to finish before my paints dry. Do you mind . . .?"

I shook my head, and he left.

"So, what are we doing?" Jared asked.

My face warmed. There were a lot of possible answers to that question, but I went for the safest one. "The psychic said there were bloody secrets in the attic. I think he knew about the murder before it happened." It was hard to come across matter of fact while I was replaying finding Heather's body.

"You believe a psychic can help us?" Jared asked. If this were *The X-Files*, he was the cynical, sexy Scully. That made me Mulder, the one with the far-fetched theories.

"The police won't talk to him. Someone has to find out what he knows."

"And that someone has to be us," Jared said.

"It can't hurt if we go," I said, "but it could do some harm if we don't."

When I stood up, Jared did exactly what I anticipated. He was on his feet almost as fast as I was, though his got tangled and he staggered to right himself.

"Fine," he said. "I'm coming with you. Not because I believe him," he added. "Someone's killing young girls, and you fit the profile." That was troubling, but I wasn't going to let it paralyse me. I grabbed Armand's card from my room. If he'd finished work for the day and it was a wasted journey, at least we were moving forwards rather than pretending tonight never existed.

On the quiet street, the air was humid and heavy. The sky was black and only a pocket of light came from each house. I focused on the uneven path, but soon circled back to Heather and the girl who died at the convent.

There was no wind, and the only sound was two pairs of

footsteps. I listened out for a third. An alleyway ran alongside each house. If someone jumped us, would we be able to defend ourselves? My pulse was loud, and I grew more and more alert as we passed every inky-black space.

Jared must have read some of that from my face. "I'll protect you," he said in a deep, superhero voice that couldn't have been serious.

"Guys get murdered too, you know," I said.

"Statistically, serial killers prefer women," he said.

"Reassuring," I said, staring into the depths of an alley and hoping someone wasn't staring back at me. "Do you think that's what we're dealing with?"

"No," he said. "Most killers go after someone they know. Actual serial killers are rare."

Bleak as our conversation was, it occupied me long enough for us to reach civilisation. This street was cloaked in grey and shadows. At the crossroads ahead, the streetlights gave off an orange glow and people crossed our deserted road.

"So, what do we say to Armand?" I asked.

"We find out if he has any information and hand it to the cops," Jared said, spinning the ring round his thumb. "Mostly, I'm thinking if this guy is full of shit, how did he know about the attic?"

Chapter 9

Jared was right: how could Armand have known about the girl before she died? "Are we making a stupid mistake?" I asked.

"Wouldn't be a first for me," Jared said, drawing to a halt.

Armand's door was made of sun-bleached wood with fragments of black paint clinging to it. The number '45' was crooked and rusted.

Nobody else would come to find out what he knew. I knocked as hard as I could before I chickened out.

Armand opened the door stiffly, his nose wrinkled in the very image of confusion. He didn't predict our visit – not a good start.

"Sorry, are you open?" I asked. Jared's question had shaken me up, and the pieces hadn't quite formed a picture yet. There had to be a way

Armand could've known someone would be murdered in an attic. I could only think of very troubling ones.

"It's late, but since you're here . . ." Armand said, letting the words drag as though we were terribly dull and inconvenient. His Eastern European accent was thicker than before. "I suppose you might as well come in."

He led us through a dingy hallway that smelled of damp and into a white room. A black swirl of mould had unravelled across one corner of the ceiling, and the room contained only a lopsided table and four chairs.

There was a pile of large cards on the table. The top card had a purple geometric pattern in the background and a stark, realistic painting of a cat's skull in the centre.

"I can pay you this time," I said.

"Call it five dollars," Armand said, with a flick of his hand. "This won't take long." He had rings on three fingers and the black jewels caught the light from the exposed bulb overhead.

I opened my backpack and pulled a five-dollar bill from my purse. I placed the note on the table, and Armand ignored it.

He laid the cards out with nimble fingers. "You each seek an answer to the same question."

"Yeah, we do. A girl was found dead in an attic, which is a lot like the prediction you gave me. How did you know?" I asked.

Armand trailed his fingers over the cards. "I could have a police informant, and I do read the newspaper from time to time."

"But you knew *before* the murder."

"Or you had something to do with it," Jared added.

"If that's what you think, it makes you either very brave or foolish to approach me."

Armand gave no indication that we were getting through to him, but I kept on going. "Why didn't you . . .?" Anger snuffed out my question.

"Why didn't I prevent the murder?" His shoulders drooped. He might have cared more than he let on. "Sometimes I read minds in the present or see images in the past and future. I can't control it, and I can't always tell the difference. Besides, I've tried to warn the police before. It did not go down well."

Armand pointed a manicured finger at Jared. "You aren't convinced. Choose a card."

Jared sighed, consulting his watch.

Running a finger along the fan of cards, Armand continued, "If you don't believe me, you have nothing to lose."

Jared's leg jumped repeatedly under the table as he took a card.

It displayed a tiny battlefield, with severed heads and limbs painted in muted tones against gaudy splashes of crimson. There was definitely no good news in the image.

Armand inspected the card and then Jared. "I see death but also healing. Despite your prickly appearance, you care for people. You have declared your future, in fact, towards that end. Would you like me to share the reason with your girlfriend?"

Jared snapped before I could correct Armand, "No – you've made your point."

Whether or not Armand was genuinely psychic, we needed to find out everything he knew. "Say we believe you," I said. "What else can you tell us about the murder?"

"I saw a girl in an attic who was drenched with blood. Her life was ended by a blade, and you were there. That's why I saw it – your presence connected the two points in time. That is all."

My jaw hurt like I'd been clenching it. That couldn't have been everything he knew.

Luckily, Jared kept the questions going. "How do you know a blade ended her life?"

Armand's reply came in fragments. "She was cut from here to here." He demonstrated, sliding a finger across his Adam's apple. My throat seized up in sympathy. "She must have been alive when it was cut, as the wound continued to bleed. There were also bite marks along here." He moved his fingers down the left side of his neck, from below his ear to the jutting line of his collarbone.

"She was bitten?" I asked. I would've said what was done to her couldn't get worse, but there it was.

"As I said," Armand replied.

I didn't want him to shut down completely, so I moved on. "Do you know anything about the girl who was found outside the Ursuline Convent?"

Armand exhaled and visibly deflated. "My ability does not work on command. That's everything. I wish I could help more." His cold tone suggested otherwise.

I wanted to fling his cards across the room and demand answers, but either he couldn't help or he wouldn't. I made one final attempt. "Is there anything else that could help us?"

"I have a contact who may be helpful." Armand spoke hesitantly, and his confidence faltered with his accent. I knew it! "You can find him at a bar called Empire of the Dead. Attend their Vampires and Victims party tomorrow night, dressed as Lestat and Claudia, and I'll tell him to find you."

Armand's skill was getting to me. Surely it wasn't a coincidence that he suggested Jared's costume and the place where Della works.

"Won't other people dress like them?" I asked. Jared was especially gorgeous as Lestat, but it'd take more than a costume for me to resemble Claudia.

"I see passion and the two of you dancing close. Play those parts well, and he'll find you."

"Isn't Lestat more of a father figure to her?" I asked, trying to ignore the thrill I got at the image of me and Jared getting up close and personal.

Armand's smile was playful. "You two ask a lot of questions. That's how I see you behaving – perhaps you're doing what you want to do and not what they do."

"And you're not telling us who this contact is?" Jared asked.

"I must ask his permission. Do as I said, and he will find you."

"Fine," Jared said. "Thanks for your help." Jared wasn't quite as enthused about Armand's plan as I was.

"Be careful," Armand called after us. With his unnamed contact and getting us all dressed up, Armand was definitely playing with us. So why did I get the impression he wasn't enjoying the game?

My questions buzzed around as I tried to separate the truth from Armand's performance. Jared walked fast, eyes trained on the pavement. A definite trigger sent him spiralling. "What did Armand mean about you healing people?"

"I've decided to major in nursing," he said dully. "Any ideas what you want to study at college, or university, I guess you call it?"

"I don't even know if I'll go." Usually when I admitted that, judgment followed, like university should've been everyone's dream. Jared just waited for me to continue. "To be honest, I don't have any idea what I want to do." A lot of people went to university to branch out from home. I wanted to find somewhere to put down roots.

"Don't worry. It took me ages to work it out," Jared said.

It gave me some confidence that I wasn't the only one who was unsure about my future. That brought me back to our present. "Do you believe Armand can do what he claims?"

"No . . . Yeah . . . I don't know. I don't want to."

"He's good," I said. "I mean, he might've spotted you dressed as Lestat at the mansion, or carrying around a nursing textbook, but there were things he couldn't have seen."

"He said the girl was bitten," Jared said. "If that story comes out, it suggests he's genuine."

"That's smart," I said.

"Didn't you know that about me?" Jared grinned.

It felt good to grin back, though it didn't last. "If he's right, that's sick. I mean, biting someone is another level of disturbing."

"Yeah, it's messed up." Jared was so quiet that I almost missed his reply. "So, we're going to Empire for the party tomorrow. Let's see if Armand's friend approaches us and go from there. If he tells us anything, we can take it to the police."

This wasn't the first time I'd turned amateur detective, and it had failed before.

When Mum vanished, I'd refused to believe she left like everybody said. There were signs she went by choice: the case missing from the bottom of her wardrobe, the empty drawers and the gap on the rail where her wardrobe used to be stuffed with clothes.

There were also things she should've taken: brown pill bottles in her mirrored cabinet and expensive skincare products she'd saved up for. Armed with minor clues and stubbornness, I investigated her disappearance.

It was a long time since I'd read Nancy Drew books, but I used some of her best tricks. I emptied Mum's bin, finding only Opal Fruit wrappers and receipts. There was a stack of abandoned books on her bedside table, with titles like *Understanding the Undead* and *Vampires through History*. There were also vampire novels by Laurell K. Hamilton, Anne Rice and L.J. Smith.

My friends' mums mostly read books with big-haired couples on the front or gossip magazines. It never bothered me what mine read, until she left because of it.

When I flipped through the books, no evidence fell out. Her coats had empty pockets, and handbags contained only the same blunt lipsticks and screwed-up tissues you'd find anywhere. There were no clues at all. Everything in her room smelled faintly of lilies and cigarette smoke. It was like she'd just left.

Libby was furious when she found me digging around in Mum's drawers. She told me our mum had given up on us, and we should do the same. If she found out Jared and I were investigating Heather's death, there was no telling how bad her reaction would be.

The memory faded, and I noticed Jared was watching me. "You OK?" he asked.

"I was thinking Libby will be pissed off if she finds out where we've been."

"You think so?" Jared asked.

"From previous experience? Yeah."

"I guess some people would rather wait for trouble to pass than face it head on," Jared said.

"That's a nice way of putting it," I said. In less than a year, he'd got a good handle on Libby's character. "Any ideas how to deal with that?"

"I tend to let her be." That was what Libby wanted people to do. If we left her alone, she didn't have to face up to anything.

We were almost back when the air began to feel stuffy and thick, crackling with unspent energy. The streets were quiet, but the remaining people picked up the pace. Jared walked faster as well. "There's gonna be a storm," he said. In Whitby, the temperature dropped before a storm, and wind whipped in from the bitterly cold North Sea. Only the swollen sky was the same here.

The first spots of water splashed on my arms. It was almost pleasant compared with the relentless needles of rain at home. Soon, the water hammered on my skin and poured down my face. Jared set off at a clumsy jog, laughing with pure joy. Elated, I skidded over the slippery pavement.

Eventually, Jared unlocked the front door. I followed him into the hallway, shivering.

Jared closed the door and we stood there in silence, looking at each other while water dripped onto the wooden floor. His hair was flattened against his head, wet curls looping over his forehead. The T-shirt was moulded to the slim, defined shapes of his chest and abs. I didn't dare check on my clothes.

Our breathing was loud, and even Jared's eyelashes were spiky from the rain. He headed for the bathroom, watching me.

I stood there, listening to the steady drip of water onto the floor and hoping to recapture that connection. He returned with a towel around his neck. He could've tossed mine at me like a big brother but he wrapped it around me, letting his hands fall on my arms.

With his fingers curved around my bare forearms, I felt a new spark. This wasn't just my feelings. The soft eyes and lingering touch were all him.

The door crashed open, and Jared leaped back. Libby stood there in the doorway, dripping and fuming. Even wet as she was, I smelled the alcohol.

She squinted at the towels and asked with all of the slurry, indignant anger that drinking brings, "Where the hell have you two been?"

Chapter 10

Della followed Libby inside. By the time the four of us sat at the kitchen table with towels and steaming mugs, Libby was calm enough to speak. She stank of beer, and there was the slightest slur to her question. "Well? Are you going to tell me why the two of you went out at night?"

"You went out too!" I said. "I'm almost eighteen – you don't have to wrap me up in cotton wool."

"Maybe I should!" Libby shot back. "I'm responsible for you!"

"Mina wasn't alone," Della said. "Jared went along."

"Why did the two of you go out?" Libby asked, so withering that Jared opened his mouth but nothing came out.

Sensing this was going to cause another eruption, I kept it brief. "The police weren't planning to follow up on the fortune teller, so we did."

Libby let out a bleak laugh. "You went to see a stranger about a murderer."

"We were going to hand whatever we found to the police, but he didn't give us anything new." Jared's eyes shifted towards me, and I agreed with the small lie. There was no use telling Libby what we'd discovered if this was her reaction.

"There's a surprise," Libby set down her mug and coffee sloshed onto the table. "It's obvious you're not safe here." She rose unsteadily and marched out.

I followed her into the hallway as she snatched the phone off the hook. "Who are you ringing?"

Libby dialled roughly with the phone wedged between her ear and shoulder. "Aunt Sandra."

"She's somewhere in—"

Libby held a hand up to silence me. "Hi, it's Libby. We're both fine, but could you give me a call when you get this? Thanks."

Letting the phone clatter down, Libby said, "It was her answer phone. She said she'd listen to her messages."

"Do you want me to leave?"

"I want you to be safe!" Libby fired right back, raking her hands from the roots of her hair. They got stuck halfway down, and she tugged them free.

"I feel safe," I said, which was strange but accurate. "I couldn't sit around and wait while the police test our hair."

"We didn't do anything!" Libby said. "It'll all be fine." I knew that vacant look from Mum. It was the dismissive one, where nothing was serious and I was at fault for caring. "Anyone want food?"

I shook my head, mostly because Libby's cooking was terrible, but also because I couldn't be around her when she was like this.

"It's been a long day. I should get to bed."

Libby could've taken the opportunity to open up after the day we'd had. "Night."

Footsteps followed me into my room, but they didn't belong to the person who should've come. Della entered and closed the door. She leaned against it. "Wanna talk about it?"

"I'm not the one you need to check up on," I said, sitting on the bed with my legs crossed.

"You're both strong and stubborn," Della said, and it wasn't the first time I noticed how much she loved my sister. Whenever she mentioned Libby, she gave a particular smile that put lights in her eyes.

"I'm glad she has you."

"You do too, if you need me," Della said, and this time her affection was for me. "Libby doesn't like talkin' about emotions – I don't have to tell you that. Even though we don't know each other too well yet, you can come to me."

"Thanks." Libby's first serious girlfriend never showed an interest in me. My friendship with Della had potential. "It's hard . . . she reminds me of our mum when she's like that."

Della took a deep breath and let it out. "Libby told me about her. I get it. I lost my mom . . . She died a few years ago."

"God, I'm so sorry."

Pain made Della's face drawn. "It is what it is. I only brought it up 'cause I wanted you to know I've been there. I never met your mom, but I know one way Libby's not like her. She's not goin' anywhere."

That was where Della was mistaken. Libby had left me once, and this time she was prepared to send me away the second things went wrong. What if the summer ended without us mending our broken relationship?

Della left, and I grabbed the diary from my bedside table. Whoever wrote it understood how fraught sibling dynamics were.

May 24th 1932

I write this with hands too strong and quick to be my own, and a body overcome by new urges. Not the least of these is potent loathing towards my brother. Though I have my thoughts and feelings, he has stolen my life, and for this I can never forgive him.

John was gone all night and swore at me this morning when I tried to wake him for work.

He was in my room when I returned home. He did not say a word, only smiled coldly before he grabbed me. He bit down hard on my neck, holding my arms to my sides when I struggled.

The pain was so severe that I almost fainted, like the tip of a fish hook plunging into my throat and gouging through muscle and sinew. When he tore his mouth away, I collapsed to the floor. I held both hands against the wound and my fingers slipped between ribbons of flesh. Blood cascaded through them, spilling onto my floor. I knew death was imminent, before I discovered why John did this to me.

He crouched down, blood dripping from his gashed wrist. I knew not what he planned until he let the salty drops fall into my mouth. The taste was foul, worse than maggots squirming in rotten fish. He released me and my recollection of the night ends there.

I awoke in the throes of indescribable anguish, a stabbing in my gut akin to a knife cutting from the inside.

Staggering back to bed, I was overwhelmed by the aroma of salt and metal. I clamored to touch the place my brother had ripped apart. My skin was unbroken, though gummy with dried blood.

Understanding came over me with a surge of hysteria, though my heart did not race. My breath did not come fast. I laid a hand on my chest and all was still. John had become a vampire and consigned me to the same fate.

This body is too powerful. Every noise is so loud that even the click of my own bones and the swish of hair against my ear could drive me mad. Worst of all, a clawing sensation dwells in my stomach: a creature that will not let me rest until it is satiated.

I stopped reading mid-entry, distracted. That put my problems with Libby in perspective. Wayne had believed his brother would kill him. Instead, John had violated him. I shuffled down lower into bed, wide awake. The diary wasn't the best bedtime read on top of the day I'd had.

I tried every position, threw my bedding off and back on, and then ended up lying on my back with an exhausted headache threatening to punch through my forehead.

I must have drifted off because I woke with cold sweat gluing the sheet to my skin and the nightmare lingering. Heather was in the chair how I found her, except for some crucial differences. In my nightmare, she clung to the last shreds of life, gasping through a mouth bubbling with blood. Libby stood over her, long strands of hair hanging over Heather's terrified face.

I threw the sheet back. There was no way I could stay in bed. I planted my feet on the cool, wooden floor, leaving condensation prints as I padded across the room. Heading into the hallway, I was drawn to the line of light along the bottom of the kitchen door.

The light hurt my eyes when I stepped into the brightness. They adjusted quickly, so I could focus on Jared reading at the table. There were rings under his eyes and a haunted shape to his features. "Yeah, I couldn't sleep either," he said, closing the book. It was a thick volume about New Orleans.

I sat across from him, noticing the clock. It was after three, so I got some sleep. "Suppose it's understandable." Meanwhile, Libby slept peacefully.

"Since you're here, I have to show you this. What happened in the attic was familiar, so I went through my books. It took a while, but I found it."

Jared thumbed through the book and turned it for me to read. I understood why he didn't want to tell this story aloud. It was about a socialite called Madame LaLaurie, who was famous for her lavish parties and fine home. She and her husband once held a party when a fire broke out upstairs. When guests rushed to extinguish the flames, they found victims chained in their attic. Some were dead and had experienced horrendous torture. There were people with eyes gouged out and mouths stitched shut, others with bones broken and reset in impossible positions. Madame LaLaurie's husband was a doctor, so it was possible they did it all as twisted experiments. I couldn't bear to think about what the living victims must have suffered, waiting in terror and starvation as the others rotted, fearing which awful fate would be theirs.

"OK." I closed the book. "So, two people have died in the same way as New Orleans myths . . ."

"Three," Jared said glumly.

He removed a neatly trimmed newspaper article from the back of the book. I scanned it and recognised the story – it was about Betty Watson, the girl who was murdered with an axe in her own home. "I read this when I first got here. Is that from a myth?"

"The Axeman of New Orleans – a serial killer who was active around 1918. This one is well-documented." Jared told this story without his usual enthusiasm. "He broke into people's homes and murdered them with an axe, usually married couples. Newspapers published a letter, which was supposed to be from him, saying he'd kill again on a particular date in a home that wasn't playing jazz music."

A killer was turning New Orleans mythology against the people who lived there. "You're right, that's three girls," I said. "Betty Watson, Heather and the girl at the convent."

Jared looked washed out and exhausted. "Do you think the police have worked this out?"

"I have no idea," I said. "You saw how they reacted when I mentioned Armand. Could the same person have killed all three girls?"

"Seems that way."

"We could still see if Armand's contact knows anything," I said.

Jared's smile was a ghostly moon compared to its usual brightness. "I was always down for that."

"But we're not telling Libby?"

"She hasn't given us any choice," he said.

"I suppose not. We should try to get some sleep," I said, and we stood at the same time, leaving no table or other barriers between us.

I noticed a hole down one side of his vest where a sliver of bronze skin showed. His hair was in the snarl of sleep and his eyes were heavy, as if we were in a dreamy place where things could occur that we'd never explore in the day. I remembered how it felt when he wrapped the towel around me. This time, Libby wasn't there to derail us.

"You can borrow the book if you want. Night, Mina," he said, drifting out of the kitchen. Great. We had a moment and Jared missed it.

Chapter 11

Back in my room, I saw the Carter diary on my bedside table. I should've left it there – I'd had enough nightmares. Still, I wanted to read what happened next.

> When the sun descended, I sprang from my bed and met John in the hall.
>
> "You feel it too," he said. A youthful smile brightened his face and I despised him less. My brother did this to me because he would have us spend eternity together. "Come, brother."
>
> I must be weak, as I went with him without questioning it. The only way I can

justify what I did next is that the human writing this slumbered whilst I fed. I draft this confession as the potency of stolen life sings in my veins.

We went to Bourbon Street, the beating heart of New Orleans. Tonight, it pulsed with life.

John has varied tastes and his first victim was a beautiful boy, fine-boned and full-mouthed. He beckoned with one finger, and the young man went willingly. John has always charmed people, and this attribute is all the more potent now.

When he and John wandered down a side street, I did not follow. Soon, I caught the ever enticing aroma of spilled blood, but I could not rely on John for this. His method is too savage. I must seek my own.

A woman caught my attention, dressed in an emerald green that glowed in my newly keen vision. Her head was held high, though her fingers twined nervously through her chin-length curls. I do not possess John's charm, and her fate was decided when she changed course for a quiet side street.

I followed. Away from the hubbub of Bourbon Street, her heartbeat was loud, replacing the one I no longer have. She quickened her step.

My conscience clouded my need, but it was not to last. In a few long, quick strides I had grabbed her arms and pushed her to the alley wall.

She begged, gasping and crying so hard that she could not scream. I recalled the first vampire we ever saw: the young woman who took a man's life in front of us. Sickened, and feeling rather like her, I placed a hand over my victim's mouth. The need for her blood crushed all others and I bit down hard.

No sensation compares to it. My fangs sliced through her flesh so effortlessly that I could have been gentle, and spared her some pain. I did not. I tore and maimed, driven by her sobs and the enthralling elixir that surged from her body and into mine. We were connected, and she gave herself to me.

The worst outcome is that I know not if she lived. I must learn to be more careful.

John came to my door just now, laughing until tears fell. They left bloody tracks from his eyes. "You mourn for her? They exist for us to feed, and without their sacrifice, we would die."

"And if I would rather die?"

John leaned on my doorframe. "Brother, I will not

allow it. Ours is a story worth telling, and I have plans to make it legendary."

There were two brothers by the name of Donner, who led a group of travelers from Illinois towards California. Trapped by snow, members of the party resorted to cannibalism to survive. Only half their group reached California the following year. The facts always repulsed me, but now I understand a hunger that vanquishes morality. I dread our story becoming as infamous as the Donner party.

I stopped there, or I might have read into the early hours. The conflict Wayne went through was impossible to face. What would I have done if I had to drink blood to survive? I might have made the same choice as Wayne – trying not to hurt people and taking only what I needed. That was the mark of a talented writer. Whoever put this diary together almost had me convinced.

A few hours later, two unpleasant sensations woke me. My right shoulder was throbbing, and a burnt smell seeped under my door. The pain wasn't much of a mystery. A reddish-purple bruise had blossomed near my shoulder blade, where I lost that fight with Jason and the meat locker door yesterday.

In the kitchen, the mystery of the smell was solved. Libby stirred a mixture that appeared to contain every breakfast ingredient thrown into one pan. She must have been hung-over for that to have seemed like a good idea.

"Morning," she said. "Did you sleep well?"

I'd found a girl who'd been murdered, and she thought there was a chance I'd slept well. If I called her on it, all I'd get was another argument. "Not really," I said.

"Load up on coffee then," Libby said. Nothing cured trauma like caffeine. "We have to pick our costumes for the party at Empire."

It was the opening day of Fang Fest. Recent events had overshadowed it, but the buzz of anticipation returned. Today was all about dressing up and hanging out with my sister.

Libby filled two bowls with the sloppy eggs, beans and bacon. I was glad she didn't bring up phoning Aunt Sandra again. I wasn't ready to leave New Orleans.

I grabbed two spoons, and we sat beside each other. Libby tucked in, and I scooped up a mystery lump with a few beans. Jared's protein shakes were becoming more appetising by the minute. I took a wary bite. Libby's cooking hadn't improved. If anything, it had got worse.

With the breakfast sloshing in my stomach, I left the kitchen. A newspaper fell on the mat, so I grabbed it and retreated to my room to read.

The headline was about as rational as I expected: *Vampire Killer Strikes Fang Fest*. They'd write anything to sell papers; a disturbed individual with a thing about biting wasn't automatically a vampire. I read the facts of the crime scene fast, gaining a fresh supply of flashbacks. The new details made it much worse. Heather was killed somewhere else, brought to the mansion and posed, then covered in blood that wasn't all hers. And at some point before her death, she was bitten.

As I finished reading, there was a knock at the door.

"Come in," I called.

It was Jared, and I was wearing ratty pyjamas again. He came in and shut the door. "I knew you'd have it. Any updates?"

I offered him the paper because it was too early to use words like 'vampire' and 'psychic'.

He accepted it and stood over me to read. Done improbably fast, he dropped onto the bed. He was so casual about it that he had to have no clue how it felt to have him there.

"Armand called it – Heather was bitten," he said. "If you root around long enough in bullshit, you're bound to find the truth eventually. And she wasn't killed at the mansion . . . It's so weird that she ended up back there."

"We should see if there are any updates about the other girls." I'd almost got to the end of the paper when I found a small article about the girl who was attacked outside the convent. There had been no progress in solving her case, but they found out who she was. She was called Ella Tinton and was only Libby's age when she died. The image of her was tiny and it was all her parents had left, along with memories and the chance that the police would find out who killed her.

"Is that all there is?" Jared turned the page. "What about the other girl . . . Betty?"

There was no article about her at all. They must not have come up with the same theory we had – the myths that bound the girls together.

There was another knock on the door, and I took in the sight of Jared sprawled on my bed.

With him in here, that meant Libby was probably out there.

Chapter 12

Libby leaned on the doorframe of my room, her eyes narrowed and devious.

"I was getting this," Jared said, jumping to his feet with the newspaper in his hand.

"Uh-huh," Libby drew the syllables out. "With the door closed."

Jared left so fast he tripped over the metal strip along the bottom of the door. "So, we'll catch up later and head to the mansion?" he asked.

"Yeah," Libby said. She waited until Jared closed his bedroom door. "You and Jared? Why didn't you tell me?" Through the lightness, there was a scrap of hurt.

"There's nothing to tell." Fantasies didn't count.

"But you like him," Libby said.

Other sisters shared secrets and plaited each other's hair. It wasn't natural for us anymore. "I hardly know him."

"Good – he's a little old for you."

"You're both only two years older than me!" I said, making myself look guiltier.

"Whatever you say."

Libby flounced off to her room, and Jared was hiding in his. I was tempted to read more of the diary but opted for human interaction. Music and intriguing rattling came from Lucas's open door, and I hovered there awkwardly. He was playing a song by Silverchair. I'd heard it on the radio. The lyrics were pretty grim – all death and execution – but the singer's voice and repetitive guitar rhythm were mesmerising in the way they came together. Still listening, I tapped my knuckles on the door.

"Hey," he said, smiling up at me from the floor. He pushed back a loop of blond hair that immediately fell down again. His face was drawn and sallow, like he got even less sleep than I did.

There was an open toolkit in front of him and a grey games console in a snarl of wires. "It's Jared's. He got carried away with the controller, but I fixed it. Want to try it out?"

"What are we playing?" I asked, sitting on the floor with him.

"How about *Mario Kart*?"

Lucas turned off the music and battled with the tangled wires, while I took in his room. I hadn't absorbed much during the paint scare. Every surface was covered with artwork: sketches, chalk and different kinds of paint. Each one had the subject's name written in blocky capitals at the bottom. There was one of Libby sticking her tongue out and Jared reading, more of actors like Michael Keaton, Jack Nicholson and Christian Slater. Some I'd never heard of, like a guy with serious cheekbones called Richard Chanfray. There was even one of Leonardo DiCaprio, squinting with a cigarette dangling from his lips. Each piece captured the vibrancy within the subject, not exactly like a photograph but somehow more alive.

Mario Kart was therapeutic, even with the tortoiseshells and banana skins flying all over the place.

"How are things with Libby?" Lucas asked quietly.

I glanced at the door. The tinny game music should have covered most of the conversation, but I wanted to keep Libby out of this. Lucas took the opportunity to snipe me with a red tortoiseshell, and his kart raced by. "Hey!" I said, watching mine spin out of control, and my green dinosaur, Yoshi, with it. "We're fine. She was pissed off at me and Jared for going to the fortune teller."

"You've had a year away from each other," he said. "Give it time."

"You're right," I said. "I'm trying."

"She said your parents aren't around. That puts a lot of pressure on the two of you."

While Lucas chose another racetrack, I checked the door again. Talking about our mum was enough to send me and Libby straight into an argument. Dad was a subject that could tear us apart. Whereas losing Mum was a tragedy, we were better off without him. Libby had two extra years of life with Dad and we remembered things differently. He moved back to America when I was nine. Mum's fascination with vampires slowly descended into an obsession after that.

"Yeah, it does," I said finally. "Do you talk to your parents much?"

Lucas's hands clenched the controller and his toadstool character veered off the racetrack. "There's no point. I used to want to be an actor, and we butted heads over that, but it didn't work out. Then I found art, and that was it. My dad doesn't understand. He wants me to be a carbon copy of him."

"Sorry," I said. Now I knew why people struggled when they consoled me about Mum. It was impossible to make it better.

"I've dealt with it," Lucas said. "That's why I'm sure you and Libby will work it out. I know what fucked up beyond all recognition looks like."

Lucas's kart sped over the line, with his toadstool at the wheel looking very pleased with himself. Most of the other karts zipped past before mine. "Thanks for the races," I said, getting up. My left foot had gone to sleep, and it prickled with pins and needles.

Lucas nodded, selecting his next race. Perhaps he was one of the few people who understood how hard it was to think about the past.

❧

It was dusk when the four of us arrived at the mansion, meeting Della by the door. She gave Libby a hug and we headed inside. The bear-trap chandelier gleamed overhead, and the atmosphere inside was dull and mournful. The last time we were here, the police took samples of our hair. Surely they would've contacted us if the results meant trouble.

"I'm in here." We followed the rasp of Thandie's voice into the kitchen, where she was sipping a drink the colour of pond water.

"Would anyone like some tea?" Thandie was the perfect hostess, even though a murder victim was found right above us. It was hard to predict how it'd affect her business. Events like this were hard to scrub off a place.

"No thanks." Jared answered for us. "Did the police leave?"

"For now. They said we could open tonight, but I think we need a break." Thandie set down her teacup. "What can I do for you?"

"If you don't mind ma'am . . . Can we borrow some clothes for the party at Empire?" Jared asked.

There was an uncomfortably long pause, and then at last she said, "You know where they are. And Mina, the meat locker job is yours if you want it."

"Great," I said, though playing a victim didn't sound as fun anymore.

We traipsed up the stairs slowly, and I ended up in the middle of the group.

When we entered the changing room, Libby took charge. "Let's pick our clothes."

Jared and Lucas went to the boys' side of the room. I followed Libby and Della to the rail at the back of the girls' side. I pushed away the image of Heather's body in the attic right over our heads.

Libby flipped through the coat hangers, pausing occasionally to inspect an outfit. "It's a Vampires and Victims party, but I bet you've had enough of being a victim. How about Norma Bates?" She held up a saggy dress with a lace collar.

"She's not a vampire. But if you want to wear it, go ahead," I said.

"Too lacy." Libby yanked out a hanger with a flowing, black cape and red velvet underneath. "Dracula's more my style."

I sifted through a few outfits, not seeing the one I was supposed to take. "Is there a Claudia costume?"

Libby whipped a blue dress in a clear wrapper off the rack. There seemed to be a blond poodle stuffed in the bag with it.

She dangled it in front of me like when we were kids and she'd held my toys out of reach. "You want to make a matching set with Jared? Are you sure there's nothing going on with him?"

"No! I mean yes, I'm sure. Claudia's my favourite – you know that."

"Why won't you talk to me about this? I've seen how you look at him."

Libby's whispers always carried and only a wooden divide separated us from Jared and Lucas. "Can we not do this now?" I asked, pointing at the flimsy wood and willing Libby to understand.

"Fine. I just want to share this with you." Libby handed the Claudia dress over, so sincere that I felt in the wrong.

Even if Libby wanted to be involved now, where was she for the past year? I could've been in any number of back seats or bedrooms with the curtains closed. I hadn't, mostly, but that wasn't the point.

Della came up and brushed her hand down my plastic-wrapped dress. "That colour'll suit you. Don't know 'bout that wig though."

Libby brightened, though the conversation definitely wasn't over. "Mina'll make it work. Wait until you see Della in her outfit."

The boys joined us with their costumes and hopefully complete ignorance of what we'd been discussing.

"Hey, we'll match," Jared said, gesturing at my Claudia outfit like it wasn't the plan all along.

My sister pursed her lips but kept quiet.

Downstairs, Libby opened the front door before she noticed Jared stayed behind. He hovered by the door next to Thandie's office. "I was planning on showing Mina the museum."

"Right," Libby said, with a hint of suspicion. "We'll see you outside."

Jared led the way into the museum. The floor was black, and the walls were bleach-white. The room was full of glass cabinets with displays of artefacts, from weapons like an axe and crossbow to a delicate perfume bottle with a metal flower blooming over the glass. The only break in the rows of glass was a closed door across the room.

The nearest case had a ragged piece of wood on one shelf and a bowl of bones beneath it, with no labels for explanation.

"What's that?" I asked.

"The trigger finger bones from a pirate named Jean Lafitte and a piece of his ship. Thandie's a . . . collector. She lets people come in here after tours sometimes."

The next glass case got my attention. A book bound in brown leather was open on a stand, so the yellowed pages and old-fashioned handwriting were exposed. "Is this the original diary?"

"If you can call it that," Jared said. "Thandie copied the best pages. Mostly, he spends a lot of time complaining about his brother."

I was on Wayne's side there. Jared had made it clear he was sceptical about the brothers' existence, let alone believing the diary was real. I couldn't help thinking about them like they were historical figures, with the diary as proof.

"As much as I like history, I'm guessing that isn't why you brought me here."

Jared approached a cabinet halfway down one wall. There was a thick chain coiled on one shelf with a rusting metal ankle cuff. Crusty, red smears lined the cuff. On the next shelf was an ornate photo frame that contained a portrait of a dour-faced woman. She leaned on a chair and an opulent, black dress cascaded down.

"That's Madame LaLaurie . . . the woman who kept her victims in the attic," Jared said. And a chain she used to trap one of them.

"You might also wanna scope out the axe in the cabinet behind you," Jared went on.

The reason he brought me here was as final as a guillotine blade coming down. I looked back at the dull axe I noticed before, putting it all together. I had to be sure. "So, there's an exhibit about Madame LaLaurie and one about the Axeman. What about the convent?"

"Right over there."

Three murders. Three methods in this room.

Chapter 13

If the killer happened to take one or two stories from the museum, it could have been a coincidence. Three was a pattern. "Do you think the murderer got the idea here?"

Jared ran a hand down his cheek with the sandpaper rasp of stubble. "It's possible, but they're some of New Orleans' most famous myths; the idea could've come from anywhere. There are plenty of tours and books about local mythology."

"Except one of the victims was found here."

Jared cleared his throat. "There are twenty stories in this room."

I picked up his thread fast. "That's twenty ways to kill somebody."

Jared flipped open a low cupboard underneath the nearest cabinet. He removed a thick booklet and handed it to me. "We used this to give tours of the museum, until the movie tour took off."

I flipped through the pages, seeing some stories I knew and a lot more I didn't. The Comte de Saint Germain, the Sultan's Palace, Civil War ghosts, a fire that destroyed the whole of New Orleans...

"Let's get out of here," I said.

I reached for my bag, but I'd not brought it. Libby wasn't on board with our investigations, and the booklet would only give us more material for arguments.

"Want me to hold onto that?" Jared lifted up the back of his shirt, pointing to his jeans. Golden-brown skin flexed over lean muscles. "I have big pockets."

"Thanks."

I handed the booklet over and he rolled it up, tucking it into his back pocket.

The others were waiting outside on the dark street. Della and Lucas chatted quietly. Libby jangled the keys at us. "I'll lock up. Can we talk on the way back?"

Our mum taught Libby the art of the nuclear meltdown, so I prepared myself. Libby locked the door with a snap of her wrist and stuffed the keys in her bag.

The air was humid, and breathing soon became difficult. The other three got a safe distance away but Libby didn't lay into me.

"I planned for this to be a fun trip," she said, her mouth twitching into an almost smile.

"It has been. Well, at least five minutes have been halfway decent."

"Halfway fucked-up, you mean." Libby let the hanger swing from one finger and the plastic wrapper dragged on the pavement. Hair fell over her face and her eyes gleamed through the curls.

"How are you holding up?"

I needed her and this conversation yesterday, but while Libby was up for talking I had to make the most of it. "I'm OK. Last night was . . . Finding Heather was awful, but I'm dealing with it. How about you?"

"You know me." She shrugged and her hair fell back. "Let's talk about something else."

Sharing time was over.

"Can we talk about Mum?" I asked, immediately regretting it. I had to bring up another source of discontent when she'd already shut me down.

Libby gave a hollow laugh. "Anything but her – she left us."

Libby left me not long after Mum did. Until we discussed that, I knew we wouldn't move on. Even if I was ready, Libby wasn't. "So what do you want to talk about?" I asked.

"I don't know . . . what about Jared? Sorry I said he was too old for you – he'd actually make a great boyfriend. I mean, he's fatally clumsy, but you can't have it all. He was one of the first people I met here, and we clicked straight away."

"He's great. He's also not the least bit interested in me, so don't get ahead of yourself." It stung to admit that out loud.

"But you like him." Libby was teasing but seemed invested in this fictional relationship.

I could have lied, but she already knew. "It's fine. I can live with an unrequited crush."

She pushed her hair back, and her face opened up. "He was happy that your outfits match. Maybe it's not as tragic as you think."

I felt a flash of guilt that I wasn't telling her the reason for our costumes. I was doing this for us. Tomorrow, we'd give everything to the police and be done with secrets.

"Doubt it, but it doesn't matter. I'm going home in a couple of months." The idea of leaving sent a pang through me. I didn't want to get on a plane and watch Libby and New Orleans disappear behind me.

"Let's not think about goodbyes." Libby slung an arm around me. Our skin stuck together and it was too hot to be near any human, but comfort settled deep in my body.

Going back to Whitby itself wouldn't have been so bad. I loved the town, with its ruined abbey on the cliffs that inspired Bram Stoker; 199 steps that left you breathless and tiny jewellery shops that sold shiny, black Whitby jet. After our mum left, Aunt Sandra moved us from our cosy end terrace into her too tidy, sterile house with shiny chrome and no personality. Even though she wasn't the caring type, I was grateful to her. I just didn't want to go back there.

In the hallway, Jared slipped me the museum booklet with a wink. Libby left me to read in my room without questioning it. She wouldn't have been so chilled if she knew the subject matter.

The booklet was printed on cheap paper and the images were grainy. After a few minutes, I was so engrossed that I hardly noticed. There was a property nearby called the Myrtles Plantation, which was supposedly built on a Native American burial ground. About ten of its past residents had been murdered. In one story about the place, a servant had tried to poison her employers, accidentally killing their children. The myth of the *loup garou* was about a bogeyman that some people believed was a werewolf. There was a patch of road near New Orleans where there'd been a series of car accidents allegedly caused by the creature. The killer's myths of choice about the Carter brothers, the Axeman of New Orleans and Ursuline Convent all made appearances.

Della knocked and popped her head round the door. "Hey, you want some dinner?"

"Sure, thanks. Wait, Libby's not making it, is she?"

Della gave a throaty chuckle. "You're good." She ducked out, returning with a plate of sliced meat, cheese and olives with a swirl of nuts and honey.

"This is incredible – thank you!" I filled a circle of ham with olives and dipped it in honey.

"No problem. Brushin' up on mansion stuff?" Della leaned in to see what I was reading. She tugged on a braid, wincing when she pulled too hard. "I love the horror movie scenes at the mansion, but these stories used to keep me awake. My mom . . ." Della closed her eyes for a moment. "She was superstitious, and she wanted me to know what was out there."

"How did you stop being afraid?" I asked.

"I don't know that I ever did, but MMA helped."

"I get that," I said.

"Guess I should leave you to it." Della closed the door.

After reading about the Carter brothers in the museum booklet, I dipped into the diary.

June 7th 1932

I assumed John's actions could not be worse than what

he has done to me. He has sentenced me to become a monster and yet this was not sufficient for him.

Tonight, I returned home to find a young woman bound and gagged in our parlor. She blinked at me, long and hard, her mouth slack and her eyes struggling to adjust. He has drugged her: another disgraceful habit of John's put to morbid use.

I was so repulsed that I was unable to speak. Is it not enough that we rob humans of their blood? John would steal their liberty as well. "What is this?"

"My new plan." John opened his arms wide. "Imagine arriving home and having your choice of flavors. She is only the first; I will find more."

"That is repugnant. I'll have no part in . . ."

"Stop. Talking!"

John's wrath has been known to render me mute, but this was different. I stopped mid-sentence and was unable to continue. I tried to speak and only a rasp escaped.

John watched me with gleeful calculation. "Well . . . This is a curious development. Speak. Tell me what you think of me."

*"You are a monster!" The confession escaped without
my will, without even a thought.*

*I hurried to my room before he could instruct me in
anything else. I thought he would follow but perhaps,
like me, he is trying to make sense of this. I have
always been weak when it comes to my brother and
now it appears I am entirely at his mercy.*

*John's new plot is to collect humans for his own
amusement, and I will not be able to stand in his way.*

Jared had told me the Carters captured humans and fed on
them. I hadn't known that John controlled everyone, including
his brother. I couldn't think of anything scarier than someone
overcoming my willpower and using me like a puppet.

Shaken, I picked up my pen. I'd enjoyed spending time with
Jared and exploring New Orleans, but we had to give up our
investigation.

I made brief notes on each myth from the museum, fleshing
them out with information from Jared's book. After that, I wrote
down what Armand told us about the crime scene. The final part
would be our upcoming visit to Empire.

It was time to get ready, but someone beat me to the shower. I
tapped my knuckles on Lucas's open door. "Can I come in?"

I realised he had a canvas set up. Though disrupting an artist
was likely a big no-no, Lucas said, "Sure. Wanna take a look?"

His canvas was propped up on a wooden easel with a place to
rest the paints underneath. Reds and oranges smeared the pallet,

though there was no paint on the canvas. Those were the bloody shades on his hands the other night.

The faint outline of a woman's face was visible in the centre of the canvas. Even though the pencil marks were simple, he'd captured a whole personality in the sad shape of her eyes and the downturned pout of her mouth. "It's beautiful," I said. There was a photograph of the woman on the drawers behind the canvas with a luminous sunset behind her.

Colour spread across his cheeks like paint blooming in turpentine. "Thanks. It's my mom." His expression shifted, revealing how similar they were. He had her slim frame and delicate features as well as her sadness. "I almost forgot – I made you this."

Lucas picked up a white, folded top from the bed and offered it to me.

I accepted it, examining the fitted T-shirt. There was a hand-painted image of Winona Ryder with long, black curls pinned off her face and the blood-red dress she wore in *Dracula*. Underneath, 'Mina' was written in swirling text. "Lucas . . . You made me a Mina Harker T-shirt!"

"Do you like it?"

"No one's ever done anything like this for me before. Thank you!"

One side of his mouth came up in a small smile. "You're welcome."

I took my new T-shirt and folded it carefully, putting it in my top drawer.

Della came out of the bathroom wearing a fluffy, blue dressing gown. "It's all yours," she said.

The cool water rinsed the stickiness of the day from my body and ink from my fingers. Libby went in after me with a handful of bath pearls and a stack of magazines. That was the bathroom out of bounds for over an hour.

Back in my room, I pulled down the zip on the dress bag and freed the blond wig. Who knew I'd miss wearing the victim outfit? This dress was even further from my taste, but at least I could wear shoes.

It took a while to wriggle into the stiff fabric and I got my head stuck in an arm hole. Finally, I was in and managed to pull the zip halfway up before it jammed. Inspecting the damage in the mirror, there were two main problems. In the New Orleans climate, I was going to melt like the Wicked Witch of the West. Claudia also didn't have to worry about boobs, so I was exposing a lot more flesh than I was used to.

Jared decided to knock on my door then, looking like he should've been cast as Lestat.

Chapter 14

"Fine dress, my lady." Jared bowed with a flourish of one hand, offering an eyeliner and an English accent. In his other hand was a pot of fake blood with a brush sticking out of it. "Would you be so kind?"

"Stop trying to sound like me and you have a deal," I said, accepting the make-up while nerves skittered around my stomach. "Isn't this usually Libby's job?"

"Have you tried disturbing Libby when she's in the bath?"

"Good point. Close your eyes." This was the worst time for a shaky hand, and I watched the eyeliner tip wobble all the way to his eyelid. "I'm not as good as Libby."

"You'll do better than me." We were so close that his breath brushed against my hand.

Oh so carefully, I glided the point over his eyelid, my hand grazing the apple of his cheek. Somehow, I managed to draw a straight line along the roots of his eyelashes. It was too neat, so I smudged the line with the tip of my middle finger. He shivered, which didn't help my concentration. "Stay still." I moved on to the other eye. He smelled of mint and woody aftershave, and delicious warmth unfurled in me.

"Your eyes are done."

He opened them, and it was so much more intimate now he could see me. His eyes blended between three colours: earthy brown around the pupil faded into green, with a ring of hazel around each iris. "How do I look?"

"OK, I suppose. Your eyeliner, on the other hand, is perfect."

He chuckled and pouted. It was too much: the thought of touching his mouth with him watching me.

Every part of me tightened as I loaded the brush and painted his lower lip. The bristles sank into his lip as the fake blood glided over the cracks, glossy and inviting.

I applied the last stroke of red. I could've done with a lie-down in a dark room but Jared stayed. "So . . ." His mouth quirked into a heartbreaking grin. "Are you willing to do whatever it takes to track down Armand's guy?"

I pushed my shoulders back and lifted my chin, mimicking Claudia's spirit. "We wouldn't want to waste these outfits."

Jared was different when he was dressed as Lestat. His posture was more upright and there was a predatory quality to the angles of his body. I was so drawn to this version of him. My senses were on red alert, catching hints of his scent and craving more.

He peered over my shoulder. "Want me to fasten that?"

I turned slowly and he pinched the fabric together with one hand, zipping with the other. At the top, his hand lingered on my exposed back.

The impression of his fingertips remained when I faced him. He was a head taller than me, and I had to tilt my head back to make eye contact. Our outfits created magnetism that drew our gazes together at a single heated point.

I inched closer and his shoulders slackened, bringing his face closer to mine.

"Hey, do you want me to—?" Libby broke off as she appeared in the doorway. Her towel slipped a couple of inches, almost giving us an eyeful. Hitching the fabric up, Libby recovered. "Never mind!" She skipped out, and Jared followed almost as fast.

He paused in the doorway and gave me a look loaded with meanings I couldn't decipher. Then he was gone.

For the next few minutes, I wrestled with the blond wig, getting even more hot and bothered. Every time I tried to smooth it or work out where my head went, it became more matted.

"Need a hand?" I was relieved to see Della at my door.

"You look incredible! I didn't know there was an option to be Buffy."

Della took the wig from my hands as I admired her outfit. Her braided hair was pulled back in a high ponytail. She wore a black leather jacket over a white prom dress that was hacked short at the knee. A wooden stake stuck out of her pocket.

"Thanks," she said, teasing out the wig with her fingers. "She's not a vampire or victim, but I love the movie."

"Me too." Buffy was my favourite movie character. She was strong and she had purpose, but not in a way that cut her off from other people. "Where can I get a stake?"

"They sell them in a little shop downtown," she said. "Now, let's fix this wig. You got pins?"

Della pinned the wig in place and went to retrieve Libby's make-up bag. Soon, she returned and dusted my face and arms with light, vanilla-scented powder. She dotted my cheek with a beauty mark and loaded my eyelashes with mascara. "You're all set."

With powder over my tanned skin and a wig of blond ringlets hiding my brown hair, I could've been anyone. If we were going to hunt down Armand's mysterious friend without my sister noticing, a secret identity had to help.

"I don't know how you did this, but thank you," I said.

"You're very welcome," she said, glancing at the open door before murmuring the rest. "You know, sometimes dressing up makes people braver, like if they want to make a move on the cute boy who lives across the hall."

"I'll remember that," I said, fidgeting. "Before you go," I added, as she made a move for the door. "Are they going to let me in? I'm not even eighteen yet." That hadn't occurred to me until I saw myself in the mirror with Della.

"OK, so the Louisiana drinking age hasn't been twenty-one for all that long, and they'll serve anyone on Bourbon Street. Anyway, you'll be with me. You won't get carded."

After the epic bath, I expected Libby to hold us up, but she appeared minutes later, with her damp hair scraped into a bun and lips matte with red lipstick. She'd cinched the Dracula suit in with a belt round her waist, and the cape draped low so her tanned shoulders showed. She didn't mention walking in on what almost happened between me and Jared, whereas I went over and over the memory. All the signs said he was about to kiss me but there was always the chance he was crouching down to brush an eyelash off my cheek or point out food stuck between my teeth.

We all met in the hallway. Lucas had his hair gelled flat on the sides and pushed back into a faux mullet. He wore a black leather jacket with the collar up and fingerless, black leather gloves. He held a bejewelled silver bottle. "David from *The Lost Boys*?" That was my third favourite vampire movie, and Lucas wore the costume much better than Kiefer Sutherland.

He smiled, flashing plastic fangs. "You got it. I'm obsessed with that movie." The fangs made him lisp, and he was back to cute again.

Jared's eyes shifted from the wig to my powdered shoulders. I tried not to get too excited – it was just a costume.

"Come on, y'all," Della said, jabbing Jared's arm with her stake.

He rubbed his arm. "Hey, watch the heart!"

Bourbon Street was heaving with people dressed like us and the ambiance was intoxicating. The warm air smelled of booze and felt pleasant against my skin. Some people were dressed as characters I recognised: a bald, pointy-eared Count Orlok from *Nosferatu*; a frilly-shirted Louis and also Star from *The Lost Boys* in her floaty, white dress.

Other people were basic vampires with plastic capes and fake blood around their lips, or their victims clad in flimsy nightwear.

We stopped at a shiny, black door. The windows were covered from inside and a sign above the door read *Empire of the Dead*.

"Cheerful." When I saw the name in print, it tickled at my memory.

"It's from the warning inside the Catacombs of Paris: *Arrête! C'est ici l'empire de la mort*," Lucas said. "A lot of French people live here, and they brought the story with them."

I read a book once about catacombs around the world. In Paris, a labyrinth of bones was set up underground to deal with the lack of cemetery space. Now, visitors wandered the claustrophobic corridors to see bones arranged in grotesquely beautiful patterns.

The bouncer nodded at Della and stepped aside. Giddy, I tried to strut past him like a sophisticated twenty-one-year-old.

Jared led us through a pair of velvet curtains and into a packed room. There was a small stage in the corner with a woman hunched over a microphone, her breathy voice carrying over a dissonant blend of cello and electric guitar. She sang a fluid, sultry melody about a Transylvanian concubine.

Smoke hung thick with the unpleasant mixture of beer and sweat. Pockets of people danced in the swollen crowd and everyone drank from test tubes of thick, red liquid. Along one wall, there was a bar with bottles displayed behind it and a white sign with *Vampires and Victims* daubed in red. The customers had done their best to live up to the title. Nearby, a girl was draped in a black cape, dancing with a guy in a white shirt splashed with red. I turned away when she licked his neck.

I noticed then how the place earned its name. Countless cages were suspended from the ceiling, and all of them were inhabited by complete animal skeletons. Above us, there was a bird with fragile bone wings outstretched. Beside it was a rodent with a shrunken tail.

I got left behind our group. People pushed from every side, and I had to angle my shoulder to part them. A ball of anxiety swelled in my chest. Me and Jared had a plan, but it wouldn't hurt to enjoy myself.

We broke away from the crowd, and I breathed more easily. The music diminished as we found a table. Lucas sat and put down the silver bottle alongside a candle in a blood-red jar. He took a packet of cigarettes from his pocket and turned the box over and over, exposing a pale wrist with a network of blue veins.

"I'll get drinks," Della said.

"I'm coming." Libby kissed my cheek as she passed.

"You have lipstick right here." Jared reached over and smoothed a thumb over my cheek. I froze, hyper-aware of the roughness of his skin.

After that, I couldn't think of anything to say while Della and Libby were gone. I pretended to watch the dancers and admired Jared instead. His eyes never stopped moving from the cages on the ceiling to the packed dance floor. Considering how clumsy he was, his whole body moved to the beat with an impressive amount of rhythm. While Jared seemed at ease in the chaos, Lucas shrank down in his chair, rattling the cigarette box. I was somewhere between the two of them, willing Armand's contact to find us without Libby noticing.

She and Della returned with test tubes of thick, red liquid that smelled of strawberries. "You get *one*," Libby said. I accepted the drink, silently telling her I'd drink as much as I wanted.

"On three!" Della called, holding the tube out in front of her.

"One, two, three!" I chorused with them and knocked the drink back.

It burned on the way down and tasted more like lighter fluid than strawberries. It lit me up inside.

"Anyone want to dance?" Libby asked as the music cut out and a blond guy stepped onstage with the band. He was tall and well-built, with a long, black leather jacket and sculpted cheekbones. "I spoke too soon."

The guy tapped the microphone, licking his lips. He seemed too timid for this job. "It's time for the dance contest." He gave a dry, nervous cough that the microphone sent booming around the room. "Anyone not participatin', clear the floor . . . please."

Libby grabbed Della's hand. "Who's coming?"

"I'm game," Jared said. "Mina?"

Was this happening because Armand predicted it, or would we always have ended up in this situation?

Chapter 15

"I'll sit this one out." Lucas snatched up the cigarette packet and tapped it on the table to a nervous rhythm. "Dancing's not my thing." I was starting to understand Lucas. He wanted people to notice his artwork but not him.

"It's not really mine either," I said.

Libby and Della had their arms wrapped around each other while they watched me and Jared. It wasn't at all awkward.

"Shall we?" Jared asked, offering a hand and dipping his head so a curl fell across one eye.

I knew we were only doing this because Armand suggested it. That should have kept me grounded, but I was all fidgets. Our hands slotted together, and Jared pulled me into the throng. The music returned and the ragged, deep refrain of strings hummed through my body. My vision sharpened, but I was blurry and unreal. I channelled Claudia, haughty and self-possessed, willing myself to believe it.

We reached the centre of the swell of dancers as the woman's low, strange voice joined the strings. I lost sight of Libby and Della, and they left my thoughts. Jared's eyes fixed on me, circled with the make-up I put there. I remembered the brush of my hands against his face and wanted him to touch me like that.

Jared slid an arm around my waist and held up my other hand. He pulled me in until our bodies connected. "Is this OK?" he said into my ear.

That wasn't how I would've described the keen sensations. I was aware of every point of contact: our joined hands, where his palm rested gently on my hip and the hard press of his body against mine. "Yes," I said.

He looked not at me but into me, and his tongue swept over his bottom lip. I wanted him to do the same to mine. He buried his mouth in my neck like at the mansion, but this time it wasn't playful. His lips moved tenderly over a sensitive spot in the crevice of my collarbone. My whole body was loose and pliable, but doubt whispered to me. Was he only playing the role so Armand's contact would find us?

Jared nuzzled his cheek against mine. The rough stubble sent pleasurable shivers coursing through me. Surely it wasn't all for appearances. I didn't have to wait for him to make a move. When would I have another chance to act out of character?

A cold hand fell on my arm, and Jared released me. At first, I thought we were cut from the competition or I'd been exposed as underage.

The blond guy from the stage blinked fast, rubbing both

hands on his leather trousers. "Marsden's waitin' for you in the back."

"Della's boss," Jared said.

The guy set off across the club, and we followed. Jared's hand was my anchor. Was he aware of how close I came to kissing him?

The blond head veered around the crush of bodies by the bar and through a red curtain. It may as well have been a red flag. 'Don't follow a stranger into the back room' was a basic survival rule.

I slowed down, and Jared knocked into my back. "Ready?" he asked, releasing my hand. "Let's see if he knows anything and get out."

Too nervous to speak, I nodded. Libby's description of Della's boss had me picturing a mob leader behind a desk, about to make the kind of offers we couldn't refuse. We found a storeroom and a guy gutting a box with the paper-thin blade of a box-cutter.

Marsden had a face like an aging prince, with a jawline that was all angles, sloping cheekbones and unusually blue eyes framed with thick lashes.

The storeroom was full of boxes, so there was barely space for four people. The blond guy edged around the boxes into the far corner, like he might duck behind them.

Marsden's smile was bright as his blade. He used the box cutter to trace a lazy loop in the air, then stabbed it into the nearest box and slashed towards us. "You must be Armand's friends." His open-armed gesture might have been welcoming if not for the box cutter clenched in his right hand. He clicked the side of it and the thin blade extended.

I got a fierce instinct to turn around and forget all about why we came, but we'd made it this far. "Armand thought you could tell us more about the recent murders – the girl who was killed with an axe, the mugging victim at the Ursuline Convent and the girl in the attic at the Mansion of the Macabre."

"Did he?" Marsden straightened up, smiling pleasantly. For the first time, I relaxed a fraction. He was a bar owner. I'd let blood cocktails and animal bones take me onto the path laid by Mum. She'd made morbid connections where there were none, filling pages with feverish notes about her theories.

Marsden appraised me. "Your accent's familiar. Is your sister dating one of my bar staff?"

At home, people said our North Yorkshire accent wasn't that strong. In New Orleans, it marked us out. "Yeah, she is." I was reluctant to tell him our story.

"Since I know your sister, I'll give you some advice. There are people in this town who drink blood. Some say they're vampires; others say they're 'life-stylers' – those who enjoy the vampire way of life. At least one victim was bitten and their blood was taken. There are places you can find the kind of people who drink blood, but I wouldn't recommend it."

"What places?" I asked, though I was processing what he'd said. There were people who drank blood?

"Don't tell me you want to go there. You do know the fate of the curious cat." He drew a graceful arc in the air, and it was clear what that gleaming edge could have done to a tiny cat body.

Jared said, "You don't have to—"

"It's called The Underground. If I wanted to find your killer, I'd start there," Marsden continued, as though Jared hadn't tried to stop him. I wasn't sure why Jared did that when Marsden was providing concrete information. "Is that all?" Marsden's body language was open, and his clear eyes made the smile especially dazzling.

"That's everything. Thanks," I said.

"I'll be seeing you around here with your sister, no doubt. Libby, isn't it?" Marsden said, crouching down and slicing another box.

I nodded, although I'd rather not. Jared held the curtain back and followed me out.

We wove through the crowd towards our quiet corner, but I felt far from peaceful. The killer wasn't just copying myths; maybe they had delusions of vampirism.

We paused before walking back into the alcove where Lucas sat. He blew a plume of smoke over his head, not acknowledging us.

Jared made no move to approach the table. "No way we're going to The Underground. The police can deal with this."

"People really go there to get bitten?"

"Yeah, and it's fucking dangerous. They could bleed excessively, develop an infection or catch . . . What?"

"You sound like a nursing student."

He gave a weak smile. "That's reassuring, I guess. You sure you're OK keeping this quiet, after we've told the police I mean?"

"I'm fine with it." Libby and I had enough problems without me poking more holes in our relationship.

Secretive conversation over, we approached our table and sat on either side of Lucas. He stubbed out his cigarette in the ashtray. "Giving up on the dance competition?"

"I don't think we'll be collecting any medals," I said.

"Speak for yourself. I was like Kevin Bacon in *Footloose*." Jared swung his arms in an attempt at the famous dance and clipped the candle.

It rattled on the table and Lucas caught it, blowing out the flame. Tendrils of smoke drifted around his face.

"I don't remember Kevin Bacon doing that," I said.

"Slow dancing suited you better," Lucas said. "You looked good together, like a Jack Vettriano painting."

He dipped a finger into the melted wax and watched it solidify on his fingertip. I didn't get the art reference, but my cheeks got hotter anyway. With any luck, it got lost in the atmospheric lighting.

Lucas picked lilac paint from the side of his nail, and a fleck landed on the table. "How's the painting going?" I asked, as he brushed the paint onto the floor.

"I'm working on the sunset," Lucas said, "but I can't get the colours right."

"You've never sucked before," Jared said.

A shy smile spread over Lucas's face as Libby and Della dropped into the empty chairs. Libby backhanded her glistening forehead. "It's so hot! Did you see us out there? We were robbed!"

"Of the prize," Della added. "Not actually robbed."

So, neither of them noticed our disappearing act. That was one–nil to the younger sister.

For the next couple of hours, we danced and drank colourful – and in my case alcohol-free – cocktails. It was cool by the time we burst outside, but I'd already sweated off the powder. I avoided reflective surfaces because I didn't need to see the wig. It was heavier on one side, and some of my hair had escaped around my face. It'd been such a laugh that I hardly cared when Jared didn't touch me again. Nope, I hardly cared at all.

When I got back to my room, the wig situation was as bad as I thought. I yanked out the pins, wrestling with a couple that got stuck in my hair. Finally, I set the matted, blond monstrosity down on my drawers. It was beyond resuscitation after a few hours on my head.

I packed my notebook and the museum booklet into my backpack. It was the police's turn to take over this weight.

There weren't many pages left of the diary. It was time to finish reading and let it go.

June 11th 1932

> Multiple horrors now rule my life. John has killed several of his 'guests' through overzealousness, and it falls to me to lay them to rest. As I carry their bodies, so light despite the life they once contained, I think of the families we have robbed of a loved one. He continues to grow his collection, and I must participate because he holds sway over my actions.

> If I commit to paper what he can do, perhaps I can find a way to overcome it. His compulsion fades over time, though that is of little benefit when the memory of what I have done remains. He can also give commands to carry out at a later time, though he has to be precise with his wording. Trying to best him is fruitless. How can I find a way around his ability when I must bend to his will?

He has discovered that he can control our 'guests' as well and commanded them all to be quiet. His ability appears to be quite literal, so when he bade me, "Watch silently and learn," I could not speak or look away.

He is not content with drinking their blood, but has taken to 'sporting' with them. Though he calls it sport, I would give his actions their true name: torture. I am reeling from his latest game.

"What shall I do with you today?" John mused aloud to his captives.

The young man and older woman sat there in meek compliance, whereas the lithe, athletic young woman had murder in her eyes. Before John discovered his cursed gift, she had fought at her ropes until the skin had sloughed away, forming seeping red sores. I smelled her blood from where I watched, hating my brother.

"I know," he said. "I shall give the three of you the choice." Choice? Those poor souls had no more choice than I did.

John continued, and I shall never forget the events that followed, nor my part in them. "Vote which of you will be fed upon tonight. You can be number one," he began, pointing to the boy, and then moving his languid hand to the older woman. "You are number two, and you are three. Each of you must speak one number."

"Three," the boy and older woman said immediately.

The woman who would be fed upon clamped her lips shut and did not reply. Where did she find that strength? I did not have the power to ask her, and John's next command was directed at me. "Well? Feed on her then. Be as rough as you please."

My legs jerked me forwards as if I had commanded it. Even though I fought the urge with all of my might, I prowled towards her like the killers John and I both are.

I bit down as carefully as I could, since John left me that power. She gasped and John snarled, "Stay quiet, girl."

The sweet blood filled my mouth with salt and life. The energy she gave pulsed through my body, and I became whole once more. Her blood surged through me, and it was invigorating. Only when it slowed did John say, "That's quite enough." My fangs retracted from her skin with a repulsive rip. "I am in need of a drink. Come with me, brother."

I write this entry whilst he grooms himself. What I have done haunts me, and the act of writing has not alleviated it. He calls, and I must go.

We went, and drank ale and moonshine rather than blood. John's temper improved during our outing, letting the raw energy of jazz pour over us in a smoky basement bar.

On our return, we found our door forced open from the inside. The girl with the fight in her is gone.

John is livid and I must go. Next time I write, I pray it is with better news.

There was a typed note printed underneath the last entry:

John and Wayne Carter were later caught and executed on June 13th 1932. Their bodies were interred in the Carter family tomb in St Louis Cemetery No. 1.

Jared said the girl who escaped took her story to the police, and the brothers were executed soon after. They deserved it.

The house was quiet so I got ready for bed in peace, wiping off the panda eyes and remnants of white powder. I almost missed the knock on my door; it must've been the lightest rap of knuckles.

A shifty, fidgeting Jared stood there, picking at the hem of his vest with one hand and mussing his hair with the other. He looked so good, all sleepy eyes and uncharacteristic awkwardness. "Sorry, did I wake you?" he asked.

The house was perfectly quiet around us. It felt like something was going to happen, but it couldn't possibly be what I wanted.

"No, you're fine. What's up?"

He released a slow breath. "I've wanted to do this all night . . . well, not just all night."

Desire for him uncoiled and spread slowly through my body, but I didn't show my hand yet. "Oh, and what's that?"

He rested a thumb on my chin. His eyes were still lined with black, and there was uncertainty in them. How was he unsure of me? I was so full of emotion it could have spilled out and carried both of us away.

I took a step towards him and scrunched my hand through the wiry curls at the back of his head. He smelled of toothpaste and faint traces of his woody aftershave.

A sultry smile a lot like Lestat's erased his uncertainty. He leaned in, his head tilted and mouth enticing. I kissed him first.

Chapter 16

Jared's lips were full and gentle as his fingers traced a shivering path down to my waist. With a hand on each side of his face, I pulled him closer.

The kiss was all shades of sweetness and passion. Our tongues touched tentatively at first, and then we poured everything into the kiss.

I walked us backwards towards the bed. He said, "We don't have to . . ."

"Don't get ahead of yourself," I said against his mouth and kissed him again.

There was no space between our bodies, right down to our entangled feet. I made it my mission to kiss as much exposed skin as possible, from the hard round of his shoulder to a brush against an earlobe that made him suck in a breath.

By the time we pulled away, we were both flushed and breathing fast. His eyes shone, and he gave me a brilliant smile. "Why did we wait so long to do that?"

"I don't know. Maybe we should try it again?"

For a while, we talked, kissed and kissed again. Soon, our eyes were heavy and Jared left before we fell asleep.

For the first time since I came to New Orleans, it wasn't long before sleep took me.

Libby had suspicions the second I arrived in the kitchen. She handed me tea in a mug that said 'Deadly until caffeinated'. "You did your hair, and you're . . . happy."

"I sometimes do both of those things." I sipped my tea and it was too hot. I was jittery about seeing Jared. Caffeine was a bad idea anyway.

"Not before breakfast."

"I think around midday, it's technically brunch, or lunch," I said.

"Some of us have been up long enough to hit the gym," Jared said as he came in, wearing a Kurt Cobain T-shirt over denim shorts. He gave me this adorable, awkward little nod.

He grabbed the protein powder tub and attempted to tip some into a glass. It puffed out over the counter.

"Should I ask what happened or does someone want to draw me a diagram?" Libby hopped onto the counter and brushed away Jared's escaped protein powder.

"We kissed and it was awesome – thanks for asking," Jared said. Even though Libby was in hostile mode, I was relieved that Jared was being so open about us.

Unperturbed, Jared went on, "Why do I feel like I need to say sorry or buy you a pony?"

"Keep your apologies and creepy little horses," Libby said. I waited to see where this was going. "You can kiss my little sister as much as you want." She came across easygoing enough, but her arms were still folded and she banged her feet against the cupboards.

"Is that the whole speech? I don't mind it so far." That made me want to kiss him, even with Libby in the room.

"Good – the rest is simple. I love you like a brother, but if you hurt Mina, I'll cut off an appendage you might need one day."

Jared choked on his protein shake. He jerked his head towards the kitchen door. "Oh good, that's the newspaper."

He retrieved it from the hallway and Libby met him at the kitchen door, mug in hand. "And that's my cue to leave." Libby headed out, abandoning the banter. Any talk of current events and she was gone.

Dragging a chair round the table, Jared set it next to mine. "News and then the police station?" he murmured into my ear.

The paper lay forgotten as he took my cheeks in his hands and pressed a kiss against my lips. We parted, leaving only the smallest space. I closed the gap, and my kisses weren't the least bit gentle.

Eventually, I wriggled free and unfolded the paper. A couple of pages in, there was another article about Heather's death and a photograph of her. I never got to see her alive like that.

Jared leaned his head on mine so we could read together. Slowly, the tension and nightmarish images of Heather's body trickled away.

Jared got through the article a lot quicker than me. All I'd read were rehashed details when he said, "What?"

I scanned the following paragraphs and then caught up. "The police found DNA evidence at the scene? Are they supposed to print that?" It meant the police were investigating the hair sample that looked a lot like ours.

"They'll print anything to sell papers. It doesn't mean the evidence will lead anywhere." Jared leaned his head against mine, and we carried on reading together. There was a short tribute to Heather at the bottom of the article, about how proud her family were that she went to college and how empty their lives were without her. If that was Libby . . .

I refused to let myself fall down that pit of despair. "I have to shower, then can we get this done? I'll tell Libby we're going for a walk."

I showered, then without much deliberation put on the Mina Harker T-shirt with denim cut-offs. I paused at Lucas's door, listening. There was movement inside, so I knocked.

He took a while to come to the door. His *Simpsons* pyjamas were very cute, in contrast with the unhealthy greyish tint of his skin and odour of stale smoke coming from his room. The cloud of sleep lifted when he noticed my T-shirt. "It fits!"

"It does," I said. "I wanted to say thank you again. It's great."

"You're welcome again," Lucas said, messing with the neckline of his pyjama top.

Jared surfaced and locked in on my T-shirt. "Another masterpiece, my man," he said to Lucas, turning to me. "You ready?"

A light breeze stirred the fresh morning air. We wandered into the French Quarter with our hands entwined. On this street, shop signs hung from the balconies above. The windows displayed everything from elaborate fancy-dress costumes to an array of citrus-coloured shoes. The golden, breezy day made me feel lighter. I shifted my backpack onto the other shoulder, feeling the weight of the contents. One more conversation with a detective, and we could leave the investigation to them.

"It feels easier than I thought to give everything to the police," I said.

"I know what you mean." Jared put an arm around my shoulders and kissed my forehead. I wasn't used to being this close to him yet, feeling the pressure of his body against my side and inhaling his familiar scent. "It's been a rough few days, and you're supposed to be on vacation."

That was true. It didn't cast me in the best light that I'd spent my holiday fixating on death and monsters. Both of my parents had cared more about their obsessions than us. I couldn't afford to lose the few people I had left.

After Dad left, Mum had spent every minute reading books about vampires, tucked into the corner of our increasingly messy little house. She went through novels and thick research books at an incredible rate. At first, I was glad she wasn't pining over Dad. I was the only one who was happy he was gone.

Even when Dad lived at home, he never really had time for us. Mum and Libby only remembered his charisma. I remembered our house was always packed with people, mostly women, listening as he talked endlessly about politics and freedom. When he spoke, you believed him. He had these green eyes that mesmerised me even as a little girl. They were as deep as a murky lake, where a murder victim could be weighted down and forgotten.

I wouldn't be like them, tipping over the edge of hobbies into obsessions. Mum lost her job and Dad went off travelling to spread his message – and who knew what else. Both parents lost us.

I snuggled in closer to Jared and thought about Libby.

I was going to let this case go and keep hold of the things that mattered.

The police station was an impressive, mustard-yellow building with white columns. As we approached it, I questioned how smart it was to admit we'd been snooping around the case.

Jared walked in like he wasn't at all concerned. He was all respectful and confident as we approached the counter, while I tried to act innocent and probably ended up shady. "Excuse me, sir," Jared said. "Could we please speak with Detective Boudreaux or Cafferty?"

"Can I ask what it's regarding?" the officer behind the desk asked, exceptionally friendly in a way that also suggested not to waste his time.

"Thanks Mike, I'll take this." Cafferty's friendliness made me feel no more at ease. "What brings the two of you down here?"

"We have information about the case," Jared said.

There was curiosity and mild confusion in the squint of his eyes. "All right. I'll see what interview room is free."

I'd wanted to give him my notebooks and leave, not get all official. "Do we have to . . .?" I couldn't think of an excuse to get us out of it.

"I have to take your statements, but we can skip the interview room," Cafferty said.

"OK," I said. Was he only being nice to get more out of us?

We ended up in a cramped space not much better than an interview room. The police break room had no windows, a dated kitchen counter on one side and sagging chairs spaced out around the walls. "Do you want tea or coffee?" he asked.

Jared shook his head and I said, "No thanks." The stale coffee odour of the room was making me queasy. What I wanted was to get out of here as fast as possible.

Cafferty sat down, sinking low into the seat. We sat across from him as he drew out his notebook and pen. "What do you know?"

I pulled the notes out of my backpack and handed them over. "We think the same person killed these three girls . . . and that they used New Orleans myths for inspiration. There are myths about the convent, an attic and a killer that used an axe. And I found other stories they might go for."

Cafferty flicked through my notes. "We've been investigating the myth angle. This is good work, but you really shouldn't have been anywhere near this."

Sensing a telling off, I took advantage of his pause. "There's more. We found out there might be a connection to a place . . . where people go to get bitten."

Jared clarified. "A blood bar."

Deep creases formed across Cafferty's forehead. "Where did you hear that? Do you have its name?"

"The Underground," I said.

Cafferty scrawled down the name. "Is there anything else?" he asked.

"That's everything," Jared said.

Cafferty sighed and clicked the end of his pen. "This could be very helpful, but you have to leave it to us now. You could get hurt."

Cafferty tucked the notebook into an inside pocket and patted it. For some reason, the gesture tapped into my memories and came up with a shocker. "You were at the mansion," I said. He was the tall, brooding guy who kept to himself on my first tour.

Jared's thick eyebrows shot up. "When?"

"I was on the tour the night before the victim was found there. This has to stay between the three of us," Cafferty said, "but I heard there was an exhibition about the Axeman, and we're looking into the possible connection to the first murder. We were told there was a museum at the mansion, but they left out how it was after a horror movie tour. And it was closed."

Jared let out a muffled burst of laughter. Cafferty's smile faded as he got back to business. "I'm trusting you won't repeat any of this – it could jeopardise the investigation."

"We won't," I said.

"Good. Thank you for your help," Cafferty said.

"Thank you, Detective," Jared said.

Cafferty walked us to the door of the station, and we stepped outside into the blistering sunshine. I was getting used to the heat. It worked into my muscles, and the knots slowly unravelled.

Jared grabbed my hand and swung our arms back and forth. "Do you ever think everything's going to turn out OK?"

"Yes, usually before everything falls apart. You'd better be right."

"It's got to happen at some point."

"Look at you two." Libby was in the hallway when we got back.

My impulse was to drop Jared's hand but to his credit, he kept hold of mine. "I know. We're adorable."

"True, but I'm more into scary." She waved a piece of red paper around and bounced on the balls of her feet.

Jared said, "Do we ask what she's talking about or wait for her to explode?"

I played along. "We should let her get it out. Libby . . . what do you want to tell us?"

I took the flyer from Libby, and Jared read it with me. It was exactly what I needed.

I played along. "We should let her join us," Libby said. "Do you want to roll out?"

I took the flyer from Libby and told Jared it was exactly what I needed.

Chapter 17

The flyer said, '*New Orleans Hell Tours present The Horror Quest.*' This was our chance to let go and have some fun. I wanted to recapture that feeling from my first trip to the mansion.

Jared slung an arm around my shoulder and said, "Sounds awesome."

"As long as it's not too awesome," Libby said. "Thandie said she'll pay for our tickets so we can snoop. Empire is sponsoring this event – we have to buy them there."

By that point, I was totally confused. Jared said, "Hell Tours is Thandie's main competitor. They do horror tours of the city."

"Thandie wants us to find out what they have planned for the vampire festival before her turn to host," Libby added.

Lucas appeared in his doorway, leaning on the

frame. "I'll come if Thandie's paying." Rather than being contained as usual, he was full of edgy excitement.

Libby put on a mix tape while we got ready, cranking up Wilson Phillips until the whole street must have known they needed to 'Hold on'. Libby crimped her hair and sang while I painted my nails black. Della was helping out at the bar and I missed her. Still, it wasn't often that Libby and I were alone. I wanted to make the most of it.

Libby finished crimping her hair and then reached for her bulging make-up bag. "Want me to do your face?"

"Sure," I said.

She took the opportunity to grill me while I was a captive audience. "So. You and Jared," she said, smoothing foundation over my forehead. Alanis Morissette possibly inspired her question, singing in the background about falling head over feet for someone.

"Yeah, yeah, you were right."

"I'm happy for you," she said, moving on to my cheeks. The stroke of the brush was soothing. "You guys actually have a lot in common. I think that's why I liked him when we met – he reminded me of you."

"Thanks," I said, touched and revelling in how well this was going. Libby and I were having a meaningful discussion without any tension. I wanted so badly for it to last.

By the time we were ready, it was clear that we were sisters. Her hair was wild from the crimping and mine was big from the humidity. The heavy make-up made our features more alike but there was one major difference. She was like Winona Ryder in *Heathers*, effortlessly cool and sexy in a stretchy, grey dress.

In Libby's black lace, I was more like Winona Ryder in *Beetlejuice*.

Jared's face brightened when we came into the hallway. "You look great."

"We know," Libby said. "Come on."

Jared put his arms around my back and pulled me in close.

🦇

We arrived at Empire of the Dead to buy tickets, and Libby rushed to the bar to kiss Della.

There were tables dotted around the dance floor with people eating enormous plates of burgers and toasted sandwiches. I wondered how they could eat under the audience of dead animals. It was lighter than last night, but the gloomy feel remained. 'Waterfalls' by TLC played quietly, and that only made the scene more surreal.

Jared, Lucas and I joined the ticket queue at the bar. Lucas shifted over when Libby joined us, placing himself at the edge of the group.

The blond girl behind the till considered us with deep blue, judgemental eyes. "What can I get y'all?" she asked.

She looked way too young to work here, even younger than me. Her pale hair and skin made the dark eyes all the more extreme.

"Five tickets please, Veronica," Libby said, her smile saccharine enough to come across as insincere.

"You have to wait about an hour and a half until your time," Veronica said, equally sweetly. "Real sorry 'bout that. Y'all should've gotten here sooner."

"It's not a problem," Libby said through her teeth. She hated waiting.

"Aren't you Della's girl?" Veronica asked, with more interest. She pushed five crimson tickets across the counter, one at a time.

"That's right," Libby said brightly, taking the tickets. "It's always so good to see you."

"Yeah, I bet it is," Veronica purred, spinning the bangle around her slim wrist. She had more magnetism than just about anyone I'd met, tilting her head at us and offering a smile that was hard to look away from.

"So, y'all need a map." She drew a red and yellow flyer from behind the counter, following the network of roads with one finger. "There are alternate routes and endings depending on the decisions you make and the map you got. Your first location's right here." She pointed to a red sticker on the map. "If you complete the hunt, you'll win a money-off voucher for your next tour. Y'all have fun now."

Marsden came up alongside her. He leered at each of us but lingered over Libby. Yes, definitely creepy. "So, you're braving the Horror Quest. Make sure you come on back to tell me what you think."

"We'll do that," Libby said, backing away from the bar. "We should get going."

Della came over as we walked away. "I hear the two of you got some news."

"Yeah." Jared took my hand and held it up victoriously.

"Good for you. What tour time did you get?"

Libby glared down at the tickets. "We have a couple of hours to kill."

"I'm hungry," Jared said. "Let's grab some food."

"Don't eat here. The kitchen's nasty," Della said. "I'll catch up with you guys when my shift ends. I can make Veronica tell me the tour route."

"Apparently there are 'alternate endings'," Libby said, mimicking Veronica's brittle cheer.

"I'll find you."

Jared took us on a long walk that he assured us was worth it. We arrived at a restaurant called Mother's, with a red and white sign hanging outside that said it was established in 1938. It was a diner with glass counters containing hot meats that smelled of the richest gravy. The walls were brick and covered with photographs of people who had eaten there.

"I'd never order for you," Jared said, "but you should get a po'boy called the Famous Ferdi Special. Trust me."

I went up to the counter and ordered what he said. A po'boy turned out to be the tastiest sandwich I'd ever eaten: melt in the mouth ham and roast beef in a bread bun with flavoursome gravy poured over the filling. Jared inhaled his in a few bites, gravy dripping from his fingers. Lucas ate half of his sandwich and Jared finished it. Libby ate hers slowly, with Jared watching the whole time, but she eventually demolished it.

Exceedingly full and contented, we made our way slowly to the first tour stop.

The sticker on the map directed us to a ramshackle diner with windows painted white from inside. "Are you sure this is it?" Lucas asked. The abandonment was unnerving. There would've been a time when this place was buzzing with customers. Now, it was forgotten and falling apart.

"Let's try the door," Libby said. She grabbed the handle and pushed. The door opened with an exaggerated creak, and she led us inside.

Dust coated everything and left a scratchy layer at the back of my mouth. At first, there was nobody here. Then a sinister grinding came from the back of the room. A waitress roller-skated around the booths with blood sprayed across her short, white apron. Leaning casually on one shoulder was a baseball bat twined with barbed wire. She glided by, flashing bloodstained teeth before doing another lap of the tables.

"What now?" Jared asked.

A girl sprang up from behind the hostess stand. "Hey there," she said brightly. "You got a couple options." There was a crimson slash across her mouth, stretching her smile wide. "You could stay out here and become part of the menu. Or you could head on into the kitchen to find your first clue."

Libby strode towards the kitchen and the rest of us followed. Why did this make me think of the kids in horror movies, who explore the murderer's house and end up slashed with knife-fingers or dipped in hot wax?

I shivered despite the stuffiness. The light was weak, and the whole place stank of rotten meat. Lucas and Jared shuffled behind me and Libby.

Glass specimen jars lined the counters, containing rubbery foetal pigs and greying, shrivelled organs suspended in yellow liquid. The sandwich sat heavy in my stomach, and I moved closer to my sister.

Eyeball magnets held scraps of paper hostage on the fridge. Libby snatched one and backed away as a scraping noise cut through the silence, punctuated by loud footfalls. We paused together by the humming fridge, listening. We weren't alone.

Chapter 18

H igh, wheezing breathing joined the thump of heavy feet. I conjured up hot, foul breath tinged with the stench of rotten meat and an assailant who lunged from behind.

"Dinnertime!" A huge man with a fierce beard and a chef's knife leapt into the room, letting out a shrieking cackle. He slashed and stabbed the air.

We swerved around him and raced towards the front door. Fear pounded round my body, as I heard the dragging thud of his boots. The bloody-mouthed waitress lurched into our path, dead-eyed and cackling. She had no irises, only black pinpricks in blank eyes.

A few younger kids hovered outside the door, and Libby gave them a thumbs-up. "Good luck!"

We were all breathing hard and I had to admit, the adrenaline gave a serious high.

"They're doing great so far," Libby said. "Fancy clues and plenty of scares. Thandie will be pissed off. Not sure what it has to do with the vampire festival, but it's fun."

"So I guess we put these together." Jared held out a hand for the piece of paper Libby found on the fridge.

He placed the sheet over the map we got at Empire, and we huddled around it.

"That's weird," Lucas said.

The overlay was mostly translucent with some opaque patches. "Where do we go next?" Libby asked.

"Some words are blocked out," Jared said, pointing. The labels about key locations in New Orleans were mostly covered by the overlaid sheet. Only scattered words were exposed.

"It's a message," I said. I read the visible words aloud, feeling like Mouth from *The Goonies*. "Your journey begins where archaic drugs are dispersed. Tread with care or else be cursed."

"Guess we're heading to the Pharmacy Museum." Jared removed the overlay and pointed out the location. I'd planned to visit the museum, and this was my opportunity.

We took our time walking there, watching the blue drain from the sky. New Orleans went through an odd shift around this time. The day tourists with children, 'I heart New Orleans' T-shirts and disposable cameras vanished. The evening crowd surfaced as the daylight faded, and they were much more fascinating. They wore tiny top hats, veils made of black lace and punishing corsets. One woman even wore a ragged, black wedding dress.

We found Della waiting outside the Pharmacy Museum. "Hey, you guys were fast," she said.

The museum had severe bars round two floors of balconies.

It was an old-fashioned shop, with forest green window frames divided into panes. There was no sign of its past as a place where people bought poisons, thinking they were medicine, or had their skin cut to let out the 'bad blood'.

There was a queue outside the door, and they let us inside a few at a time. The group behind us were also doing the Horror Quest, arguing quietly about the map. While we waited, I peered into the windows. The displays were jammed with glass bottles full of murky liquids, bunches of dried herbs and candles. There was a leering model of a jester called a 'gaper' with its tongue stuck out. A sign said nineteenth century pharmacies displayed them to encourage people to take medicine.

The museum was set up as an apothecary, with old, neatly labelled bottles lined up on wooden shelves and gruesome medical equipment stored in glass cabinets: bone saws, rusty pliers and a metal hook. "I don't want to know what that was for," Libby said.

We paid for more tickets, and I scanned the room for signs of the Horror Quest. The clerk gestured at the map in Jared's hand. "You'll wanna see my colleague – back there."

In the corner, there was a staff-only area with a red rope dividing it from the museum. Feeling rebellious, I unclipped the rope, and we squeezed into the back room. It felt good to be part of the group.

Sitting there was a man with a wide smile and shiny, very dark brown skin. "Welcome, friends," he said in a French accent. In front of him, there was a chest carved with symbols. "Pass my test and I'll deliver your clue. Fail and grievous pain is your due."

The man opened the chest and inside were three bottles. One was a small, red sphere, with a short neck and screw top. The

second was a black, opaque cylinder topped by a cork. The last
bottle was a vibrant yellow with gummy white marks where the
label had been peeled off. "Which of you will show your bravery?
One bottle leads to love. One leads to wealth. The other leads to
death."

"Is this a *Princess Bride* thing – like you poisoned all of them?"
Libby asked.

Nostalgia rushed through me. We watched that movie over
and over again for a month. I had a crush on Wesley, the dashing
swordfighter in the mask. Libby had preferred Princess Buttercup.

"They're not going to poison us." Jared's lip quirked into a
sneer, and he scooped up the black bottle.

"If you're so certain, be my guest."

Jared pulled the cork out and sniffed, grimacing. "Smells like
your socks, Libs."

"Get lost! Gold has to mean wealth, right?" Libby swiped the
yellow bottle and drank it. She set it down hard on the table,
retching. "Did I just drink from the piss bottle?"

A rumbling chuckle started deep in the man's chest.

Della sighed and took the red bottle. She sipped it and then
drank the rest. "Rose water."

"Damn," Libby said.

Lucas grabbed Jared's bottle and chugged it down, coughing.

Jared shrugged. "I would've taken the bullet for you."

The man reached into the chest, sliding across a hidden panel
at the bottom. Underneath, there was a beige doll made of sacking,
with white wool for hair. Detailed stitching gave the doll human
features, but the parted lips and wide eyes were off somehow. It
wasn't the bland, plastic face of a Barbie but the frozen terror of a

trapped soul. A thick layer of pins covered the bottom of the box, and their sharp points made my toes curl.

The man extracted the doll and handed it to Lucas. "Chèz Voodoo," he read from the tag. "That must be the next location."

The next group appeared by the rope and the man ushered us out, clearing away our empty bottles and resetting the doll. He took more coloured bottles from a shelf behind him.

Chèz Voodoo had three strands of ribbon across the window in white, blue and gold. Pinned to them were voodoo dolls in a rainbow of bright fabrics, with wool for hair, button eyes and stitched mouths. One particularly unnerving doll had a pink rosebud smile with black stitches across it.

From behind the counter, a girl with a chunky, black bob recited, "The store has been very quiet today. I hope nothing bad will happen."

Three groaning zombies lurched into the room, with sagging flesh and eyeballs hanging out on springy, pink muscles. It would've been scarier if they could see. Mostly, they bumped into each other and the empty shelves.

They had rubber limbs in their hands with scraps of paper sticking out of them. "More clues?" Libby asked, grabbing a couple of plastic legs and an arm.

The rest of us did the same and ducked out of the door before the zombies bumped us to death.

We removed the papers tucked between rubbery fingers and toes, but all the ones I found were blank. Lucas held up a handwritten note. "We're going to Royal Street."

We gave the rubber limbs back to the surly girl behind the till before continuing our quest.

"Why is this address familiar?" Jared asked, consulting the map and the apartment building like one of them might have the answer.

The building was so dilapidated that a kick could have brought it down. Spindly balcony rails encircled the first floor, giving an impression of prison bars. The area was poorly lit and deserted, with an oppressive, charcoal sky overhead.

"Let's go!" Libby skipped to the door, but her giddiness wasn't contagious. Lucas trudged after her, nervously scratching at the inside of his elbow.

Della and I had been with Libby so far, but Della hesitated. "Does the Horror Quest end when the building falls down on us?"

"Come on," Libby said. "Don't you want to complete the quest?" She acted playful, but there was a hard edge underneath it.

Jared raised his eyebrows at me. "Let's get this over with."

Libby pulled the door handle, and I hoped it wouldn't open. It gave in with a sigh like a dying breath.

The air inside was damp and cloying. There were no windows, and graffiti covered every surface in the dingy hallway. Rubbish was stuffed into the corners, and it smelled like someone had been using the place as a toilet.

There were a couple of apartment doors with strips of wood nailed across the doorframes. That meant we had to go upstairs.

When Libby and Lucas set off, I said, "There's nobody here. Maybe we got the address wrong. Can we go?"

Libby looked crushed but gave in. "If you want."

"I can go back with you," Jared said, taking my hand.

That decided it. I wasn't going to ruin their night. "I'll be fine."

"Are you sure?" Libby asked, but she'd planted a foot on the next stair.

"Yes," I lied.

Libby jogged up the stairs, closely followed by Della and Lucas. He seemed more invested now and fiercely determined – at least Libby had won him over.

Jared kissed my forehead and looped his arm through mine. "The sooner we go up there, the sooner we can go back to our place."

That made the decision for me. We set off together, and the wood flexed with every step. I pictured us plummeting through the rotten floor. A patch of light came from the top of the stairs, and I used that as my goal. Things were always better in the light.

At the top, one door was barred and the other was ajar, with gouges around the side where nails had once barred entry. That room was the source of the yellow light, though I had new doubts about going in there.

"Are we ready?" Libby teased, her hand resting on the door.

Where had my spirit of adventure gone? Only a few days ago, I couldn't wait to race through the Mansion of the Macabre with clowns and psychopaths. Earlier today even, we'd sought out the scares dotted around New Orleans. The horrors of the past few days had left my nerves raw and exposed.

Libby led us inside and let out a shrill scream. A lantern in one corner cast a yellow glow over what she saw.

There were three bodies tied to chairs, their heads lolling forwards. Three more people were dead.

"Fuck," Jared said. "I know where we are."

Chapter 19

Libby sobbed and Della whispered consolations to her that weren't true. We wouldn't be all right and neither would the latest victims. This time, I knew the myth. The killer had re-enacted the Carter brothers' crimes. My heart thudded fast and hard, a stark reminder that they were dead and I wasn't.

We edged towards them, and I took in the signs of death. Their skin was dull and faces were empty of life. There were none of the subtle movements that marked out the living.

Jared moved ahead and reached out a hand. "We should . . ." His tense intake of breath came out as a laugh. "They're fake! It's part of the tour."

Relief flowed through me. Calmer now, it was obvious the bodies were mannequins. I'd seen death recently, and their waxy faces were a poor copy. I'd thought we'd branched off from the make-believe of the Horror Quest. The rush of adrenaline was genuine though, and it'd left me shaky and used up.

"There's another clue!" Libby grabbed a card from a long-haired mannequin's hands and pored over it with Lucas.

"You OK?" Jared stroked the apple of my cheek with one thumb. "You're pale."

Della considered me sympathetically. "He's right. You want some of my water?"

"No thanks. I just think I've had enough excitement for today."

"Wanna ditch?" Jared raised his eyebrows, and I weighed up our options. If everyone else was here, we had their house to ourselves.

"Want me to tell Libby you're leaving?" Della asked.

"It's OK, I'll tell her," I said.

Libby and Lucas had gone into the next room. The door was a black rectangle, and my breathing was still slowing back to normal. I wanted to stay out of the darkness. "Libby?"

There was a yelp of pain, and Libby let out a ragged scream. After a crash, faint illumination came in from the streetlights.

I reached the door at the same time as Jared and Della. She held up the lantern, and there was just enough light to see the nightmarish scene. Lucas lay on his back with a knife handle jutting from his chest.

"Shit . . ." Della choked out, pushing the lantern into my hands. "I'll call an ambulance." Her footsteps got me moving, and I rushed with Jared to Lucas's side. The lantern light didn't extend to the corners. Panic surged when I realised the attacker could still be there. I took in the jagged edges of the broken window and hoped they were long gone.

Jared wrenched off his T-shirt and wrapped it around the knife hilt. Blood soaked through the grey fabric, streaking Jared's arms and bare torso. I was used to grief as a faint absence, but this feeling was wild and helpless.

Jared held himself together better than me. He murmured reassurances to Lucas with his hands around the knife hilt. Only his rigid body gave him away.

"What can I do?" I asked. Lucas needed help. His skin had turned ghostly, and the thick, glossy blood continued to spread. He groaned and his face contorted in pain.

"Did someone call an ambulance?" Jared asked.

"Della did," I said.

"Good." Jared let out a shaky breath and shifted his bloody hands to reapply pressure.

I'd forgotten about Libby until she sobbed. She sat inside the circle of light but away from the blood. I couldn't think about her for long. I kept all of my attention on Lucas. It seemed like if we cared enough, he had to make it.

Della hurried back in. "The ambulance is on the way. How is he?"

"Hanging in there," Jared said fiercely. The blood had seeped across the floor and touched Jared's knees. How much could a person lose?

Sirens blared in the distance, and Della dashed from the room. She was so alert. I couldn't think through the roar of alarm.

"Can we do anything?" I wanted to ask how Jared was, but it wasn't the time. If this was hard for me, it must have been unbearable for him to see Lucas like this.

Desperation showed through his optimism. "I have to leave the knife in. If I pull it out, it could cause more damage."

What would happen when the paramedics removed it? I couldn't think of anything to say that would help.

When I didn't respond, Jared kept going. "We just have to wait. Lucas . . . How you doin', buddy? Can you talk to me?"

Lucas's eyelashes fluttered and he moaned. Jared pressed his lips together. His hands remained on Lucas's chest, locked onto the wound.

The sirens were loud, and I willed them to arrive fast enough.

Two paramedics rushed in with Della leading the way. Jared retreated. He watched from the shadows, tense and stony-faced, with smears of blood drying on his bare chest and arms.

The paramedics were so deliberate and methodical, quietly asking Jared questions as they worked on Lucas. I wanted to scream for them to hurry. They placed padding around the knife, and the white instantly turned red. I glimpsed Lucas's strained, unmoving face before they positioned an oxygen mask.

Libby was still tucked into a ball, and she'd crept back to sit with Jared. She'd made herself so small that most people scanning the room wouldn't have noticed her. Della did, easing Libby onto her feet.

The paramedics lifted Lucas onto a stretcher and carried him out of the room. Jared followed, pausing in the doorway. "I'm going to . . ." He was gone before he finished.

"They told me what hospital," Della said. "I don't live too far from here – we can take my car."

I jogged down the stairs behind Della and Libby, flinching as the wood creaked and groaned underfoot. Della kept hold of Libby's hand, but every step was a stumble. We left the building behind us but not the devastating events.

The walk to Della's was a blur. I told my feet to keep moving, one step after another. We had to get to Lucas.

Hospital waiting rooms were all the same, antiseptic-smelling and painted in pastel shades that weren't at all soothing. The people looked the same too, tired and empty of emotion, with full cups of coffee going cold in their hands.

Jared stood when he saw us. "Lucas is in surgery. They'll update us when they have news."

The blood was gone from his arms, and he wore baggy shorts and a black *Friends* T-shirt that wasn't his. I didn't know what to say so I wrapped my arms around his waist and rested my cheek on his chest. He put his arms around me and buried his face in my hair. "Thanks. You did good back there."

"I didn't do anything," I said.

Jared's voice was muffled but emotional. "You kept your shit together. That stopped me from losing mine."

I peeled my head off his chest. "You were great."

"Let's hope I did enough."

The three of them handled waiting very differently. Jared sat in one spot, feet apart and elbows dug into his knees, hands covering his face. Libby did what I knew she would, pacing and asking a string of questions none of us could answer. "Shouldn't they be updating us? How long will this take?"

But she avoided the one question Jared threw at her. "Libs, what happened in there?"

Libby sat on the nearest seat. She tucked up her feet, wrapping both arms around her legs. Her eyes filled with tears. "Please . . .

I can't. Not yet."

Jared's nostrils flared, but he let it go.

Della's serenity contrasted the other two. Their distress was plain for anyone to see, but hers was more discreet. She sat up straight with her hands in her lap. Only the quiet despair in her eyes revealed her emotions. I wasn't sure what I gave away to other people. Inside, it was a storm of nausea and questions.

"The mannequins were set up like the Carter brothers' victims," I said. Jared knew that, but I had to keep busy.

Jared let his hands fall between his knees. Left exposed, his eyes were surrounded by swollen, angry skin. "That was their apartment . . . where they kept the victims."

A doctor surfaced and Jared rushed over. I heard only snatches of conversation, heated words like "family" and "just us". Her expression was sympathetic but unrelenting. Whatever she said, Jared couldn't get around it.

She walked away and Jared returned. "They called his dad, and she said we have to go home. Visiting hours are in the morning."

"Did they have an update?" Libby asked.

Jared's jaw clenched. "He woke up before his surgery. They said it was a good sign that he remembered things, like his dad's number. But he lost a lot of blood, and they have to repair the damage, so . . ."

Libby blinked hard. "I don't want to leave him."

Detectives Boudreaux and Cafferty walked in and made the decision for us.

Last time I saw them, Boudreaux took our hair and bombarded us with questions. This time, there was sympathy in her tone. "I'm sorry to hear about your friend. Do you have any news?"

"He's in surgery," Jared said.

Boudreaux looked disappointed, but Cafferty was on hand with compassion. "He must be stable if they're performing surgery. He's young – the odds are in his favour."

"He's in the right place," Boudreaux added, before circling back to why she was really talking to us. "We understand the four of you witnessed the attack. Would you be able to come on in and answer a few questions?"

She made that sound optional. Luckily, Della gave a rational response before I went with sarcasm. "No problem. We can take my car."

Libby sat in the front next to Della, rapping her fingers on the dashboard.

In the back seat, Jared held my hand on his bouncing right knee. When he spoke, it came out confrontational. "Libs, you have to tell us what you saw."

In the rear-view mirror, Libby's face was white and pinched. "You saw too."

"No, I heard you scream, then I saw Lucas bleeding out!" Jared said. He exhaled shakily, flexing his fingers between mine. "Did you see who did it?"

Libby shook her head. "The room was pitch black. I saw . . . Someone moved . . . a man, I think. I thought it was an actor and then his arm jabbed towards us." The rear-view mirror reflected her tears. "Lucas fell. I didn't know he was hurt until there was a crash and some light came in. There was so much blood . . ."

"What happened next?" Jared asked.

"By the time I looked up, the guy had gone. I think . . . He must have jumped out of the window."

"You couldn't have stopped it," Della said.

Libby wrapped her arms around herself and closed her eyes.

At the police station, they took our fingerprints, asking us to press each digit onto black ink and white cards. Then we waited silently in a corridor as police officers carried on their business around us.

Getting interviewed was easier than I thought. Libby was with me, and it was over fast. Back in the corridor afterwards, I tucked my feet up in my chair and went over what I said. There were no taxing questions, and I couldn't have made it any clearer what I'd seen. The worst part was describing Lucas bleeding on the floor. I wished I saw who did it and that I could've helped more.

They took Libby in after me, and she was gone a long time. Once they'd talked to Della and then Jared, the detectives went through the interviews all over again. Time went on and on, and I started to feel cabin crazy.

When the detectives took me in again, they went over the same questions until I wanted to snap that I'd told them everything. The truth stayed the same, no matter how many times they asked about it.

The last time they took Libby, Boudreaux acted different. Her feet struck the tiled floor hard, and she carried herself stiffly. "Elizabeth, we have a few more questions."

We'd been through this before, so I thought it was just another interview. Libby was only gone for a short time when she returned with Officer Boudreaux behind her. I didn't recognise how strange that was until I saw the handcuffs.

Chapter 20

They thought Libby did it. All at once, Della, Jared and I were on our feet, arguing.

Boudreaux snapped, "That's enough! I have to take Elizabeth to be processed."

"Wait . . ." I said. "Lucas is our friend. You can't think Libby did this to him! He'll tell you when he wakes up." They were taking Libby away. It felt totally unreal, but the metal circles around her wrists told the cold, hard truth.

"We found evidence. As I said, I have to process the arrest."

"I'll stay to debrief you," Cafferty said.

"I'll be OK," Libby said. She didn't look OK. She looked stunned. "I'll call Thandie – she'll get her lawyer on it." She spoke almost vacantly, and I suspected that detachment was keeping her from falling apart.

"We have to go *right now*," Boudreaux said. She led Libby down the corridor and out of sight.

I attempted to follow, and Cafferty stood in my path. He reasoned with me quietly. "If you do that, you'll make things worse for Libby. Go back to the interview room."

Worry coursed through me as I ran through the evidence they might have had. Was it because Libby was the only one there when Lucas was hurt?

We followed Cafferty into the interview room, and I sat beside Della. Her hands made fists under the table. Jared stood behind us rather than joining Cafferty on his side of the table.

Cafferty sat down, but left the camera off this time. I launched straight into questioning him for a change. "Do you really think she did it?"

"It doesn't matter what I think," Cafferty said carefully. "I can tell you what'll happen next. Libby will be taken to booking, and then the prosecutor will have seventy-two hours to decide whether to file charges."

"What if they do that?" My question came out frantic.

"She'll be arraigned. That means she'll plead guilty or not guilty in court."

"What makes you think she did it?"

"I can't talk about an ongoin' investigation," Cafferty reeled off the statement, but at least he looked unhappy about it.

Della took over. "Detective Boudreaux said they found evidence. How does that evidence connect back to Libby?"

Cafferty sighed and swept his pen off the table. "Hypothetically, if two people left prints on a knife handle, we can usually tell how the knife was used."

He mimed holding both hands round the tip of the pen. "Someone stopping the blood, for example, would hold the knife like this."

Cafferty passed the pen into his right hand, thumb on the inside and fingers curved round, like he was about to use it to slice bread. "Lucas was stabbed in the chest from the front by a right-handed person. He would've seen the person coming at him, so Boudreaux thinks he may know them." I got a flash of the scene as if I'd witnessed it. A sharp blade piercing cloth, skin and muscle. Blood flowing. Lucas crying out. Libby screaming.

Cafferty had made it clear: Libby's fingerprints were consistent with using the knife to stab Lucas. She was also right-handed, like the killer. Those things didn't clarify how her fingerprints got on the knife handle.

"Do you have somewhere to stay?" Cafferty asked. "We have procedures in place for minors, if needed." Though the words were all business, there was concern behind them.

"She's good," Della said. "I got one more question. Did you get the hair test results back?" I was so glad she was here, thinking rationally when I couldn't.

"We did. We're looking into it."

"Was the hair Libby's?" Jared asked.

"I'm afraid I've said all I can." He seemed genuinely sorry about that.

"And are there any other leads?" Jared pressed.

Cafferty hesitated, and then said quietly. "Not at this time. Now I really do have to go. I'll see y'all out."

Della drove the three of us back, and I tried Aunt Sandra's number in Whitby. The answer phone was full. She wouldn't have helped much.

We hovered in the hallway and Jared stared down at his watch. "Seventy-one hours before her arraignment. They'll drop the whole thing if . . . when Lucas wakes up." He grimaced at the slip.

"We have to help her," I said. "What do we do?" I was usually full of purpose and plans, but this time I had nothing.

"We go to bed," Della said.

"We can't just leave her," I said, even as Jared nodded in agreement with Della. "You too?" I asked.

"We can't help her if we're exhausted," he said. "We'll talk about it in the morning."

I wanted to argue again, but they were right. My eyes felt so dry that blinking hurt, and my mind was fuzzy. "Fine," I said, frustrated.

"I have to go," Della said. "My dad'll get worried if I don't show. Should we meet at the hospital at the start of visitin' hours? See Lucas, then decide what we're gonna do about Libby?"

"Definitely," Jared said. He attempted optimism, but worry made lines across his forehead.

Then it was just us. Jared stood there, hands deep in his pockets and shoulders low. I usually felt at ease around him, but all the day's events had left tension behind. Lucas was in hospital. Libby was gone, locked away from us.

"So," Jared said uncertainly, "you tired?"

"Yeah, we should go to bed." Though I was so tempted to stay up and try to make a plan to save Libby, Della had it right. Lucas and Libby needed our help, but we needed to rest first.

"Sure," Jared said, with a flash of disappointment. "Night, Mina."

After getting ready, I lay in bed and thought about Lucas and Libby. I hoped he was on the mend and sleeping off the surgery. I doubted Libby was sleeping well wherever she was.

When we met in the kitchen the next morning, Jared was swigging a protein shake and setting breakfast ingredients out on the counter. I put the kettle on out of habit. While the water boiled, I went over our plans for the day. First, we were meeting Della at the hospital to see Lucas. I had no idea how to help Libby yet.

"Pancakes with bacon?" Jared asked, opening a cupboard by the oven. "Maple bacon?" he corrected.

My stomach grumbled. Apparently, it just needed some encouragement. "All the yeses," I said.

I heard the newspaper fall on the mat and went reluctantly to collect it. The case I'd followed with fascination had circled closer and closer until it had the power to ruin our lives.

By the time I got the paper to the kitchen, I'd found the story about Lucas. The article made a lot of fuss about him being attacked during a New Orleans Hell Tours event. With such bad press, maybe Thandie didn't need to worry about competition from them.

I pushed on through the article. It didn't name Lucas, but briefly outlined the events and then ... "They said they have Libby in custody!"

Jared turned off the gas and left the pancake sizzling in the pan. "They printed her name?"

"No. It says the police have a young female from a rival company in custody. They're making it out to be some turf war!" Seeing it in print really hit home. If we or the police didn't get to the bottom of this, Libby could go to prison.

"People won't know who she is from that," Jared said, "and it doesn't mean the press think she's guilty. They just like stirring shit up. Let's go see Lucas, then we'll head to the station to see if we can talk to Libby."

"Good idea," I said, folding the paper so I couldn't see the article.

"I think I destroyed that pancake. Give me a second and I'll make you another."

I ate quickly, thinking about the article until I felt sick.

The corridor on the way to Lucas's ward had no windows, and my trainers squeaked on the linoleum floor. The hospital disinfectant failed to disguise the sickly scent.

A nurse directed us to Lucas, through a place of whispers and closed curtains.

Hands cold from the sanitiser, we entered his ward. Della was there, perched on a chair to one side of the bed. She gave us a strained smile. Lucas's bed was near the door. There were three other beds in the room, and a little girl was asleep in the one by the window.

Lucas was propped up in bed, smiling weakly. The skin around his mouth and eyes appeared fragile and thinly stretched over the bone. He wore a flimsy, blue hospital gown with loose sleeves that fell past his elbows. A needle was taped to the back of his hand and a long tube joined up to a drip. "Hi," he croaked.

His heart-rate monitor was a constant bleep in the background. Nobody else replied, so I asked, "How are you feeling?"

"I don't know. They gave me drugs." When he shifted, the top of the compress was visible over the neckline of his gown. This could've ended so differently.

"I brought you some clothes and stuff," Jared said, putting the bag down by the bed. "Did the police stop by to see you yet?"

"Not while I've been awake," Lucas said, giving a long blink.

"Did you see what happened?" Jared asked.

Lucas shook his head in a slow rocking motion. "Libby and I went into the next room and it was over so fast . . ." His eyes opened to weak slits. "Where is she?"

He didn't know she was arrested. Luckily, Della jumped in. "She got held up, but she'll be along real soon."

Lucas closed his eyes again. "Sorry guys, I need sleep . . . the drugs . . ."

"We'll come back," Della promised. Lucas nodded slowly, fading.

Della stopped in the waiting room. In the fluorescent lighting, her skin was ashen. "I'm going to stay here a while, until he wakes up," she said. "I called the police station . . ." She paused, grimacing. "They wouldn't tell me what's going on with Libby. I talked to Thandie's lawyer and she's workin' on it."

"Mina's family – she might have more luck," Jared said.

"Sure," Della said, her upbeat tone coming out forced. "I have work at eleven, so I'll stay with Lucas until then. I'd rather not go but . . ."

Jared stepped in. "You've done all you can. We can take it from here."

"He's right," I said. "You take care of Lucas, and we'll help Libby."

"Teamwork," Della said, giving a thin smile. "See y'all later."

When Jared and I walked out of the hospital, we hit a wall of heat. "So . . . back to the police station," I said.

"Yeah." Jared's lack of enthusiasm suggested he had about as much confidence in our plan as I did.

We sat in the air-conditioned police station reception for almost half an hour with no updates. The officer behind the desk had said she'd tell Boudreaux and Cafferty we were here and then studiously ignored us.

"What's taking them so long?" I asked, adopting the role of the impatient sister since Libby wasn't here.

Jared pulled the ring off his thumb and jammed it back on over and over again. "Must be hard work trying to prove an innocent person did it."

Boudreaux came through the front door, cool and immaculate even though she came in from the sun. "I don't have long," she said curtly. "What can I do for you?"

"How's my sister's case going?" I asked.

"You're aware that I can't discuss an ongoin' investigation," she said with some patience. "Your sister's fine."

"Where is she?" I asked, my composure slipping away. I couldn't bear her being locked up.

"She's in a holding cell," Boudreaux said. "Now, if you'll excuse me."

Before we could say anything else, she'd hurried away.

"That went . . . well," Jared said. "What now?"

"I suppose . . . we regroup with Della," I said.

"We'll figure it out," Jared said, holding my hand as we went from the air-conditioned reception into the brutal sunlight. He must have seen the apprehension on my face because he continued with more feeling. "We will."

We arrived at Empire of the Dead just before opening time. A cluster of black-clad customers were waiting for the bar to open. They must have been melting in this weather.

Jared came up behind me and wrapped his arms around my waist. Even though it was boiling and I was sweaty, I leaned into him.

When Empire opened, we headed inside, with Jared's hand on my lower back.

Della was behind the bar, and she deflated when we approached. "Don't take this the wrong way, but I didn't wanna see y'all so fast."

"Yeah, Boudreaux sent us away," I said.

"Can't say I'm shocked," Della said. "Take a seat. You want a cold drink?"

"Can I get a grape soda?" Jared asked, reaching into his pocket. "It's on me," Della said. "Mina?"

"I'll have the same, thanks," I said, perching on the rickety bar stool.

Della turned to grab our drinks, and Marsden sidled up to the bar. "We can't get rid of the two of you."

I agreed with Libby; he gave me the creeps, despite his old Hollywood appearance, with high cheekbones, sweeping hair and those clear blue eyes. He was charismatic but in a syrupy way.

"We came to see Della," Jared said evenly.

Marsden's response had a sting in the tail. "Don't you feel like talking? I thought we connected at the party. I'll leave you to your drinks."

Della came back as he left. She set down two glasses of fizzy, purple juice with plenty of ice. The three of us watched Marsden walk past tables of sleepy people consulting laminated menus and into the storeroom.

"You talked to Marsden at the Vampires and Victims party? How come?" Della asked.

"It's a long story," Jared said.

"We asked him if he knew anything about the murders," I said. Della had to be fully informed if we were going to rescue Libby together. "He said . . ." I paused, realising we had a clue to follow. "He said there are people who drink blood, and they go to a place called The Underground. It might be a good place to try."

"The Underground? I've heard of it." Della's tone was wary.

"I know it sounds sketchy, but we could ask around to see if anyone has information," I said.

"I don't know . . . I've heard pretty bad things about that place," Della said. "If we do this, any ideas how we're s'posed to get in?"

Jared had stayed unusually quiet while I negotiated with Della. He turned his glass slowly, condensation trickling down his fingers. "I have. It's the one Lucas uses."

Chapter 21

"Hold up," Della said. "Lucas lets people drink his blood?"

Jared let out a whistle of air, slouching down on the bar stool. "Yeah, and I couldn't stop him, if that's what you're asking. I tried."

"We're not accusing you," Della said. "I just . . . don't get it. Lucas is more scared of death than anybody I know. Why'd he do that?"

I had some ideas. I understood pushing yourself right up to the edge of what scared you. It wasn't Jared's job to stop him. "Our mum went through it," I said. "She had . . . addictions. Sometimes people resist being helped."

Their silent concern and understanding almost pushed me to tears.

Mum had gone out late all the time, sometimes staying away for days. While she was gone, Libby and I would curl up and watch horror movies. We got lost in the horrors of possessed dolls and masked killers and forgot for a short time about our mum being away.

Each time, she tried to sneak past us. The next morning, we'd find blood on tissues or the wall of the shower. She always had an excuse. We should've pushed harder for the truth.

Right near the end, she came home with a compress taped over her neck. It was on the right side, the one unmarked by scars. "What happened?" I asked.

"I'm fine." She sounded even more broken than I did. "It's nothing."

She was gone days later, before the wound even had time to heal. If Lucas survived this, we'd help him without taking no for an answer.

"So, we're going to the blood bar." Della and Jared gave each other a look like parents bargaining over who had to discipline the child.

"Girl, it'll be a lot safer at home," Della said. "We'll go and come right back."

I thought she'd be on my side. "You won't let me try to help Libby? Why keep me out of it now?"

"You're only seventeen. Those places are dangerous," Jared said.

My dad hadn't been much of a father figure, and I didn't need Jared to step into that role. "So I'm old enough to kiss but not to be helpful?"

Della took Jared's empty glass and tipped the ice into the sink behind the bar. "She's got you there. Be right back." She went to empty the glass washer.

Jared rested his forehead against mine. "Jeez, you're stubborn."

His head pressed hard against mine, but neither of us backed down. "I am, and if you don't let me come with you, I'll go by myself."

"Fine." Jared kissed me hard. He slid off the bar stool and extended a hand to me.

Agreeing to catch up with Della when her shift ended, we left her to work.

Outside, it was even hotter than earlier. "Should we go home?" Jared asked. "There's plenty of food."

"As long as you're cooking it," I said. We'd exhausted every avenue of our investigation for now. Eating Jared's cooking was a reward for the small progress we'd made.

"Not a problem," he said, kissing the top of my head. "Hey, I'm sorry I didn't tell you Lucas had been to the blood bar."

"It's OK. It wasn't your secret to tell."

"I know, but if I'd spoken up sooner . . ." Jared rubbed a hand over the back of his head.

"It wouldn't have changed anything," I said. "We have to keep moving forwards."

We put the news on when we got back. They were cycling through the same old facts, and I didn't like being in Libby's room without her. After that, Jared headed for the kitchen. "Can I do anything?" I asked.

"Nah," Jared said. "You relax." Ordinarily, I would've jumped at the offer. With everything that was going on, sitting still wasn't very appealing.

Rather than being in the way, I went to my room and took out my copy of *Interview with the Vampire*. I usually read about two books a week, but I'd hardly touched it since I got here.

After a while, meaty smells drifted through my open door, but I stayed where I was. Louis had fed on Claudia. I knew what was coming and read faster. Lestat was about to turn her, dooming her to spend eternity as a child. Every so often, I lost the plot of the story and thought about the kind of people who entertained themselves by drinking blood.

"Mina!" Jared called.

Entering the kitchen, I was hit by the smell of gravy and other things I couldn't identify.

"You ever tried *loco moco*?" Jared asked.

"No," I replied, but I loved how he said it. "From Hawaii?"

There was a bed of rice, a hamburger and gravy on my plate. Jared carefully laid a fried egg on top of the burger. "Sure is. You got your rice, homemade gravy, hamburger patty and obviously the egg right on top."

"It looks amazing," I said, cutting into the burger and making sure I got a bit of everything on my fork.

"Forgot the salad." Jared grabbed a bowl from the fridge and then we feasted.

The gravy was salty and flavoursome against the sticky rice, and the combination was delicious. We hardly spoke over the food, and I ate way too much. Sitting back on my chair, I was sorry Libby couldn't share this with us. Every time I did the simplest thing, it came back to her.

"I should wash up – you did the cooking."

By the time I grabbed the plates, Jared had the empty oven

dishes halfway to the sink. "We'll get through them faster together."

Jared washed, wearing a pair of yellow rubber gloves that came almost to his elbows, and I dried. The routine of it was calming, and I unwound for the first time since the police took Libby.

At first, I thought he did it by accident. A splash of bubbly water landed on my hand, and I wiped it away with a towel, picking up the last mug.

I'd set it in the open cupboard when a slash of water soaked my left arm and the sleeve of my T-shirt.

Jared was the picture of innocence, wearing the rubber gloves that were now covered with a telling white froth. I reached a hand into the water and flicked upwards, soaking his chin and the front of his shirt.

It could've turned into a full-on water fight. Instead, Jared slid a gloved hand around my back and pulled me close.

The wetness from his shirt soaked into mine, and he looked down at me. He kissed my cheek and cupped it in his hand, then let his rubbery fingers settle on my neck.

"I really like you," he murmured against my mouth.

"You're OK too," I said, kissing his stubbly cheek and enjoying his mock outrage.

"I need to up my game," he said. He pulled off the rubber gloves and held my waist, leaning in slowly.

He kissed a sweet spot behind my ear and moved on to teasing my earlobe lightly between his teeth.

I caved. "Fine, I really like you too."

We ended up sprawled on my bed together with a thick book of

New Orleans myths apiece. Though we couldn't guess which one the killer might choose next, it felt like we were arming ourselves.

Over an hour must have passed when my eyes grew heavy and both of us slouched down on the bed. Jared wrapped his arm around me, letting the book fall off to one side. He closed his eyes and I rested my head against his chest. He wrapped his arms around my back and pulled me closer. It was so cosy that I let my eyes shut.

A loud knock on the front door woke me. I felt sluggish and my eyes were gritty. Jared stirred, his curls standing out from his head.

"I'll get it," I said, but Jared sloped out of bed with me.

We went to the door together, and Della was standing there. She eyed our mussed hair. "Sorry, am I interrupting?"

The street was dusky behind her. We'd slept through a good chunk of the afternoon. "We fell asleep," Jared said.

"Right . . ." Della said, strolling into the hallway.

Getting dressed up was a lot less entertaining than usual. I borrowed Libby's black cotton dress, and Della helped me to twist my hair back with Libby's bat clips.

Jared grabbed a red token from Lucas's room to get us in, and then we set off into the oppressive evening. The air was too thick, and the clouds were swollen like another storm was coming. A headache brewed behind my eyes. Della and Jared had a quick back and forth about our best approach at The Underground. We had to tread carefully. The idea was to find someone who knew about the murders, not bump into the killer.

With that decided, Jared held my hand and kept patting his pocket where he'd placed the red token.

We passed a park that might have been a great place to spend an afternoon, though at night it was eerie. Silvery water gleamed beyond massive trees. Anything could have been lurking behind them or the low fences.

A shadow shifted by the lake. "Did you see that?" I asked. The shape went still as a tombstone or a creeper who'd been busted.

"See what?" Jared's upbeat question shifted to concern. "Oh, that weird guy watching us."

"You don't know it's a guy," Della said, "and it's possible they're out for a walk . . . alone in a pitch-black park. OK, let's pick up the pace."

That was when the shadow moved, cutting through trees and over grass in a straight line towards us. We did as Della said, walking so fast that I did an occasional skip to match Jared and Della's long strides. I had to look back. It was definitely a person, with broad shoulders and a long coat flapping around long legs. It was also closing the distance.

We got to the edge of the park, our feet striking the pavement hard and fast. When I checked again, the pursuer was gone.

Della did the same, shaking her head. "We need to get a grip. It was prob'ly some jogger."

Jared slowed the pace with Della, putting his arm around my waist. I couldn't relax, going over and over what could've happened. The chance of it being the killer was slim, but that was probably what murder victims once assumed. I couldn't shake the thought that if the murderer had set their sights on any of us, we could've been dead.

We approached the unlabelled door of The Underground on a side road a short walk from Bourbon Street. This area was seedier, with crumbling shop fronts and boarded windows. The only person in sight was a hulking doorman, but I heard the thump of bass. With the experience in the park behind us, I decided to let it go as a bad case of paranoia.

The club was tired, with only a scattering of customers. Our feet stuck to the floor, and pulsing lights illuminated the room in snapshots. The only thing the place had going for it was that 'How Soon Is Now?' was playing. Libby was obsessed with The Smiths about three years ago, and she used to walk around the house swinging flowers like Morrissey.

Jared tugged my hand and pointed towards the back of the room. The music was so loud that the beat vibrated through me, as Morrissey sang about being human and needing love.

Lethargic clusters of people occupied tables and a girl manned the empty bar, her chin propped up between her hands. A guy at the nearest table had a bandage knotted round his wrist. Was this whole place a front for the blood bar?

We crossed the dance floor and broken glass dug into the soles of my shoes. Jared led us to a door that said 'Staff only'. It was interesting that a staff area required another enormous doorman, this one equipped with a clipboard.

Jared drew the token out and held it up to the burly guard dog. "I'm on the approved list and they're clean – paperwork pending." Jared lied smoothly. What test were we supposed to . . .? We were in a blood bar. They had to check we didn't have a contagious disease. But why was Jared on the list?

Jared gave his name and the man consulted his clipboard. He assessed each of us sternly, and I was sure he was going to say no. Shaking his head slightly, he withdrew three red ribbons from his pocket and gave them to Jared. It was unclear what swayed him, but I was grateful Jared didn't have to face the blood bar alone. Jared accepted the ribbons and pushed through the door.

The air cooled as we ventured down a long staircase, with black walls and naked bulbs spaced out along the sloping ceiling. There was a sickly fragrance of roses, and the concrete stairs were worn down the middle.

Jared stopped halfway down and gave out the ribbons. "We're supposed to tie this to the place we want to get bitten," he whispered another thing he shouldn't have known, pausing as a rowdy group passed. There were red ribbons tied around necks, elbows, wrists and even one thigh.

"We have to fit in," Della whispered, taking two ribbons and passing one to me, "but nobody's biting us."

Della tied the ribbon around her elbow. Anticipation ran through me as I tied mine around my neck, drawing it into a loose bow with fraying ends that tickled my collarbone. I was curious what it would be like to be bitten. There must have been some pleasure if people gave their blood willingly. Did Mum get bitten in a blood bar back home? I'd made a similar assumption when she came home with her neck taped up, but I didn't want to believe it.

Jared caressed my ribbon. "If anyone's going to bite you, it's me."

"Only if you wear your Lestat outfit."

"I knew you liked it." He winked, crouching down to tie the ribbon round his left leg. "Let them try to bite behind my knee."

Inside the blood bar, two bodyguards were the only visible

people. The circular space was edged with booths covered by red velvet curtains, most of which were closed against prying eyes. Down here, the rose scent was eye-wateringly strong and the carpet was a very specific shade of red. The walls between the booths were plain, and there was no music. People didn't come here for the ambiance.

Between the folds of velvet, I caught glimpses of motion. It wasn't a place to throw back the curtains and quiz people about their drinking habits.

Jared approached a bouncer with a shaved head and a thick neck. I followed with Della. Her eyes hadn't stopped roving around since we arrived.

"Excuse me, sir," Jared said.

A moan escaped from behind the nearest curtain. I couldn't tell if it was motivated by pain or pleasure.

The bouncer didn't flinch. "Are you here for someone in particular?" There were criss-crosses of scar tissue on both sides of his neck. One mark above his white collar was livid red, as if newly healed. The bite mark formed a lopsided circle, with the imprints of individual teeth visible.

"Is Elvira working?" Jared asked. That was a made-up name if ever I'd heard one, unless her parents named her after *Elvira: Mistress of the Dark*.

Either Lucas had given instructions about his exploits, or Jared had been here before. I knew which option I preferred.

"She's occupied right now, but you can wait."

A tall, graceful guy about my age glided down the stairs. He approached me, his light grey eyes locked on my ribbon. "Would you care to join me?"

"Not likely." Jared stepped in front of me. He ripped the ribbon off his leg and stuffed it into his pocket. "She's with me."

The guy shifted his attention to Della. "I wouldn't," she said.

With a condescending smirk, he reached for her arm.

Impossibly fast, Della caught his hand and bent his wrist back with a loud crack. Retracting his hand, he flexed it backwards and forwards. "You've only made yourself more intriguing, but I will respect your wishes."

The bouncer appeared. "Are we going to have a problem?" he asked, quiet and menacing.

"No problem, George," the guy said. "Ladies."

He drifted to a pair of closed curtains to the right of the room and slipped into the booth.

"Elvira's free," the bouncer added. He managed to say her name with a straight face.

A young guy shuffled out of the nearest booth, with a compress taped inside one elbow and a face that was equally happy and spaced out.

We stepped into Elvira's lair. Her hair was dyed black and her top was black fishnet over a purple vest the same colour as her lips. Thick make-up ringed her eyes, and her skin was pure white. "Close the curtains," she said.

Della and Jared took a curtain each, and then we sank into the plush seats around the circular booth. In the middle, there was a table with a row of shiny scalpels, a basket of bandages and a small bin labelled with instructions about disposing of sharp objects.

"My name is . . ." She narrowed her eyes at Jared. "We've met before. Where's your beautiful friend?"

"In the hospital." Jared's jaw twitched. "Have you heard anything about the people who've been murdered recently?"

"Funny, you're a little young for cops," she said, stroking the handle of a scalpel.

"We just want to know if you've heard anything," I said, trying not to stare at the sliver of blade.

"I might have," she said. "My memory's not what it could be. Blood helps."

"That's not why we're here. You like Lucas," Jared said, annoyingly smooth and charming. "If you tell us something useful, we can help him."

"I don't know who did it, just that they're old ones. There are supposed to be *humans* helping them as well." She said the word disdainfully, as if she wasn't one of us.

"Real vampires?" I asked. Did she seriously believe that?

"If you're not giving me any blood, you can get out. That's all I know."

We stepped through the curtains, and I turned straight to Jared. "When were you here?"

He froze in place, lips parted. The truth shouldn't have been so difficult. "I'll tell you everything . . . later."

Della's sneering upper lip suggested she was forming a new opinion of Jared. I was with her. There was no excuse for keeping this from us.

I almost laid into him as my attention wandered to a space where the next two curtains parted. Despite my anger, I wanted to understand why Lucas, Jared and possibly Mum came to places like this. As we walked past the booth, I looked.

Through the velvet curtains, Thandie's face was serene as she took a young woman's slender arm. She had no scalpel in her hand, and she made no cuts. She just lowered her mouth to the girl's exposed wrist.

Chapter 22

Thandie's eyes were closed and the repetitive pull of her mouth against the girl's wrist mesmerised me. The young woman's face was happy, almost ecstatic, and she bit her lip. A morbid place inside me awoke at the sight.

Della grabbed my arm, but Thandie spotted us. Her mouth detached from the girl's wrist, leaving neat puncture marks. Blood covered Thandie's teeth, though not so much that I missed the curved fangs retracting into her gums.

The girl sagged to one side as Thandie whipped an adhesive compress from a tray on the table and applied it to the wound. The girl looked drunk and very contented as she ambled away.

"Come with me," Thandie said to the three of us, scrunching her hair with an agitated tug.

I replayed the incident as we followed Thandie up

the stairs. There was no convincing myself it was elaborate role play. I saw her fangs.

We followed her out of the club. Thandie lit a cigarette, blowing the plume of smoke away from us. "I suppose I should explain. Are we going to your place or the mansion?"

"Ours," Jared said. He extended a hand towards mine. I made no move to take it, so he let it fall.

Thandie watched me over the glow of her cigarette. "You have nothing to fear from me."

Whatever she read from my face, she had it wrong. I was more fascinated than afraid. A lifetime of questions were about to be answered.

Jared let us in and Thandie followed him to the kitchen without an invitation. Was that a vampire myth busted, or had she been here before? The click of Della locking the door stirred up my fear. Elvira said an old vampire, or vampires, were responsible for the murders. We could've brought one home with us.

Though Jared and I sat at the table with Thandie, Della leaned against the counter, flexing her fingers at her sides. A vein throbbed at her temple, and I thought about the pulsing blood. Did Thandie notice it?

"Now you know." Thandie's emotions were impenetrable, and she wasn't visibly breathing. I'd never noticed before. What other ways were there to spot a vampire? I had to know everything.

"You didn't kill them," Jared stated.

"If you're referring to the young girls who've been viciously murdered these past weeks, I did not. Why would I leave a body in my own house?" She made a good point.

"You're a vampire." Jared raised his eyebrows. Was I the only one who believed her? She'd fed from a human right in front of us.

"Yes." Thandie went motionless, and it was unnerving. She'd never given off much human warmth, and now she'd shed it completely. She didn't blink. Her chest was unmoving, and there were no human fidgets. I was an example of that, tracing my hands back and forth over the smooth wood of my seat.

"How . . ." Jared trailed off and tried again. "How old are you?"

"That's an impudent question, but I'll let it go. I'm older than I look, and than you'll live to be."

I took over. "You're telling us vampires are real. Immortal vampires – like in the stories."

I expected her to lie or be evasive. She said, "I suppose so, though not exactly like the stories, and not everyone at The Underground is truly like me."

I wanted to crack her open and let the secrets pour out. This was the truth my mum wanted, and it was within my reach. "Did we just invite you in? Do you have to be invited?"

"I've been here before," Thandie said. "As a rule, we have to be invited into homes, apart from our own." That was some comfort. If vampires were responsible for the murders, we were safe here. Except this one had an invitation. "Public places or residences with dead owners are fair game," Thandie added, sharpening the edge of my anxiety again.

"Do you know who's doing this?" I asked.

"Of course not, and you shouldn't try to find out."

"What does that mean? Libby's locked up because they think she did it!"

Thandie gave no reaction to my outburst. "My lawyer is working around the clock to get her out. No good comes from digging into matters you don't understand."

"Why don't you spell it out for us?" Della asked, bristling. She'd been quiet through all of this, but her anger came through loud and clear.

Thandie pressed her hands hard into the table. "Do I need to explain that you should let the police do their jobs? I want to help Elizabeth as much as you do, but it's not our place. You're not prepared for this discussion. I can let myself out."

She moved so fast that we couldn't argue. Seconds later, she'd unlocked the front door and shut it behind her.

With her gone, my thoughts spun out of control. "Vampires exist . . . She's a vampire. They've been around all this time . . . God, how many have we met and not even realised?"

Jared scraped his hands up and down both cheeks. "This is insane. I'm not hallucinating – you guys saw that."

"We did." Della was the coolest person I'd ever met because she gave no reaction, while me and Jared were in a meltdown. "Don't either of you think she could be the killer?"

I was too busy wrapping my head around living for ever but I went back to her question. "I hope not."

Della pushed her chair back. "I have to get home – you know what my dad's like."

She wasn't as fast as Thandie, and we caught up with her in the hallway. I understood that her dad was protective, but we'd had our worlds shaken up. I wanted her to stay and talk about it.

"Should we meet tomorrow?" Jared asked.

"That's fine," Della said, her hand on the door. She left us alone with a heavy conversation looming.

Jared gave a low, humourless laugh. "I don't know what to say."

"How about we sit down?"

I followed him into his room. Although I'd sneaked a few peeks through the open door, this was my first time inside. It had the same wooden floor and whitewashed walls as mine, with a year of living on top. In the corner, there was a rack of silver weights. Posters covered the walls: *Pump up the Volume*, *The Crow*, *True Romance*, *Hellraiser* and so many other good movies. He also had a shelf of books and action figures, mainly *Transformers* and WWF wrestlers.

He sat on the bed and kicked his trainers off. I did the same, crossing my legs. Part of me wanted to curl up with Jared and forget the drama, except that he caused some of it.

He read me well. "I should've told you I'd been to The Underground."

"You think?" He must have heard the sarcasm, but he couldn't have been aware of how deeply he'd hurt me. If I couldn't trust him, what did we have left?

"I messed up. I'll try to explain . . . Lucas is the reason I decided to major in nursing. I went to The Underground with him to try and understand. I watched . . ." He swallowed. "Elvira cut inside his elbow and drank from him, and I could tell it wasn't a phase. He's addicted to the feeling, and I want to help people like him. I'm not explaining this very well."

"Your explanation's not the problem," I said. "I don't understand why you didn't tell me you'd been there. Didn't you think it was relevant when it came out that Heather was bitten? Or when Marsden told us about The Underground?" I was struggling to keep a lid on my anger, which was partly aimed at myself for trusting him so easily.

"I didn't know it'd be relevant, and . . . I didn't want you to think differently of me."

He should've thought about that sooner. "And you didn't know about vampires?"

"No! Not until we saw Thandie. I just thought some people had a thing about drinking blood."

I was already accepting it. Thandie was a vampire. Vampires were real. The more I thought it, the more normal it seemed. "Is that what this is? A . . . vampire is the killer?"

"Elvira thought so," Jared said, "although it could be a human biting people and then killing them, some kind of sick fanatic."

"I suppose so," I said. It was safer to leave this alone, but the police were no better prepared to deal with vampires than we were. Libby needed someone to rescue her. Lucas was in a hospital bed because there were monsters out there.

That was it. We'd explored everything, and while we'd talked, the knot of anger towards Jared had slackened. He hadn't technically lied; he'd held things back. With everything else falling apart, I wanted things to be good with Jared. "Is there anything else you're not telling me?"

He ran a hand through his hair. "I think that's it."

"No more holding back?" I crawled forwards on the bed until our eyes were level. I needed to be sure of him.

"I'm sorry," he said, reaching into my hair and weaving his hand through the lengths.

"I know."

I slid into his lap and wrapped my legs around his back. My

dress rode up, so there was little more than the thick, black denim of his jeans separating us.

I placed a hand on his chest. His heart was beating fast through the fabric, and my fingertips skimmed the downy hair above his T-shirt.

Jared's lips curved into an irresistible smile and he leaned in, leaving a tingling path of kisses under my jawline. His lips skimmed my neck and I closed my eyes, savouring it.

Then we were kissing and he kneaded my hips through the thin dress, his mouth insistent against mine. The last traces of my annoyance urged heat into the kiss. I ran my hands down his sides. My fingers reached the bottom of his T-shirt, and I slid them underneath the hem. He gasped against my mouth as my fingertips found smooth skin, and his muscles flexed at the touch.

Guilt niggled at me. I shouldn't lose myself in him when we had so much to solve. I disentangled myself. "We should get some sleep."

He peered up through his curls with a disgruntled grin. "You're right."

I headed straight to the bathroom and locked the door, cleaning my teeth too hard. I went back to my room to put my pyjamas on and heard Jared moving around. I almost got into bed when I changed my mind. I wanted to see him.

Chapter 23

Jared's door was open, and I had no plan when I walked through it. Without a word, he flipped back the thin quilt. He was wearing pyjamas, a black vest and matching shorts, but there were a lot of ways this could go.

"I know how this is going to sound," he said, "but will you sleep in here . . . with me?"

The space on his mattress was tempting, and I didn't want to be left alone.

"If you snore or talk in your sleep, I'm out of here." I climbed into the bed, facing away from him.

The spot he'd left was all toasty, and I snuggled down into it. He shuffled across the mattress and slid one hand under my pillow. The outline of his arm was reassuring. His lips touched the skin above my pyjama top, a sensitive spot between my shoulder blades. Tomorrow held plenty of challenges but being close to him left me almost content. "Night," he whispered.

Jared fell asleep quickly, but my brain wouldn't slow down. If Thandie was telling the truth about inviting vampires in, she was the only one who could enter. Still, only thin glass protected us. I strained to hear even the smallest sound. There was nothing.

Soothed by the quiet, I felt the pull of sleep. Then I heard something. A quiet but distinctive tap. I listened, and there it was again: a deliberate clack, clack, clack like fingernails hitting glass. Shot full of adrenaline, I sat up. Jared grumbled in his sleep, burrowing his face deeper into the pillow.

We were perfectly safe: even if a vampire was outside, they couldn't get in without an invitation. There was another clack, and I jumped. All I had to do was check outside the window and get back into bed with Jared.

I was halfway there when a realisation stopped me. Libby, Lucas and Jared had lived here for almost a year. They could've invited more vampires than Thandie to come in without even knowing. Any of those vampires had an open invitation. The door was locked, but a window could easily be broken. A hand could punch through and drag me out over the broken glass.

Before I lost my nerve, I flung back the curtains. An empty black space yawned back at me.

Not feeling particularly encouraged, I retreated to bed. Mumbling, Jared folded his arms around me, and I tried to find that relaxation again. For seventeen years, I'd fallen asleep when vampires were out there. I knew more now but refused to spend the rest of my life afraid. I scooted closer to Jared, curving into him so our bodies slotted together, and tried to sleep.

No monsters came for us. I woke an inch from Jared's sleeping face, with the golden light of morning stealing through a crack between the curtains. He was definitely not a vampire, squinting against the sunlight.

"Morning," he murmured. "Not awake." He nuzzled a stubbly cheek against mine and wrapped his arms around me. It felt so comfortable with the sheets bundled around us and warmth radiating from him. It was a novelty to rest my head in the nook under his arm, getting as close as possible.

We lay like that, with Jared's face buried in my hair, until I really needed to get up. I had a quick shower and then tiptoed across the hallway in my towel.

The daylight made me feel slightly more optimistic, mostly because we were safe from creatures with a taste for our blood. Libby had over a day before they could charge her. The main problem with her case was that the police would never think a vampire did it, if that was what we were dealing with.

Jared was serving two plates of scrambled eggs and toast as I got into the kitchen. "Good timing," he said, setting them on the table.

"Are we going to see Lucas again this morning?" I asked, tucking into the eggs. At some point, I wanted to cook for him or ask him to teach me.

"Can we stop by Thandie's first?" Jared asked. "I have a feeling she hasn't told us everything."

"That's fine," I said. Thandie was the only one who could give us information about the monster who was behind all of this. I just wasn't sure where we stood with her. The others had known her longer, but how much could we trust her when we were part of her only food group?

Jared phoned Lucas to see if he needed anything. When Jared asked how Lucas was, the response made his shoulders relax.

It was good to hear Jared having a normal exchange with Lucas. Maybe things could go back to the way they were.

Jared knocked hard on the door of the mansion before he unlocked it. Thandie stood back in the hallway, wearing a silky, black dress with low shoulders.

"Fortunately, we don't burst into flames at the sight of daylight, though there is quite a degree of agony. I must say, your concern is touching."

"Sorry." Jared closed the door.

That answered one question. "What does happen if you go out in the day?" I asked.

"Our skin blisters and then we die after prolonged exposure. I'd rather not have this conversation in the hallway. I'll make tea."

That explained the twilight shades of the house; she was always waiting for the night.

This time, the tea was lilac, with violet petals floating on the surface. She served it in fragile teacups that were scalding to the touch. It smelled flowery, a little better than the previous one.

"What brings you here?" Thandie sipped from a large stone-ware mug. I sat up straighter and Thandie covered the top. "It's coffee."

I tried not to stare, but everything about her was intriguing.

Where were her fangs? How much blood did she drink? Remembering how fast she shut us down last time, I asked the crucial question, "How do we identify vampires?"

Thandie leaned back in her chair. "Not very well, apparently."

"Lucas is hurt." Jared said. "If we can't spot them, we can't protect ourselves."

"Oh good. Your lives are in my hands." Thandie sipped her 'coffee'. "Sunlight blisters the skin, as I said, causing us to become so weak that we perish if left exposed. Covering or sheltering us can work, though at great risk if the shelter is disturbed. Let me see . . . We do not eat. Blood and fluids work quite well to keep us alive. Crosses and holy water do us no harm. That's wishful thinking on the church's part."

"What about garlic?" Jared asked.

"You wouldn't catch us eating it, or anything else for that matter, and it smells terrible. That's all."

Jared continued with the questions. "How do you kill a vampire?"

Thandie became very still. "Fire. A stake through the heart. Decapitation. But any human foolish enough to attempt it would be dead before the vampire."

I hoped it wouldn't come to that. "Do vampires have powers?"

Thandie's fangs flicked into place, retracting just as quickly. "As a rule, we are fast and strong, unless we haven't fed. Human diseases do not ail us and injuries heal fast. Many of us possess other abilities, but those vary depending on the traits we had as humans."

I wanted to ask if she had any abilities, though I decided against it. Remembering John's power to manipulate people like puppets, I asked, "Can all vampires compel people to do what they want?"

Thandie stiffened. Was that her ability too? "Some can, but not all."

Jared fired off another question. "Do you kill people?"

"I'm going to assume you mean me, as opposed to my kind. I'm not sure what you want me to say. I have to take blood from a living . . . donor. Refrigerated blood is as good as dead to us. Going to the blood bar allows me to take what I need consensually and with minimal harm." Thandie must have finished sharing, as she asked a question of her own. "Has there been any news about Lucas or Elizabeth?"

"I talked to him this morning. He's doing good." Jared's tone was optimistic for someone who was slouched low, scrubbing a hand over his tired eyes. "There's no news about Libby. We're going there next."

"Keep me informed."

"We will," I said.

We stepped out into the sunshine. "That was . . . a lot. What did you . . .?" I didn't get the chance to finish.

A black van was parked outside the mansion and the door opened. Someone wearing a balaclava leapt out and swept my feet from under me. I hit the ground hard and my head smacked the pavement. Lights and black spots swam in front of my vision. I wanted to get up and help. Everything hurt. Jared and the guy were tussling . . . he needed me. I couldn't lift my head. My sight wavered as the man shoved Jared into the van. After that, there was nothing.

Chapter 24

The back of my head pounded, and pain shot down my back. Why was my bed so hard?

My memory returned with a wave of sickness and I rolled onto my side, retching. The pavement scorched my cheek, so I sat up slowly. Everything lurched, and I put my head between my knees. Jared was gone.

I heard footsteps as people walked around me, muttering about drunkenness and being a tragic waste.

I stood, wobbling. My eye sockets ached as I let my blurry vision settle. On shaky legs, I stumbled to the door of the mansion and knocked.

It opened an inch, and Thandie retreated as I pushed it wider. I closed the door against the deadly sunlight as my legs buckled. Impossibly, Thandie caught me before I hit the carpeted floor.

Her hands were more like stone than flesh, too hard and cold for the living. "Someone took Jared."

"Come sit down."

Thandie walked me into the kitchen. Her arm around my back was as cool and unrelenting as a band of steel.

I crashed into a chair and used a hand to support my head. With my eyes closed, the dizziness eased. I cautiously poked the bump at the back of my head and was rewarded with a spike of pain.

Thandie set a mug in front of me with green leaves floating on the water. "Tell me what happened."

I breathed in the minty fragrance. "There was a black van. A man in a balaclava tripped me, and he took Jared." I tried to remember more: any features or what he was wearing. "Could it have been a vampire?" Pain and concern for Jared roared in my head, obliterating everything else.

"It's possible," Thandie said. "Though not every misfortune is because of us. Most serial killers and mass murderers are human, so I really should call the police. Will you be all right?"

"I'll manage." The tea helped. As I listened to Thandie's husky voice from the hallway, drinking the tea, my headache shrank to the spot where my head hit the pavement.

"The police are on their way." How did she do that? Thandie was back at the table without making a sound. "Do you need medical attention?"

What I didn't need was a two-hour wait in a hospital. They'd only tell me not to go to sleep, and that wasn't happening. "I'm fine. Can I have some more tea, please?"

Boudreaux and Cafferty arrived quickly. There was only one good thing about Jared getting taken: Libby was in custody, so the police couldn't blame her. "How's my sister?" I asked.

"She's coping fine," Boudreaux said. "Can you tell us what happened?" Both detectives opened their notebooks and waited with their pens ready.

I repeated what I'd told Thandie, the scanty fragments I remembered. Boudreaux wasn't satisfied. "You couldn't see the perpetrator's face or any distinguishing characteristics?"

"I think it was a man. He was pretty big, and tall . . . all dressed in black." That was everything I knew, and I had to make the most of this time with them. "Someone has taken one of my friends, attacked another and my sister's been arrested. Could they be targeting us?"

"We're lookin' into every eventuality. Rest assured, we're taking this very seriously." I appreciated Boudreaux's sentiment, though it didn't exactly put me at ease.

"And you know Libby didn't take Jared." Someone took him. All of the horrible options played out: what they were doing to him or if he was even alive. He couldn't be dead.

Boudreaux's lips twitched. "We've ruled out her involvement on this occasion."

That was something: the slightest indication she believed us.

Boudreaux rose. "Please call the station if you remember anythin' else. We'll update you with any news about Jared."

"And Libby," I added.

"For now, we're recommendin' that people travel in groups in the day and remain somewhere secure at night."

Her advice was sensible, even if she didn't know vampires were the reason for it.

I followed them into the hall, since Thandie couldn't let them out into the daylight. I took some satisfaction from slamming the door behind them.

Despair made everything muddy. How was I supposed to find Jared? They could have driven him anywhere. I had to tell Della; she'd help me.

There was a hard knock on the door. It took more effort than normal to get the heavy wood to shift, and the sunlight stung my eyes. Straight away, I knew they had bad news. Cafferty's lips tilted downwards, and Boudreaux fidgeted with her hands. She let them fall to her sides. "We just received a call on the radio."

Did they file charges against Libby? Or find Jared?

"Lucas passed away a few minutes ago."

Chapter 25

Lucas was dead. They said all the right things, about how sorry they were and how tragic it was. Those three words remained: Lucas was dead.

"Can we go to see . . . him?" I asked. Not *his body*. Not *it*, never *it*.

"I'm afraid not," Boudreaux said. "His family will have to be notified."

Did they even get to see him in hospital before he died and make amends for how they treated him? Boudreaux was waiting for an answer, but I missed the question. "Sorry . . . What did you say?"

"I asked if you want us to take you home. Is there someone who can stay with you?"

"I . . . ." I was lost. Lucas was gone, Jared had been taken, and Libby was locked away from me.

"I'll take care of her, Detective. Thank you," Thandie said from the hallway behind me.

I slammed the door again, the crash vibrating through my hand. Thandie materialised from the shadows. "Would you like to call your aunt?"

I shook my head. "She's travelling. I can't get in touch with her."

"I'll call Della at work. She'll take you home."

There was a knock at the door in next to no time. It was Della, and we collided in a hug that was fierce with all of the grief and loss we put into it. "Thandie told me everything," she said. "Let's get you home. You got a key?"

I fumbled in my pocket. "Yeah."

As soon as we got into the car, it was time for plotting. I had plenty of aches and not a lot of ideas, but we had to try.

"What are we going to do?"

"Let's talk at home," Della said, pulling out onto the road. "For now, rest."

I could tell from the set of her expression that there was no use in arguing. I rested my aching head back and closed my eyes.

The journey lasted only a few minutes, so I wasn't particularly refreshed. I followed Della into the kitchen, and she opened the fridge. "You should eat," Della said.

"OK," I agreed. If I behaved, she had to work on this with me. "How are we going to find him?"

"We can't," Della said, kind but firm. "He could be anywhere by now. The police are on it, and they'll keep us updated. You want me to fix you a sandwich?"

She was right. What were we supposed to do, wander the streets of New Orleans on the hunt for black vans? "Sure . . . thanks."

We carried our plates to Libby's room. "Let's get a movie on," Della said, sitting on the floor to consider the stack of videos by Libby's bed.

I knew she was trying to keep me occupied, but it felt so wrong to be in here while Libby was locked up and Jared was gone. Tears of frustration fragmented my vision and I sat on the bed, biting into my ham sandwich. Della had put mustard and salad on it, but the bread got stuck and I had to choke it down.

"Found one," Della said, carefully freeing a video from the stack. I recognised the cover of *Buffy the Vampire Slayer* even before she held it up. Buffy wouldn't be sitting back and eating sandwiches if she was in our shoes.

As Della fast-forwarded the adverts, I asked, "Did you hear any more about Libby?"

Della shook her head. "I called the police station and Libby's lawyer again. She was nice and all, but just said she's workin' through Libby's options."

I was sure the lawyer was doing her best, but the non-news was another setback. The movie came on, with the cheesy voiceover giving the history of vampire slayers. It usually lulled me into comfort, but I couldn't relax. "Are you working today?"

Della swallowed a mouthful of sandwich. "I called in sick. We're good as long as I don't run into Marsden."

I was fine with that. "Thanks," I said.

A single loud bang outside made me jump. "Was that the door?" Della asked. "What kind of person only knocks once?"

We hurried into the hallway. Della opened the door cautiously.

No one was there.

She almost closed it again when we spotted a sheet of paper attached to the door with a small dagger, driven deep into the wood.

"Don't touch it," Della said. She stretched the sleeves of her shirt down over her hands, taking the dagger's handle in one hand and the note in the other. She pulled hard and the fine, deadly tip of the blade came free.

Della set the dagger on the kitchen counter and placed the note on the table, avoiding contact with both. Libby's experience had taught us to be wary.

The folded note had my name written on one side in flowing handwriting. Della flipped it open with her sleeve and we read together.

> *Dearest Mina,*
>
> *Your friend Jared and I request the pleasure of your company. You will find us on the street named princess, where a false prince lost his too-short life. Come soon, and come alone, lest your friend arrive at the same fate.*

Jared's nameless kidnapper was tormenting me with riddles. It was like a fairy tale, the old, grisly kind where the prince was blinded by thorns or the girl's hands were severed.

"What's that s'posed to mean?" Della asked.

I read the note again. A street named princess, where a false prince died . . .

"I might have a way to find out," I said, hurrying to Jared's room.

Della followed, pulling off a few thick books from his shelf when I did.

We retreated to my bed to read them. At first, I flicked through unseeing, feeling the pressure. When that failed, I read the contents page, concentrating on every word. None of it was familiar. I flipped through the book again, reading a few lines of each story.

Finally, I had it: another myth from Thandie's museum. This was the story of a young sultan from a faraway land who held lavish, secretive parties and kept his home surrounded by guards. There were rumours he'd taken his brother's harem of women and his brother had chased him to New Orleans. One night, the women in the harem were found slaughtered. The sultan was buried alive.

"We're going to Dauphine Street."

Della called an ambulance while I waited, full of impatience and doubt. The note said to come alone, and I'd told her and the emergency services. She kept it vague, saying our friend was badly hurt to keep the police away for a bit. I hoped our actions weren't putting him in more danger.

Della's car was like an oven until I cranked my window open. She flew down the narrow roads as I told her the sultan story. Since the killer bothered to send a note, he had to be keeping Jared alive. There was no other option.

Within a few minutes, we were there and had beaten the ambulance. The mansion was on a corner, with three stories surrounded by balconies decorated with a repeating fleur-de-lis pattern. It was painted a bright cream, but the story of the sultan and the women cast a bleak shade over the house.

"The note said I should go alone," I said, as Della pulled up.

"No way. I'm coming with you."

The second the car stopped, I was out and running. There was a wall to the right of the house with an open door set into it. Broken glass glinted along the top of the wall, keeping intruders out or someone inside.

My feet hit the tarmac hard as I ran towards the house. I heard Della running behind me.

Slipping through the door, I paused. How did I know Jared's kidnapper wasn't waiting for me? There was no sign of anyone, but I was alert.

The garden was surrounded by walls, with a closed door that led into the house. All of the plants were dead and the churned up soil was parched.

In the centre of the shrivelled grass, there was a mound of dirt. I rushed over and discovered a hole the size of a grave. Jared was lying at the bottom, blood seeping from a wound on his neck and soil heaped over him.

"Della!" I yelled. The hole was only a few feet deep and I hopped in, sending up a cloud of dry soil.

I tugged off my T-shirt and clamped it against his bloody neck. The skin was mangled and blood immediately soaked through the thin material. Tears poured down my face, stinging my eyes as they mixed with the dirt. "Jared," I said, pushing two fingers into the flesh under his jawbone. He had a pulse. It was weak, but I felt it. His eyes were closed, and the lashes flickered at his name. He didn't respond.

Jared was alive, and the ambulance was coming. They'd save him.

I looked around nervously. The note said 'we' would be waiting at this location. The monster who did this to him could still be here.

A figure leaned over the hole, blotting out the sunlight. I flinched, preparing for the worst. It was only Della. "Please tell me he's alive!"

"He is." He was going to stay that way.

"I'll wait for the ambulance on the street. Do we move him?" Her head jerked up at the faint note of sirens.

"Let's wait for the paramedics." My T-shirt was wet with blood, and it had soaked through to my hands. What was I supposed to do? If anything happened to him . . .

His legs were covered in a thick layer of soil, but there was only a scattering above the waist. I might have interrupted whoever tried to bury him. What if I hadn't come in time? Panic bubbled up again, so I took in the scene.

The most bizarre thing was that he was dressed in beautifully made, old-fashioned clothing – a gold shirt with fine beads and twisted cording along the edges. Someone stripped and redressed him.

Blue lights flashed through the garden door, and the sirens cut off. Two paramedics appeared on either side of the hole. One slid down, a white woman with close-cropped hair. "I'll take over, could you clear the area please?" I clambered out of the hole, the earth at the edge giving way under my feet. I accepted a hand from the other paramedic, a guy with big arms.

I sat on the dirt, head down, and breathed. I heard Della telling someone I wasn't hurt and forced calm in through my lungs. They couldn't waste time on me. They had to help Jared.

Shakily, I stood up. Della answered the male paramedic's barrage of questions: no, Jared didn't have any allergies or medical conditions she knew of; yes, he'd been unconscious since we arrived.

I stood over the hole to watch what they were doing. The paramedic put a mask over his mouth and his chest rose and fell. I breathed more easily knowing he was doing it with me.

The paramedics put Jared on a stretcher and lifted him out. I was so grateful for their efficiency and speed. They were giving him the best possible chance.

Once Jared was safely in the ambulance, the female paramedic addressed us from the open doors at the back. "Do either of you want to ride along?"

"I will," I said.

"I'll follow in the car," Della said. She peeled off her checked shirt and handed it to me, leaving herself in a black vest. She hugged me and jogged away.

I slipped into her shirt and fastened it with shaky hands, as I climbed up the ambulance steps. That had to be the shock; I hadn't even noticed I was sitting there in my bra.

I hadn't been in an ambulance before, and I never wanted to do it again. I needed a quiet, safe life, where Jared was all right and our only worry was that I had to leave at the end of the summer. I fastened my seatbelt as the sirens wailed to life.

The paramedic handed me a white towel, then got to work on Jared, cutting off the bloody, golden shirt. The wound on his neck had a compress taped over it.

I almost asked the paramedic why she'd given me the towel when I noticed my hands. They were plastered with Jared's blood. Revulsion clawed inside my stomach as I scrubbed my skin with the dry fabric. By the time I finished, my hands were pink and sore but free of blood.

"You doin' OK?" the paramedic asked, reaching out a gloved

hand for the bloody towel.

I gave it to her, nodding. There were no windows, and travelling sideways brought on hot, queasy travel sickness.

"Are you Mina?" she asked.

Hope surging, I glanced at Jared. Did he wake up and tell her my name? There was an oxygen mask over his face, and he was unconscious. I hated seeing him like that.

"Yes . . ." I said at last.

"I found this in his pocket. I'm guessing it's yours."

It was another note, with my name on one side of the folded paper.

I unfolded it. There was a strip of tape along the bottom, and the handwriting was the same as the note from my door. I'd been so careful with the other note and managed to put my hands all over this one.

Dearest Mina,

Our game nears its close. I do hope you're enjoying it as much as I am, and that poor Jared is getting the help he needs. Until we meet again, I will leave you with this small favor. Look closely at the tape. Planting evidence and forging fingerprints are easy when you have the means.

John Carter

Taped at the bottom of the paper was a strand of long, curly dark hair.

Chapter 26

I paced the hospital waiting room, too agitated to sit. The note was in my pocket, signed by a long-dead Carter brother and attached to hair a lot like mine and Libby's. Then there was Jared to think about, so recently left bleeding at the bottom of a hole.

Della burst through the doors. "Where is he?"

"Through there." I pointed out the entrance to the emergency department. "They said they'll update me."

"OK," Della said, releasing a long breath.

A nurse came straight for us. "Jared is asking for the two of you," he said. "Would you like to see him?"

Some of the stress eased. He was well enough to ask for us.

We followed the nurse into a ward full of whirring machines. Curtains hid each patient from view as we followed the nurse to Jared. He reviewed the machine by Jared's bed and ducked out.

Jared's skin was pasty and his eyes were sunken, but they brightened when he saw us. I sank gratefully into the plastic chair beside him. Della stood by the bed, smiling. Jared was hooked up to a drip through a needle in his hand and a machine monitoring his heart rate. A repetitive, high-pitched beep had never been so comforting.

Tears poured down my cheeks, all the relief and worry flowing out of me. "Don't cry," Jared said, taking my hand. "I'm alive and kicking, thanks to the two of you. It wasn't as bad as it looked."

"Good," I said.

"Did you go to see Lucas?" Jared asked.

Oh God, he didn't know.

Della stepped in, her voice trembling. "Lucas didn't make it. There were complications after his surgery . . . I'm so sorry."

The smile hadn't quite left Jared's face but the light in his eyes dimmed. "No . . ."

"I'm sorry," Della said again, tears breaking up her words.

Jared ripped his hand out of mine and covered his face. The tube attached to it pulled taut, but the needle was held in place by medical tape. "We did this to him." Jared's certainty landed like a blow. If we'd stayed at home, stuck together or done any of a thousand things differently, Lucas could have survived.

"We can't think that way," Della said quietly. "A twisted person," She dropped her voice, "or *thing*, did this to him."

Even though Della had a point, the guilt remained. There were tears in Jared's eyes, but he concentrated on me again, softening. "You were there when the guy took me. Did he hurt you?"

"I'm fine. I hit my head, but I have a thick skull."

"You said it." Even though Jared's smile lacked his usual wattage, he was trying. "I should get some sleep."

"Are you all right?" I asked.

"I will be," he said.

I was so sad for Jared that I really didn't need to find Detectives Boudreaux and Cafferty in the waiting area.

"I take it Jared's resting." Boudreaux said. There was a bulging carrier bag in her hand, though I couldn't see what was inside it. "Are you two available to come down to the station again?" That was a nicer request than we'd received before. I was reluctant to stray far from Jared, but there'd been too many developments to keep them to myself.

We'd handed the evidence over, and it was waiting in clear bags on the table of the interview room: two notes and the dagger. They were with the blood-stained outfit Jared was wearing. So that was what Boudreaux was carrying at the hospital.

"I assume you're gonna explain all of this," Boudreaux said drily, waving a hand over the morbid collection.

I told them about the note on our door and finding Jared in as much detail as I could remember. Della interjected at key moments, filling the gaps in my story. Boudreaux's blank expression flickered at two points: when I explained the Sultan's Palace story and how Jared's kidnapper signed the note John Carter, another mythical reference.

When I finished, Boudreaux leaned back in her chair. "Thank you," she said. The story they'd crafted around Libby was disintegrating, unless she'd kidnapped Jared and sent me two notes from inside a cell. "We need to process all of this, but I have one more question. Assuming John Carter is a pseudonym, since he died sixty years ago, can either of you think of anyone who'd want to cause harm to yourselves or Jared?"

"No." It was so disturbing that someone could have chosen us for this.

"There's nobody," Della said. Who would have wanted to hurt a group of college students? Except the killer in every horror movie, but even they usually had a reason.

"For the time being, we have the go ahead to place you under police protection. Detective Cafferty'll escort you home and wait until the protective detail comes. You'll stay there unless you hear otherwise. Both of you. Is that clear?"

"Crystal," I said.

"Yes, ma'am. Now can we see Libby?" Della asked.

"Not yet," Boudreaux said. "Call if you think of anything else. We'll need to speak with both of you again."

Cafferty insisted on driving me back, with Della following in her car. His car was large and gun-metal grey, with a badge on the back that said Crown Victoria. Apart from a quietly crackling radio and a few extra buttons, it was like a normal car.

"How're you holdin' up?" he asked, checking his rear-view mirror. "It can't have been an easy time for you."

"No, it hasn't been," I said.

"I have a sister Libby's age," he said. "Between you and me, I understand you puttin' yourself in harm's way for her. I don't condone it, but I understand. I'd have done the same thing in your position."

After that, Cafferty made no attempt at another conversation, and I watched the people we drove past. With night falling, any of them could have been a vampire.

That was when we found Armand waiting by our door.

Chapter 27

We watched Armand from inside Cafferty's car.

"Friend of yours?" Cafferty asked.

"Sort of. He won't be staying." Not after what I was about to say.

I was aware of Cafferty watching as I approached Armand. "Have you been arrested?" he asked. The car wasn't as discreet as I'd thought. Armand's hair was greasy, and his clothes were crumpled.

"No, not that it's any of your business. What are you doing here?" Even the sight of him made me furious.

Armand was suddenly fascinated by the pavement. "I came to offer my services."

My anger spilled over. "Have you had any visions about us this week? Do you have any idea what's going on?"

Armand finally looked at me, full of sorrow. "That's why I'm here. I'm sorry about your friend. I saw what happened to him, though not in time to prevent it."

"Which one?" I'd got loud, but kept enough control to notice him contradicting himself. "You said before that you weren't sure if your visions had taken place or not."

"I . . . It's complicated," he said.

I was only just awake enough to stay on two feet, let alone go around in circles with Armand. "Do you have *anything* that can help us?" I asked.

Armand eyed Cafferty's car and shook his head. "I'm sorry to have bothered you. I should go."

Della pulled up as he bolted in the opposite direction. "Who was that?"

"The fortune teller," I said.

"What did he want?" Della asked as I unlocked the door, watching his shrinking silhouette.

"Nothing helpful," I said.

The little house smelled of sun-warmed wood and my bedroom called to me. The reality of Lucas's closed door really hit me this time. His things were still there, but he'd never come back to claim them. The painting of his mom would stay unfinished.

Della gave me a one-armed hug. "I miss him," she said.

"Me too." The small sentiment didn't do Lucas justice. His loss was a keen twinge under my ribcage. I needed Libby and Jared to come back and for all of this to be over.

"I have to call my dad, then I'll be right next door in Libby's room."

"Night, Della. And thanks . . . for being here."

"Any time," she said. "Night."

My room was cool, and I'd never been so drained. Sleep should have been right there for me to take. I stared up into the darkness, too wired to even close my eyes.

A police officer would have taken over from Cafferty, but how much could one person do? Della and I were the only ones left personally untouched by all of this. If the killer was obsessed with us, what would stop them from coming while we were asleep and helpless?

I dozed in and out, never going under. Then there was a sound. I lay still, listening. I heard it again: the loud click of the front door. Someone was inside.

Fright pinned me in place. While I lay there, shoes squeaked on the wooden floor outside my room, and the floorboards creaked.

I sat up and scanned the room for a weapon. Picking up Jared's heavy New Orleans book, I tested the weight in my hand. It could do some damage if I swung hard enough.

Quietly, I let my feet land on the cool floor and took a cautious step.

My door handle turned and I gripped the book, prepared to strike.

Jared smirked in my doorway. "What did I do now? Except overpay for a cab."

He clicked the light on and I dropped the book on my bed, dazzled. Squinting at the light, I threw my arms around him. His arms closed around me, and I tilted my head back to see his face. "Am I hurting you?"

"I'm bruised, not broken. Well, and scratched a bit." He gestured at his neck.

I traced the edge of the tape with my fingertip. "Does it hurt?"

"Yeah." His mouth was tight.

"What if I distract you?" Standing on my tiptoes, I brushed my lips against his. He kissed me hungrily, our mouths pressed together and his hands rooted deep in my hair.

He broke away first, bringing a hand up to his neck. "They said I'll need a lot of rest. I should get to bed."

"Yeah, that makes sense," I said reluctantly. "Good night, then."

"Night," he said, landing a clumsy kiss on my forehead. His door was closed before I could ask if he wanted to stay. It wasn't about me, so I shouldn't have felt offended. He needed to heal.

The next morning, I awoke to a headache but also joy that Jared was home. I touched the lump on the back of my head, and it throbbed back at me. I was lucky that was my only battle wound.

After a quick bathroom detour, I burst into the kitchen. Della was eating cereal at the table with a mug of coffee steaming by the bowl. "Sorry, did you think I was someone else?"

"I thought Jared might be up. He's probably sleeping it off."

"How does it feel to have your boy back?"

"He's not 'my boy'." I poured some cereal and dug into it.

"You didn't have the talk yet. But I saw y'all at the hospital – you'll be having it soon. I was thinking of stopping by the police station to see how Libby's case is goin'," Della said, heading to the sink to wash her bowl. "Want to come with?"

"Definitely," I said, eating faster.

Jared hadn't stirred by the time I'd showered and dressed.

"Should we make sure he's OK before we go?" I asked. "Or feed him a protein shake?"

"He went to the bathroom earlier – he's fine. We should let him be."

There was a hard knock at the front door, and I reached straight for the worst case scenario. It had to be the police with more bad news.

Reluctantly, I got up and edged into the hallway. Then I saw the outline through the frosted glass.

I crossed the long hallway in a few steps and wrenched the door open, throwing myself at Libby.

Chapter 28

I ended up in a crush with Della and my sister, shaking with tears and laughter. We crashed down on Libby's bed.

There were so many things I wanted to say, but the worst ones had to go first. "Do you know about Lucas?"

She nodded, and her eyes glistened. "I don't believe it. I wasn't there, and now . . . he's gone. And Jared's hurt . . . How is he?"

"They told him the wound on his neck isn't too bad. He's in bed."

"And they let you out," Della said, running a hand down Libby's head until it rested on the back of her neck. "How'd that happen?"

"My little sister gave some massive clues to the police." She leaned against me. "I'm not a hundred percent clear on the details, but my lawyer is a star and made them see they didn't have enough evidence to charge me – for now. I had to fight my way through an army of reporters on the way out, but we all know I look good on camera."

"So, what do we do?" I asked. As far as we knew, the police's only suspect was sitting on the bed with us. Their investigation wasn't going well.

"How about you two catch me up?" Libby asked.

"What about you?" I asked. "What was it like in there?"

Libby twined a piece of hair around her finger, the skin purpling. "I don't want to talk about it. I'm out – we're all good. Just tell me what I missed."

"Thandie's a vampire," Della said. I respected how she got to the point, even if I would've sugar-coated it. "A real one."

Libby's mouth slackened. It took her so long to reply that I thought she might not speak at all. Eventually, she got it out. "That explains a lot!"

"That all you have to say?" Della asked, quirking her eyebrows.

"I'm harder to shock these days. But wow, vampires are real . . ."

I took advantage of the stunned silence. "Do you think Mum ever found out?"

"We'll never know," Libby said, suddenly evasive, biting the skin around her left thumb. "What else did I miss?"

We told Libby about how the murders and myths in Thandie's museum were connected. She listened intently, nodding at key points.

"We have to talk to Thandie," Libby said as soon as we finished.

"You're right," I said, but I wasn't convinced. Were we sure Thandie was innocent?

Libby stood up, flexing her legs. "I'll see if the cop outside will let us go."

She went into the hallway and Della turned to me. "You hangin' in there?"

I appreciated the concern, but I wanted everyone to stop thinking I was going to break. "Like the kitten on the poster."

"OK, we're on," Libby called as she came back through the front door. "Rent-a-cop radioed for permission and Cafferty's coming to pick us up."

We waited outside for Cafferty, and he pulled up behind the police car. He opened the window. "Welcome back," he said to Libby.

"Thanks," she said. "Hate to say I told you I was innocent."

"I believed you."

"Good to know," Libby said, though I could tell she was pleased through the flippancy. "So, you're taking us to the mansion to see our boss?"

"That's right. I want to visit the museum while we're there. One of you is welcome to sit up front."

He closed the car door, and Libby walked around to the front. "Shotgun," she said.

"Might not be the best thing to say around a cop," Cafferty suggested.

"I like him better than Boudreaux." Libby reached to open the car door.

"My window's open," he said.

✸

Thandie emerged from her office when the front door closed behind us.

"What can I do for you, Detective?"

"Good morning, ma'am," Detective Cafferty said. "I was hoping I could see your museum while these three speak with you."

I expected some snark from Thandie about seeing a search warrant, but she didn't deliver. "How can I say no to that? Second door on the right."

Cafferty gave a polite nod and Thandie took us into her office.

With the door closed, she said, "I'm very pleased to see you, Elizabeth. I assume you talked to your sister and girlfriend about me."

"I'm all caught up. Can we sit down?"

"Oh dear, it's that kind of conversation."

Thandie produced a crystal decanter from beneath her desk and poured a generous measure of amber alcohol. "Why do I think I'll need this?" she asked.

Libby carried a chair over from the corner, and the three of us sat down. Della leaned back in her seat, broadcasting hostility from her scowl down to her tightly folded arms.

"Why didn't you tell me you're a *vampire*?" Libby whispered the last word.

"Don't take it personally," Thandie paused to sip her drink. "I don't tell anyone. Your friends caught me with my fangs out, as it were."

"So, you wouldn't have told us if they didn't catch you." Libby gave Thandie no chance to respond. "Mina and the others worked out that the killer's been copying New Orleans myths, and a lot of them are in your museum."

Thandie took a long drink and set the glass down with a dangerous crack. "Have we not had this conversation before? I've had it several times with the police."

"Lucas has died." Libby said. Her body quivered, but she

kept talking. "Jared got buried alive, and the police only let me go because some psycho calling himself John Carter wrote a confession note. You might have said this before, but now I'm asking you. Do you think all of this is linked to the mansion?"

Somewhere during Libby's rant, Thandie flinched, though at what I couldn't tell. She waited until Libby finished. "I assume it's about me, not the mansion. You see, the Carter brothers turned me into a vampire."

Chapter 29

L ibby squeezed my hand too hard and I yanked it free.

"What?" I blurted.

A fraction later, Libby said, "They did what? When?" For once, we were on the same page.

Thandie pressed two fingers against one temple. "I suspected it was him . . . I hoped not."

She let her hand fall. "I believe John Carter is fixated on me because I reported him and Wayne to the police in 1932. Why John took over thirty years to act on that revenge, only he knows."

The Carter brothers were supposed to have been executed, so I'd never thought my note writer could really be John Carter. Jared's story did end with sightings of them after their execution date. The monster from the diaries could be alive.

"You were the girl who got away from the

brothers," I said. And John Carter was sending me notes. That couldn't be good.

"They were executed soon after the police arrested them, and I thought them long dead by the 1960s. That was until John Carter left me bleeding to death on the street, and Wayne Carter made me one of them."

"Why would Wayne do that?" I asked. He was meant to be the more reasonable brother, who hated what they were.

"Regret, perhaps? Or atonement for his brother's actions? He was the kinder one, from what I recall of my time with them. He did not feed to kill, which is a philosophy I too have adopted. That's why I bought his diary. I heard it was up for auction and wanted to learn more about the person who saved me, or cursed me, depending on your viewpoint. At the time, it was a curse. Not long after I turned, I suffered almost a year of the most terrible pain. I thought I was going mad. My head felt like it was about to split apart and my stomach . . . You don't need the details. Suffice it to say, my early experience as a vampire was especially unpleasant, but my tea that you're all so fond of eased the pain."

I'd never heard Thandie talk so much or seen her so relaxed. Perhaps it gave her some release to tell her story.

"My main regret was leaving the other victims all those years ago. He'd subjected us to such torment, and I didn't want them to suffer any longer. I tried to untie their ropes, but I was too weak. I decided their best chance of survival, and mine, was telling the police."

"You did save them. The police came and got them out," I said.

"That's very kind of you to say," Thandie replied. Her eyes were wet with pink-tinged tears.

"Have you seen the Carter brothers since you were turned? Could you point them out in a line-up?" Libby asked.

"They were ordinary men: medium build, average height, brown hair . . . I could identify the brothers if I saw them, but I haven't since I was bitten. I scarcely leave this building, except to feed."

"I'm sorry this happened to you." It wasn't her fault she'd been forced to drink blood since then.

Thandie brushed her hair back stiffly. "You make of life what it gives you."

"Why are you so sure this is him, and not someone using John's name?" I asked, wanting so badly for her to be wrong.

"John has a reason to bear a grudge against me, and this certainly has his signature cruelty. Now, if I'm not mistaken, there's a young policeman lingering outside the door, and I have one more thing I would like to say to you. If there's anything I can do to finally put John Carter in the ground, it will be my pleasure. I implore you not to put yourselves in his path before then."

"Thanks for telling us all that," Libby said. She seemed to have forgiven Thandie for keeping secrets from her.

I was too captivated by Thandie's story to notice Della hadn't said a word. She'd gone from angry to emotionless. There was usually no up and down with Della; she was the level-headed one. Yet all this talk of vampires had brought out a sullen side of her.

Cafferty dropped us at home, where another police car was waiting. He talked to the officer as we went inside.

"I need to sleep for about seven years," Libby said. "We'll be in my room."

Della sighed. "I guess that means I'm going with her. You need anything?"

"I'm fine," I said. They deserved some space.

Jared and I needed that too, but he had to heal before our alone time got too strenuous.

I knocked on his door, and Jared croaked, "Come in."

Worried, I pushed the door open. He sat shirtless on the edge of his bed, with the wound on his neck still taped up. Defined arms and the outline of his toned stomach distracted me, until I noticed he was shaking. His head lolled forwards.

I slid to the floor at his feet. His eyes were angry red, like he'd been eating chillies, while his skin was ghostly pale and coated with sweat. "What's wrong?"

"I'm fine," he said, hardly opening his mouth to speak. The shaking worsened, and his whole body tilted towards me.

Rising onto my knees, I took some of his weight, straining to push him back onto the bed. I reached up and held a hand over his forehead. It was cold through the sweat. I had to push my fingers right into the curve of his collarbone to find a weak flutter of a pulse against my fingertips. "I'm calling an ambulance."

"Wait!" He caught my hand and stood on shaky legs. Releasing me, he staggered out and threw up in the bathroom.

I raced after him. By the time I got there, he was slumped over the toilet.

Hurrying to the kitchen, I filled a glass of water. I sat next to him and gave him the drink. "Thanks." He took a sip and rested it against his forehead.

"You should see a doctor – it might be an infection. Can I see under your bandage?"

"No!" The glass fell from his hands and bounced on the linoleum floor, splashing both of us.

I retrieved the empty glass and put it by the sink. "You can show me, or I'll tell the officer outside that we need to go to a hospital."

Jared closed his eyes, the black lashes highlighting his chalky complexion. "I wanted to protect you from this."

He ripped off the square of fabric with one tug. The skin underneath was smooth, with no bite marks at all.

Chapter 30

recoiled and hit the tiled wall. Less than a day ago, his neck was bitten by a vampire.

"Did you drink blood?" That sounded ridiculous, but I wasn't laughing.

Jared dragged both hands through his hair. The curls were stringy with sweat. "I was blindfolded, and they gave me a bottle. I don't think anyone even spoke to me . . . It's hard to remember. They held my nose and poured it into my mouth. I tried to spit it out, but they kept going until I swallowed." He shuddered, scraping a hand over his face like he could erase what happened. "It tasted . . . rotten . . . dead even."

It was like a scene from *The Lost Boys*. "You might not turn. We don't know how this works."

"I know." There was unfamiliar darkness in Jared's eyes, with none of his openness and humour. "I can hear your heartbeat." His tone was flat and unfeeling. "It's getting faster right now. And I can smell you. I'm pretty sure there's no going back."

My heart was loud in my ears. It must have tortured him. "How do you feel?"

"You don't wanna know."

He was going to have to say it because his usually animated face was empty.

"I can handle it. Just tell me."

"I feel hungry!" His lips flared, exposing his teeth. They were normal, though there was no telling how long that would last. "So you should get away from me."

I couldn't leave him in that state. "Why don't we phone Thandie?"

"Just leave me alone."

Jared sprang onto his feet, too lithe and quick for someone who looked as bad as he did. He rushed out of the bathroom, and I heard his door close.

We couldn't work through this. There was no going back. Daylight lost to him, living a miserable existence on the blood of his victims. He was going through all of that, and I let him leave.

I thrust his door open without knocking, and the lights were out. I stood there while my vision adjusted, detecting the bulky outlines of furniture but not him. A shape moved by the window. "Jared?"

"Who else would it be?" His cold sarcasm reminded me of Lestat.

I reached for the light switch, heart pounding. It beat harder the more I tried to slow my breath and calm it down.

My eyes ached at the brightness and red spots blotted out my vision. When they went away, Jared was there in front of me. Livid red circled his eyes, and his face was white. The veins on his throat protruded, and he couldn't seem to turn away from mine. There was no sweetness on his face, only hunger.

"Thandie said you need blood from a living source, so take mine." I turned my wrist upwards. I came here to do this, even if it wasn't going to plan.

There was nothing in him I recognised as he snatched up my wrist, cradling it in his hands. I came in here believing there was a part of him left to reason with. If he wasn't in control, I had to leave fast. I tried to yank my wrist free, and his fingers dug in harder. I jerked my knee up between his legs and he dodged, hanging onto my wrist.

The whites showed around his irises, and his lips shrank back. Fangs slid over his canines, as elegant and deadly as a snake's. The fine points left twin pricks of blood on his lips. His tongue swept them away.

My time ran out. I pulled on my hand with all my weight and he held on tight enough to crush bones. His mouth came down, and I screamed.

Chapter 31

I touched a hot iron once. Mum had let it steam on the ironing board while *Dark Shadows* was on TV. I brushed the silver surface with my left index finger and snatched it back. The pinch of agony brought tears to my eyes. I had a scar that showed when I tanned. It could've been worse if Libby hadn't rushed me into the kitchen and run cold water on it. Mum never even noticed.

But this was a new level of pain: a fire that burned white hot. There was no euphoria. Why did people want this? It was an incessant tugging as Jared drew the blood and strength out of me. I attempted to drag my wrist back, but my arm was too weak.

The bedroom door crashed open. Jared let me go a second before Della kicked his legs out from under him and pinned him to the floor.

"Get a kitchen knife," she ordered Libby. "No, the stake from my Buffy costume."

Libby skidded away and returned with the stake. Della grabbed it and pointed the wooden tip at his heart.

"Go get the officer outside!" Della said, sneering at Jared with pure loathing and disgust. She drove the tip of the stake harder against his chest. His eyes were closed, and his expression was pained.

Jared wasn't fighting, so I had to do it. "Don't!" I held a hand over my torn wrist. Blood leaked between my fingers and dripped onto the floor. "I told him to do it!"

Libby skirted around Jared and Della, yanking the case off my pillow and wrapping it around my wrist as we sat on the bed. "We have to get you to a hospital – you might need stitches."

"I'm fine," I said automatically, though it wasn't true. My head was light, and the room tilted on its axis. Did rooms have an axis?

"You should get him," Jared said, a bloody tear falling from one closed eye. "I deserve to be locked up."

"He needed blood . . . I told him to bite me." I said, and Libby put an arm around me.

"He shouldn't have done it." Libby sounded like she was speaking from underwater. "Mina, you've gone pale. Are you OK?"

I woke in Jared's bed. My wrist throbbed, and there was a bandage tied messily around it. That had to be Libby's work. Jared was sitting further down the bed, staring at my arm.

"Unlike what it says in the movies, having a vampire watch you sleep isn't a turn on," I said.

Jared grimaced. He now had a healthy glow to his complexion. The feral hunger was gone, leaving regret and worry in its place.

Libby and Della watched from the doorway. Della gripped the wooden stake, poised to use it.

"If I even think you're gonna hurt her, I'll kill you." Della's threat was chilling. She'd have killed a friend because of what he was, for making a mistake that wasn't even his fault. From the murderous scowl on Libby's face, she wouldn't have stopped Della either.

"I won't hurt her," Jared said.

"It's a little late for that," Libby shot back.

"I know." Jared pulled a green plastic case from the floor and opened it to reveal medical supplies: bandages, plasters and syringes that made my stomach churn. "I persuaded Libby to let me clean and dress your arm. If it's . . . If the damage is too severe, I'll take you to hospital."

"I'll have to do it," Della said, "although I don't really care if you burn up in the sun."

"Won't this be hard for you?" I asked him, trying to ignore the hatred coming off Libby and Della.

"Yes."

Slowly, he unravelled the clumsily wrapped bandage. Every time his fingers touched my wrist, pleasure rippled down my arm. My nerve endings weren't aware that he attacked me.

Underneath the bloodstained fabric, my arm was a mess. Two deeper holes were framed by chewed-up flesh, with a fringe of dried blood. Jared held my hand and squeezed his eyes shut, as if that hid what he did to me. "Remember I came in here. I offered. We both made mistakes," I said.

Jared ripped open an antiseptic wipe. He'd gone into nursing mode. "I'm going to clean off the blood and disinfect the wound. That part will sting."

He cleaned the ragged skin in a couple of deft motions. The disinfectant's sting ripped into me, and I wanted to yank my hand away. I kept it in place, shaking. Afterwards, he poured liquid fire into the wound. I looked away while my arm burned.

"Sorry . . ." he said. "The bleeding's stopped. I don't think you need stitches. There can be an increased risk of infection but reduced scarring if you get them, so it's up to you."

"I don't mind scars."

He peeled the back off an adhesive pad and carefully positioned it over the wound. I was glad to have it hidden. That made it easier not to think about him hurting me.

He retreated to the opposite end of the bed, taking his time rearranging the contents of his medical kit. "I'm going to stay with Thandie."

"That makes sense," I said. My body was weighed down by everything that had happened. I wanted to latch onto him and not let go or kiss him and promise it wouldn't separate us. I couldn't do it. I was too scared of what he might do and how it might torment him. "She'll help you adjust."

"Maybe then we can . . ."

"Yeah." How could he be right there but so far away?

"I should pack," Jared said.

I swung my legs out of Jared's bed and rose slowly. My head was clear, but I was so very tired. "Drink plenty of fluids," Jared said, as I followed Libby and Della out of his room.

My legs were unsteady as Libby steered me towards my room. I flopped into bed, pulling up the quilt.

Libby sat on the mattress with me. She stroked my hair from the scalp right down to the ends. That was exactly what Mum used to do. "Don't worry," she said. "He'll be out of here soon."

"It's not his fault," I said, turning my attention to Della instead of what Jared did. "Thanks for saving me. You were amazing."

"I've been doing MMA for five years," Della said. "I didn't know that was what I'd use it for."

"I think you need to train me," I said.

"Us," Libby corrected.

A wave of pain flooded my arm, and I hugged it against me. "You want some paracetamol?" Libby asked.

She was gone before I decided, returning with a glass of water and two white pills. "Here," she said.

I swallowed the pills with a gulp of water. They tasted chalky. Eventually, they dulled the pain in my arm but not over what Jared did to me.

I woke to my mattress sinking down on one side, and my eyes flew open.

"It's just me," Libby said. "How are you feeling?"

I sat up cautiously. "Not bad," I said. My arm felt tight and sore rather than agonising. "I need tea."

The glass between my curtains was black. "Did Jared leave?"

"Yeah, he's gone," Libby said. She didn't say "good riddance", but it was implied.

Della must have heard my request for tea because she was putting the kettle on when I came into the kitchen. When the water boiled, she poured it and Libby added milk. They made a good team, and it was sweet how they moved around each other with such ease. Jared and I would never get to that stage.

Libby asked, "Did you know about him changing?"

"About two minutes before he bit me . . . before I let him bite me."

Della's face had been strained with anger, but relaxed as she let out a long breath. "I'm glad you're all right. Jared is . . . he's our friend, but he's different now."

"He was our friend," Libby corrected.

Della went on hesitantly, "There's something I want to tell you, both of you actually. This is hard . . . I've never said it out loud before. I think a vampire killed my mom."

Chapter 32

"**M**y dad told me she was murdered by a mugger," Della said. "He still thinks that, but I'm not so sure. A while ago, I wanted to find out more, so I found the old articles at the library. There was a ton of similar cases . . ." She ran a hand through her braids. "She died from blood loss, and some of the papers said it was an animal attack . . . that she was bitten. Some of them said her blood was taken, and some even used the word: vampire."

"Why didn't you tell me?" Libby asked.

"I didn't tell anybody. I didn't want people to think I was crazy. And after we found out they exist . . . I needed to work through it."

Life was cruel and yet, it was fitting that we found Della. All three of us lost our mothers to vampires.

Libby reached under the table for Della's hand.

"It feels good to get it out," Della went on, "and now I want pizza. Anyone with me?"

Less than an hour later, we'd piled into Libby's bed with junk food. "Should we try *Buffy* again?" Della asked.

"Why not?" Libby said. "I mean, we just found out vampires exist. We might as well embrace the weird."

"Sure," I said.

The hot pizza and equally cheesy movie were comforting, but I couldn't relax entirely. Though Libby was back, Jared was gone again, forever changed, and John Carter was out there. Could one police officer outside the house stop him?

Libby bounced into my room with an envelope in her hand. I'd slept in, and the mid-morning light streamed in with her.

"Aunt Sandra finally got in touch – better late than never."

It wasn't like Aunt Sandra's looping handwriting, with the name and address printed in neat capitals. The envelope also had a New Orleans postmark.

I tore the envelope along the flap and pulled out the pages. I recognised the handwriting immediately. It was more diary entries, and the first date was from last year. These were written on new paper that had been torn from a book, with a ragged edge to one side. I flicked hastily through the other entries. There were four dates, the most recent from a few months ago. So now we had notes from John and a new diary from Wayne. The Carter brothers were alive.

Last time, I read the diaries out of interest. This time, I read as if our lives depended on it.

April 19th 1994

After over six decades, we've returned to live in New Orleans, not without much trepidation on my part. Our fleeting visits over the years haven't satisfied John, watching Mardi Gras from balconies and picking revelers off the side streets. We've waited long enough that those who were alive for our execution will be long dead by now.

Our previous trips were too quiet for John and yet, they provoked much suffering in me. Every place brought back the horrors we'd inflicted and that had been inflicted upon us. A quiet square was the location of our hanging, where a mob heckled and threw rotten fruit despite the late hour. I was haunted by the pop as my neck snapped and the scrape of my toes dangling on the floor.

There was the graveyard where we were entombed, where tourists now flocked with cameras and a morbid fascination with death.

Even the glorious Garden District, with its perfume of flowers and gentile mansions, holds grisly memories. Someone once told me the flowers were planted to disguise the stench from local slaughterhouses, and that was an appropriate backdrop for our purposes. It was there we stalked John's sire through her garden after we were freed from our tomb those decades ago. He separated her head from her body with a single swipe of a machete.

Though it brought me great regret, her death was a necessity. A friend of John's told us a vampire's progeny cannot stray far from their sire so soon after they are made, often for as long as a year. On trying, they hit a wall of pain so excruciating that it will certainly lead to madness. Yet another reason why I could not leave my brother at that time. A sire can leave their progeny, inflicting lesser symptoms upon them, but I knew he'd never leave me. And here we are, still together sixty some years later.

June 3rd 1994

John brought us back here with dreams of our former glory, and I dreaded what that would entail. In lieu of inciting mayhem, he's fallen in love, and with a human no less. This can only end in death for her, though perhaps it indicates that my brother is redeemable. If he can fall in love, perchance some kindness resides in him.

He insisted on introducing me to Emma, in a grimy bar that she didn't seem to mind. The looks they exchanged certainly suggested they are in love. She is fierce and beautiful. Her hair is a cascade of curls black as the night, and there's a ruthless streak that would make her a fine vampire. She is also unafraid of what we are. I know my brother, and I'm sure it's his final goal to have her become a creature like us.

July 30th 1994

Emma is gone. My brother is out searching for her and I don't dare tell him what I know in my heart. She obtained what she wanted and left him. It can't be a coincidence that he made her like us and she vanished hours later.

I don't know what to make of this. John returned with his mouth daubed with blood and his clothes drenched in the arterial spray of multiple victims. Unlike them, the flame of his spirit is very much alive.

Emma must be here in New Orleans. As his progeny, she cannot leave while John stays. I'd predicted that would eat away at him and my brother would wallow in his suffering. A new plan has consumed him instead, with no word about Emma. He's acquired a business, by some illicit means I'm sure, but this development gives me cautious hope. If John is diverted by a new endeavor, I could pursue my own.

June 5th 1995

I assumed John had spent these months combing the city for Emma. I didn't dare to ask, but he doesn't relinquish a grudge easily. As always with John, it is worse than I could've foreseen. He's been searching; I was right about that. But he's also been plotting.

He came home tonight spouting ideas I could barely follow: talk of blood and settling past scores with her and the woman who reported us to the police so many years ago. It appears he knows the woman who reported us is not dead, though perhaps not my part in her survival. I'm undecided whether I should have let her be rather than making her one of us.

A year has not passed, so his bond with Emma remains intact. That means she must be close, when I assume she would prefer to be far away. He insists he has formed a plan to lure her back and that mine will be a crucial role. My concern is that he can force me to participate, whether I want it or not.

There was so much to absorb from the new entries, but one word changed everything. Emma was our mum's name.

Chapter 33

The new diary held information that could help the police, even if they wouldn't believe the brothers were vampires. I had to talk to Libby first.

I knocked on her open door. She and Della were sitting up on the bed with mugs in their hands. "How you feelin'?" Della asked.

"Better," I said. There were bigger problems than my aching arm. "The letter wasn't from Aunt Sandra. I think it's more pages from Wayne Carter's diary."

Libby slopped tea over her hand and set it down on her bedside table. "Seriously? Who sent it?"

"I'm not sure, but I need you to read this."

"Sit down," Della offered, and they shuffled along so there was space next to Libby.

Libby held the pages in the middle, while

Della and I read from either side. My sister whitened as she read about the woman John Carter fell in love with, who tricked him into turning her into a vampire and left. The more times I read it, the more it resembled Mum.

By the time we finished, Libby's teeth had left tiny imprints in her bottom lip.

"And you think that's Mum," Libby said.

"I do," I said. "Big hair and big desire to leave. If it's her, that means she was in New Orleans less than a year ago." The diary said Emma met John in June 1994, and our mum left Whitby in early May of that year. The dates lined up, assuming it only took her a couple of months to find a vampire. Again, she demonstrated her spectacularly bad taste in men.

The diary said she couldn't stray too far from John for a year, so she could be nearby. Wherever she'd gone, she was alive. Or sort of alive, after her encounter with John Carter. She got what she wanted anyway.

Libby was unusually silent. "What do you think, Libs?" I asked.

"It's her." Libby was hunched over, biting the skin round her thumb. A bead of blood welled up from the cut, smearing her lower lip.

"And . . .?" I asked.

Libby shrank down on the pillow. "I knew she was here."

My thoughts raced so fast that everything was jumbled. Della got in before I did. "What the hell? You told me your mom left you last year." So Libby didn't tell Della a damn thing either.

"She did! And I never went looking for her, I swear." So she coincidentally travelled halfway around the world to the same city as Mum.

Libby levelled a pleading look at me, but it rolled off. I'd spent a year thinking Mum was gone, possibly dead, and Libby knew where she was. "When did you find out? How?"

"I'll leave the two of you to talk," Della said. She took off, braids swinging.

I moved further down the bed, waiting to see how Libby was going to justify this. She was so mad at Mum for leaving us when she did exactly the same thing to me. "Not long after I accepted my place at York University, I found a letter addressed to Aunt Sandra in her room, and I read it."

"A letter from Mum?" All of this was throwing me off balance.

Libby nodded. "She apologised for leaving and thanked Sandra for taking care of us." A tear crept down her face. Mine was wet too. "It said she was never coming back to England, but she wanted to tell Sandra she was fine. She didn't . . . want us to find out. It was easier to think she was gone."

"And she got to decide that." My fury was an ugly red fire that burned away everything else.

"It said she went 'back where they spent the summer that changed everything', or whatever. So I asked Aunt Sandra about it."

Libby continued into my furious silence. "Sandra said they went to New Orleans in their early twenties, not long before Mum had me. That was where she got bitten the first time."

The scar. I'd blamed Dad for making her obsession worse by leaving, but it was always inside her. It all made sense. She was bitten by a vampire in New Orleans and got hooked.

When she left us a year ago, she had a fresh bite mark, and she went back to the place where she met her first vampire. Mum always told us she met Dad on a plane back from visiting America, when he was moving over to England. No wonder she was so vague about the rest of the holiday.

Though Libby hadn't finished her explanation, there was one thing I knew about Mum: I'd had enough. The worry and obsessing about her were over. She was here in New Orleans or long gone. Either way, I didn't care. Finally, it all came together. "That's why you came here for uni."

Libby nodded. "I was feeling uncertain about moving to York, especially not knowing where Mum was, and then . . . the letter felt like a sign. She was never coming back, so I had to make the decision." That was so Libby – moving to another continent because of a sign. "I went straight to the mansion when I got here. She used their letter-headed paper."

"*Thandie* knows about Mum?"

"No! I just talked her into giving me a job. I asked around about the paper, but they used to sell it in the museum. Thandie didn't know anything about Mum."

"Good. That means I can trust *her* when it comes to Mum." Libby flinched and I was past caring. "Did you find her?"

"No."

From the defeat on Libby's face, I believed her, but I had to be sure. "Honestly?"

Tears trickled down Libby's face. Mine had all dried up. "No more lies."

"So, Mum found a vampire to turn her and ran out on him – at least she's consistent. We probably got dragged into all of this because of her!"

"You're probably right." Libby inched down the bed towards

me and tried to take my hand. I hid it under my leg. "I should've told you, but I didn't want to stir everything up again. All of this is my fault."

"It isn't either of our faults. It's hers, and John Carter's." I put the pages back into the envelope. "We have to give this to the police. There could be clues that can help them track the Carter brothers down." That came out normal enough, as if quiet resentment wasn't thrumming behind every word. Libby could've told me the second she found Mum's letter but she ran away. Who did that remind me of?

"I'll take this to the officer outside." I launched myself off the bed and away from her.

The sun beat down on my head as I approached the police car. The officer was an older man I hadn't met before. He accepted the diary and my explanation without questions. "I'll call it in. Someone will be in touch."

He closed the window, and I returned to the cool hallway. Libby was on the phone.

"Are you sure?" Libby said. "OK. I'll speak to you soon."

Della came out of the kitchen. "What was that about?"

"Thandie told us to stay away from the mansion."

"Are we fired?" I asked.

"No, it's just for tonight." Libby picked at the skin around her little finger. "I don't understand – it's our turn to host Fang Fest. The place'll be packed."

"John Carter hasn't been caught," I said. "I bet she's trying to protect us."

"You're right," Libby said. She'd been very agreeable since shattering everything I knew about Mum's disappearance, and her.

"The officer outside said the police will be in touch. We have to wait until then."

"Can we talk?" Della asked. It was her turn to find out what Libby had been keeping from her.

"Sure," Libby said, less than enthused.

I decided to give them some time and headed to my room. The phone rang before I occupied myself.

"Hello?" I said, assuming Thandie wanted us again.

"Mina? It's Detective Cafferty. Can you and Libby come in to answer a few questions?"

Libby appeared in the hallway with Della. "Can you hang on for a second?" I said to Cafferty, covering the phone. "He wants us to go in."

"We can go right now," Della said. Their talk had to wait.

"That's fine," I said to him.

"Great. Officer Trenton will bring you in."

On the way to the car, we agreed not to mention vampires. They had to take us seriously and stop John Carter. I was worried we could hurt them by hiding the truth, but the police managed to take the Carter brothers down once in the 1930s. This time, they had the advantage of Wayne's diary.

🦇

Boudreaux and Cafferty met us in the reception area. She held up a copy of the new diary pages.

"That was a real interestin' read," she said, changing direction when she spotted my wrist. "What happened?"

"I burned it on my curling tongs." With a head of frizzy curls, it wasn't my best excuse, but she asked no more questions.

The detectives took us to another interview room. I was less nervous when they switched on the video camera this time. We had no secrets: none they would've believed anyway.

Boudreaux set the diary copy down in the middle of the table.

"How did these journal entries come into your possession?" Cafferty asked. "They're a lot like the diary I saw in the museum, only that ended in the 1930s."

It threw me off that he took the lead instead of Boudreaux. "Someone sent it to me. It came today."

"Do you know who might have done that?" he asked.

"I wish I did," I said. "Have you read it?"

Boudreaux took over. "We have. Our working theory is that the individual masquerading as Wayne Carter has written a fictionalised account of the murders. We see a lot of strange justifications people use for killing, and events like the vampire festival tend to bring 'em out. What we're unclear on is why this account made its way to you."

"We have an idea." I was glad Libby took over, now we'd come to this part. "There's a woman that could be our mum. She went missing last year."

"Where did she go missing from?" Cafferty asked.

"Whitby, in England. The police investigated, but they didn't find her."

Boudreaux flipped through the photocopied diary, stopping near the end. "You believe this Emma is your mother."

"I found a letter from her last summer that said she was coming to New Orleans. And it sounds like her, from the description," Libby said.

"Do you believe your mother is involved with the recent crimes?" Boudreaux asked.

"I don't think so," I said when Libby faltered. "It's just . . . I have to wonder if she's the reason we got mixed up in this. If she made John Carter mad, or this guy pretending to be him, maybe he's taking it out on us."

"That's one theory," Boudreaux said, conveniently avoiding the vampire angle of the journal. I might have done the same if my arm wasn't aching where a vampire bit it.

"I need to speak with my captain. I'll leave you with Detective Cafferty."

She left, and he filled the silence with reassurances. "You're doing great. This is really good information. I think we're close to wrapping it up."

Boudreaux returned, brimming with jittery energy. "I have a big ask of you, Elizabeth and Mina. The perpetrator, or perpetrators, have committed most of their crimes during the vampire festival, and we believe they'll attend the Mansion of the Macabre tonight. If they're targeting you, your presence may draw them out. We'll make sure you're heavily guarded by armed undercover officers and detectives, ourselves included, and we'll subdue the perpetrators and remove you if they arrive at the scene."

"You want to use them as bait? There's no way!" Della said, all fired up. "You don't even know who these . . . people are, and they've killed before!"

"That's why this operation's been approved." Boudreaux said. "I understand what I'm askin' y'all to risk, but it's the last night of the festival, so we might not get another shot. I can't force you to take part. All I ask is that you think about what's at stake."

I kept down a nervous giggle. This wasn't the time to appreciate accidental vampire jokes. "I think we should do it," I said. "They're going to keep coming after us and anyone else who gets in their way. We're no safer at home."

That sounded brave and selfless, but mostly I wanted this to end. Lucas and those girls had died. Jared had lost his humanity. How many more people had to get hurt because of our mum or John Carter?

"Why not?" Libby said. "I'm in."

"I'm supposed to work, but if you both insist, guess I gotta be there," Della said.

"Actually, you haven't been approved for this, Della. Work will be the safest place for you," Boudreaux said, leaving no space for arguments. "Now, this is how it'll go down."

The plan was straightforward: parade ourselves where the 'Carter brothers' would see, then get locked in Thandie's office with police protection if they arrived. What could possibly go wrong?

Chapter 34

While we got dressed, there were no songs, jokes or gossip. I couldn't decide if it would be better if the brothers arrived or stayed away.

Libby had given me a Sally costume that she never returned to Thandie's, and I slipped on the colourful patchwork dress. Who cared if it was summer? *The Nightmare Before Christmas* was a classic all year round. I left off the red wig, since the whole point was to be recognisable.

She tapped on my open door with her fingernails. She had the Dracula cape on again but had made minimal effort with her hair and make-up. "Want me to draw on some stitches?"

"Why not?" I asked. As long as we didn't end up needing real ones.

Libby took the lid off the eyeliner but hesitated. "You don't have to do this. It's not your fault."

"It's not yours either." I was still pissed off at her for not telling me Mum was here, but I wasn't going to let her handle this alone.

"I should've told you." Libby's eyes gleamed and she squeezed the pencil so hard that the wood creaked.

"Yeah, you should've, but you didn't bring this on us. She did."

Libby wiped her eyes. "OK. Thanks. I should do your face."

"Stop crying first. I don't want to get poked in the eye."

Libby laughed through her tears and uncapped the pencil. "You'll have to trust me."

The police officer who greeted us in the car was young and nervous.

"Hey, I'm Officer Thorpe," he said. I'd have worried about driving us around too.

"Hi, I'm Libby and this is Mina."

The back seat was hard vinyl that creaked when I fidgeted. A barrier of mesh and thick plastic divided us from Officer Thorpe. Libby watched me the whole way to the mansion, holding my hand across the seat. I was reassured by her determination. Libby always got what she wanted. She believed we were going to get through this and so did I.

The mansion was its usual dead and miserable self on the outside. Inside, it was alive with activity. The usual staff hadn't arrived yet, but there were plenty of stony-faced police officers wearing Thandie's costumes. There were Draculas, biker vampires and a big-wigged Elvira that made me think of the girl at the blood bar who used her name. One guy even wore David from *The Lost Boys'* costume and I felt an intense pang of grief for Lucas, remembering that he'd worn the same outfit.

Jared was waiting for us in the hallway, looking super nervous with all of the police milling around.

Libby squared up to Jared. "I need to help with setting up. Remember, Thandie is right there." She gave a last scowl and jogged upstairs.

"How's your wrist?" Jared asked quietly. There was that grimace again. If vampires got wrinkles, he was working on a good set of them. The jokey thought soured. He might stay the same for ever. We moved to one side of the hallway, making our own quiet space.

"Fine," I said, after too long a pause. I held a hand over the bandage and there was a quick, sharp pain.

"I can't believe I did that to you."

I stepped slowly towards Jared, giving him time to deal with my closeness. "We've been through this. I came to you. If I'd left you alone, you wouldn't have done it. Can I . . .?" I reached my hand towards his.

He nodded tentatively, holding out his hand to mine. It was hard seeing him give so little away.

Our hands met. His skin was cooler and smoother, but his big hand still slotted together with mine. He stood there stiffly like he was counting the seconds until I let go.

I did what he wanted, taking a step backwards. "We can work this out." I wanted so much to kiss him, but going near his mouth was a very bad idea. Besides, I didn't know how he felt about me. It was impossible to tell if his emotions were hidden or he couldn't feel them anymore.

With me at a safe distance, he relaxed. "I wish I could stay with you."

"You're not going to be here?" There were so many reasons

why his presence was a bad idea, but I still felt disappointed.

Jared answered in a murmur as a police officer passed. "I have to wait for the sun to go down, then Della's gonna babysit me at the bar."

"That'll be fun for both of you. And it'll be safer if you stay away."

His brows lowered. "That's true."

The door of the mansion opened and Jared shrank away from it, but there was nothing to worry about. The sun had sunk low. "I should go," he said, heading out onto the street. He was looking at me when the door closed.

I trudged upstairs, getting halfway up when Libby rounded the corner. "Did I miss Jared? What a shame."

When she didn't get a rise out of me, Libby moved on. "Let's talk to Thandie."

She was behind her desk with two fingers against one temple. "Come in and close the door, girls."

We sat down and Libby smoothed out the Dracula cape around her. "Where are you going to be?"

This must have been so hard for Thandie. John Carter left her for dead in an alleyway, and we wanted him to come to her home. "Looking out for the two of you." Thandie swept up her glass and saluted us with it. She took a sip.

"I'm glad you're being cool about this," Libby grumbled.

"The police are as prepared as they can be. We can only stay alert and see what transpires."

Libby and I waited in the hallway with the bear trap suspended over us. One way or another, it had to end tonight.

258

I'd never seen so many visitors around the mansion. They were all in costume, and there was a lot of pleather and cleavage on display.

Libby and I handed out vampire goody bags with blood bags of cherry juice and vampire fangs of the plastic and gummy varieties. After that, the guests went inside to spot vampires before they got 'bitten', or tagged with red stickers. A prize waited for them if they 'survived' the tour. It seemed kind of bad taste to me but was pulling in the crowds.

The sky was black, and it was hard to keep welcoming customers when any of them could've been a vampire. Worse – any of them could have been *the* vampire. John Carter knew who we were, but we had no clue what he looked like beyond Thandie's description.

Detective Boudreaux was wearing a killer Morticia Addams dress. She handed out flyers, flipping back her wig of ruthlessly straight, black hair. Cafferty wore a waxy, expressionless Michael Myers mask. He'd assured us earlier that he had a gun underneath the navy blue overall, assuming he could reach it before John Carter got to him.

Libby was all smiles and patter, making people jump as they passed or sweetly warning them to be on their guard. Every so often, I saw Thandie or an undercover officer weaving around tourists and wished that was more reassuring.

An hour later, the crowd was thinning out and the Carters hadn't appeared.

"I don't think they're coming," Libby said, swiping some gummy teeth from a bag and popping them in her mouth.

"Maybe not," I said. We'd been so certain this was about us, but even the police were behaving less alert.

Soon, the staff headed out into the stuffy, starless night. Boudreaux deposited me and Libby in the kitchen while the police talked in the hall. We sat at the table in silence, listening. They had a meeting planned for the following day to go over their next steps.

Boudreaux and Cafferty reappeared, minus the wig and mask but still wearing their outfits. Morticia Addams' sultry style suited Boudreaux. "You did well, girls," she said. "Officer Thorpe will take you home." He came up beside Boudreaux, casual enough by then to give us a friendly nod.

"I can take them," Cafferty said.

"You can get some sleep," Boudreaux said, firm but kind. "Goodnight, girls. We'll be in touch."

Boudreaux and Cafferty left, and Libby approached the door of Thandie's office. "Can we say goodnight to our boss?"

"Sure," Officer Thorpe said.

"Thandie?" Libby knocked and then tried the door. Locked.

The museum door next to her office clicked open and I heard it: the faintest of groans.

Chapter 35

The museum was wrecked, with the glass cases smashed and artefacts strewn across the floor. Thandie lay among the rubble.

We flew across the room, crunching the broken glass. She was alive but only just. The shard of wood once kept on display was buried deep in her chest.

"Help!" Libby yelled, sinking down in the broken glass.

I crouched by Libby. We were too late. Blood frothed between Thandie's lips and her skin appeared shrunken. "I'm glad . . ." She coughed. "Wanted to see you two . . ."

"No . . ." Libby cried. "What should we do?"

Thandie coughed, closing her eyes. Her head tipped to one side, and she was gone.

The door on the other side of the museum

opened, and Veronica slinked into the room. "Too bad," she said in a sickeningly sweet voice. "So sad."

Veronica stood over Thandie's body with a sledgehammer resting on one shoulder. A slim crown braid framed her face and the rest of her white-blond hair was loose. The ends were flecked with blood.

"Veronica, what the hell? Did you do this?" Libby threw the questions angrily, though heartbreak ran through them. As well as standing over Thandie's body, Veronica gave us the map for the Horror Quest that got Lucas killed.

"Yes, I killed them. It was me all along," Veronica said brightly, leaning on the sledgehammer like a walking stick. She noticed a splash of blood at the bottom of her lacy, white dress and hissed, showing fangs.

Officer Thorpe pushed open the door from the hallway. Horror registered as he grabbed the radio from his pocket.

He didn't get chance to use it. A figure rushed past him and out of sight behind the door. Thorpe's eyes bulged, and a strangled gargle escaped his lips. A thin, red slash opened on his neck. He raised both hands, and blood coursed over his fingers. He collapsed on the spot.

"Don't take all the credit." Marsden sauntered into view, scooping up Officer Thorpe's gun from his lifeless hand. Fresh blood dripped from Marsden's fingernails. "I'm afraid I haven't been entirely honest with you girls. Allow me to rectify that. My name is John Carter."

All of the details clicked into place. He sent us to the blood bar and was there to send us off on the Horror Quest. Anger raged through me as I stood to face him.

There was a spatter of blood on one perfect cheekbone, and his large, blue eyes were devoid of compassion.

Libby sobbed by Thandie's body. "Why did you kill her?"

"Her death was long overdue," John said.

Libby reached for the axe that once belonged to the Axeman. She stood, shaking with fury. "So is yours, you son of a bitch."

Inspired, I scanned for weapons around me. There was a crossbow just out of reach, and I extended one foot towards it.

"Don't even think about it." John pointed the gun at my foot and swivelled it round to aim at Libby's head. "And drop the axe. It's so unoriginal."

Libby let the weapon clatter to the floor with a growl of rage.

"You're a fiery one like your mother. I almost had a heart attack when you walked into my bar, and that's quite a feat for a vampire. Emma's why I'm here, of course, tormenting you. What better way to lure her out? You know that. You've been reading my brother's diary."

"I don't know what you're talking about," I lied.

"No matter. I have your boy," he aimed the gun at me before shifting it onto Libby, "and your girl. It was quite convenient that they showed up at my bar. Perhaps you should come with me before they kill each other."

"They wouldn't!" I said.

"You're so sure of Jared, aren't you? It'd be a shame if that faith was misplaced."

"Fine!" Libby snapped. "Take us to them."

"She's got spirit," Veronica said, pointing the mallet at Libby. "I'll enjoy smashing it out of her."

Chuckling, John stalked out of the room, and we followed with

Veronica behind us. John wrenched open the door of the mansion. Armand was there.

"You," John growled. "Your part is over – you should have scurried away like a rat. What are you doing here?"

Chapter 36

A rmand was on John's team too – it got better and better. Elvira did say humans were helping. Whatever Armand came to do, he seemed to be having second thoughts. He glanced over his shoulder, and I knew what he was planning the second before his legs flexed. He sprinted down the street and round the nearest corner.

Veronica skipped onto the street, hammer raised, "Can I chase him?".

"Tempting as that is, I need you," John said.

She grumbled to herself, and soon Armand's footfalls faded. All I could hear was the hum of traffic and distant hustle of Bourbon Street.

"That was . . . anticlimactic," John said. "No matter. I can deal with him later. This part of the plan can proceed quite nicely without him."

John marched off ahead without bothering to

check we were following. Between Veronica's mallet and our loved ones held captive, we had no choice.

John led us into the packed bar. A brass band was onstage, and the frantic drums beat through my body. Following John, we pushed through the dancers, grazing sticky skin and leather. Every person pulsed with life, unaware of how closely death passed them by. The skeletons trapped in their cages stared down knowingly.

I reached for a glass on a nearby table, thinking I could use it as a weapon. Veronica's mallet clipped my injured wrist, sending jarring pain through my arm.

We headed for the curtains where I first met John, and he ducked through them. Libby said, "I'll go first. We can beat him. We just have to be smart."

"Y'all don't seem 'specially smart to me," Veronica said. "Get movin'."

The stacks of boxes had been moved to one side of the room, revealing a door. John unlocked it and set off down a long flight of stairs similar to the one at the blood bar. "Veronica's right. Try to be smart by doing what you're told and some of you might survive until morning. But there'll be no beating me."

"Stay behind me," Libby said, taking off after him.

I appreciated her effort to protect me, but I doubted he'd let us go. I'd never thought I was about to die. The idea of not existing was terrifying. The only chance we had was if our mum arrived, and that was never going to happen. He was so fixated on her coming, but he'd given us no reason why this night was different from any other.

John reached the bottom of the stairs and grinned up at us. Our mum had a type: he was beautiful and deranged like our dad. Did she ever want John or just the eternal life he offered?

The room at the bottom of the stairs was a concrete hallway, with the walls spattered brown and stinking of decay. A hard object dug into the sole of my shoe. It was a tooth with a bloody root where it had been yanked out.

"My work here is done," Veronica sang. "I'll leave you to clean up the blood!" She bounded out of the room, and I heard the door lock behind her.

"Charming as ever," John said.

He led us into a corridor with bars along one side. On the wall opposite the cells were hundreds of fishhooks. Jared said the Carter brothers used to haul fish when they were human. Angling my body, I reached for a long, curved hook behind me.

"They're nailed to the wall," John said, without even looking back at me. "You'd tear your hands to bloody ribbons and get nowhere."

Abandoning that idea with the last of my hope, I asked, "Where are Jared and Della?"

"We'll get to them." John unlocked the cell, letting the gate swing open. "In you go."

"How do we know they're all right?" Libby asked, her fists clenched and words fierce with defiance.

"You don't. Now, get in the cell. Argue and I make them suffer. It's very simple."

Libby marched into the cell. I followed, mentally measuring the tiny space. Two or three metres across. The front and dividing walls were bars, while the others were concrete. I tried to breathe steadily. Air can get into basements. We could die a lot of ways down here though not from lack of oxygen.

"What's that?" Libby asked shrilly.

John strode across the cell and plucked a bundle from the floor. It wasn't rags or clothing: he'd killed another girl. Bile flooded my mouth.

John held her up from behind the neck. Her head rolled back, revealing her empty face. It was Elvira, the girl from the blood bar.

"Oh, I do apologise. I forgot you met her." John held one of her hands and flung an arm around her back, dragging her around in a gruesome dance. "She interfered and could have exposed me before I was ready. She had to go."

Elvira died because we talked to her. John tucked Elvira's body under one arm, her black hair hanging down. He closed the gate and withdrew a key from his pocket to lock it. "The bar will close soon, and I have to dispose of her. Your mother doesn't have long before I return."

"She's never come for us before," Libby said. "What makes you think she will now?"

For the first time, John had no answer. "She has to," he said eventually. "Goodbye, for now!"

"Well, that cleared things up," I said, acting more relaxed than I felt. Elvira got mixed up in this mess and died because of it.

"We can't expect him to be rational," Libby said, "and we're not doing too well in that department. We have no weapons and nobody knows we're here." She gripped the bars at the front of the cell with all of her strength, rocking back and forth. They didn't budge.

The room shrank and I closed my eyes, trying to calm myself.

I reflected on Wayne's diary, the one insight I had into John's twisted motivations. "He brought us here because of Mum. Can we use that?"

"We could get him talking about her again . . . try to distract him and see if he makes a mistake." Libby fell into thoughtful silence.

From the next cell, there was a weak voice. "Libby?"

Libby's head jerked up. "Lucas?"

Chapter 37

Libby wrapped her hands around the bars separating our cells. "Lucas! You're alive!"

The rags in the next cell sat up. It really was him – white-faced and dressed in grimy overalls that swamped his thin body. Clotted blood covered one side of his throat and stained the grey fabric. "He got the two of you. I didn't want . . ." His head dropped.

"They told us you were dead." Libby squeezed the bars so hard that her hands turned mottled red and white.

"I think . . ." Lucas gulped. "I think he pretended to be my dad. He drugged me . . . They thought I was dead." John took what he needed from Lucas and tossed him down here, but he was alive.

"Did you see Jared and Della?" Libby asked.

"I heard them . . . I've been out of it." Lucas

held his forehead. "He gives me water, but it's making me sick . . . and he feeds on me." His skin was white, as though John took all the blood that once gave him colour.

Libby said, "We don't have long. There are three of us, five if . . ." Her mouth shrank to a thin line. "We can get out of this."

I wanted to believe her, but we'd seen the massacre John had left in his wake.

Even as I thought of him, John appeared at the cell door. "The bar is closed and with it, your window for finding someone to help you. How are we doing? Having a good catch-up with your friend? Like I said, you don't all have to die."

How was he that cheerful, when he'd caused so much death and destruction?

John unlocked the gate and stepped back, his gun pointed into our cell. "Ready to see your beloveds? I do enjoy a happy reunion."

Libby stayed where she was. "Why are you doing this to us?" She was all strength, not the least bit pleading or plaintive. "If you want to punish our mum, there are a couple of problems with that. One, she doesn't know we're in New Orleans. Two, even if she knew we were here, she wouldn't care. She left us once. She'd do it again."

"I made sure your escapades got into the newspapers. She loves New Orleans mythology, so I re-enacted her favourite myths. This whole spectacle is for her." He went all dreamy, as if he thought the whole murder spree was very romantic. His expression changed when he turned to Libby, as if finally appreciating what she said. "But if you're saying it won't work, then there's no reason to keep you alive, is there? For now, get out. I'm not sure how long your sweet girl can survive."

He'd found Libby's pressure point. We both ventured into the hallway, and John unlocked Lucas's cage. "Can you stand or should I drag you?"

Lucas wobbled to his feet and staggered. John caught him, sneering. "Take *this*, will you? I have rather a refined sense of smell, and he's offending it."

Libby and I got on either side of Lucas, looping our arms around his back to support him. So much for being able to overpower John. Like he said, Lucas smelled of blood and days' old sweat. He felt frail and cold.

John unlocked a door at the end of the corridor and stood to one side to let us into another room of cells. Passing him, I caught the lightest tang of citrus. It transported me back to the attic where I found Heather. I hadn't needed another confirmation that he did all of this, but there it was.

Lucas got heavier, and I took more of the load. How were we supposed to get out of here with a friend who could hardly walk?

We reached the entrance of another cell, and John swung the bars open. Libby let go of Lucas. The sudden weight almost pulled me down. When I noticed what Libby saw, I nearly let go of him too. Della's body lay sprawled on the floor of the cell. Jared crouched over her, blood coating his snarling lips.

Chapter 38

ibby collapsed at Della's side, fumbling for her throat. Della's skin was slick with blood, so Libby's fingers kept slipping.

"How do I do this? I can't find her pulse."

"How terrible," John said, wrenching Lucas off my arm and gripping him around his neck. Lucas clawed at John's hand, but he held on.

I lunged towards John. "Stop it!"

John batted me away and I crashed into the bars, my teeth clashing together. "Fine." John eased his grip on Lucas's throat, addressing Jared. "This wasn't part of the plan. I asked you to bring Della down here, not kill her."

It all made sense. John didn't kidnap and bury Jared to kill him. He turned him and sent him back to spy on us.

Jared stood shakily. "I didn't . . ." He touched his mouth, examining his bloody fingers.

"Can you not do any better than that? It's embarrassing," John said, adjusting his grip on Lucas's throat. Lucas moaned, not fighting anymore. "Don't demean yourself by lying, boy. I made you for a purpose. You failed to fulfil it."

"Libby . . . Mina." Blood smeared Jared's face, and his eyes were damp and bright. He was convincing. I wanted to believe him so much. "I didn't do this!"

"I wish I'd known you were such a terrible liar. You helped me fake his death, boy. You were quite happy about my plans then. I thought a protégé was the answer, but you've turned out to be a terrible disappointment. Now Jared, *stay there and stay quiet.*"

John let Lucas go. He leaned against the nearest wall, panting. Jared stood there like a statue, just as John told him.

Reaching under his shirt, John drew out a stake. "Come now Libby, you know what to do. Kill the feeble creature who murdered your lover, or I will kill Lucas."

Tears ran down Libby's face as she stood, reaching for the stake. John handed it over, looking delighted.

"Wait!" I said.

"She's dead!" Libby screamed back. "He killed her and bit you. John will kill Lucas. I have to do it."

She launched herself at Jared but paused with the tip against his chest. "Damn," she said through the tears. "I can't."

"I was afraid that it would come to this. *Stake him.*"

John's last instruction zinged with power and intent. With a groan, Libby sank the stake into Jared's chest.

Anguish clenched his face, and his legs collapsed from under him. I went down at his side as grey seeped across his skin. There was no time for last words, no final minutes together. His eyes bored into me, unseeing. How could Libby do that to him, and me?

Libby collapsed onto her knees, gasping. "How did you make me do that?"

Lucas straightened up, giving a beautiful, deadly grin.

"It appears you've made a mistake," John said.

Libby's face was blank. "A mistake?"

"It's true I made a deal – eternal life in exchange for betraying friends. Just not with Jared. Lucas, I think it's about time to wake Della."

Lucas freed a brown bottle from his pocket and tipped the contents into Della's open mouth. Nothing changed at first. Then she coughed and sat up.

Libby dissolved into uncontrollable tears. She deserved to cry. John Carter tricked her, and Jared died for it. God, he was dead. Sobs took over me too, and I couldn't suck in enough air. How was I supposed to survive this? How was I supposed to face her again?

"Urgh, my stomach . . ." Della rasped. "Whose blood is this?" She touched her spattered neck. There was no wound; John planned it all. I wasn't breathing enough, and my head was light.

"Why did you do this to us?" Libby asked Lucas, shaking and crying.

Lucas raised one slim shoulder. "It's simple. I don't want to die. And I don't want my art to outlive me." He was all sinuous grace and confidence. Was he lying to us all along?

"He played a pivotal role in getting you arrested, and I rewarded him. All it took was a few fingerprints placed on a knife handle while you slept and hairs from your brush.

Now, Mina. It's your turn to play. You get to decide who dies next."

Chapter 39

"Lucas – grab Della for me."

At John's instruction, Lucas wrenched Della off the floor. She struggled weakly, affected by whatever drugs John gave her. Lucas slung an arm around her neck and held her against him.

His shyness was gone. Hunger had overcome everything else. I knew how that felt. I'd become grief and loss. I needed to look at Jared while I still could but loathed seeing him like that.

"I'm waiting, Mina," John said.

"OK, kill Lucas," I said.

"Nice try," John said, scooping Libby off the floor. She was loose and compliant, shut down by what she did to Jared. "Let's end this now, Mina. Evidently, your mother hasn't arrived. Perhaps she isn't coming at all."

Hurt flickered across his face, and then it was

gone. So John Carter did have feelings. "There's nothing here for you, besides a girl you just met and a sister who doesn't deserve you. She's the one who's like your mother – cold and unreliable. Let Della or Libby die and you can go off and live your life. I may be 'evil' but I'm also true to my word."

The lie was so transparent that I could have laughed or cried. I looked back and forth, at Libby's placid face and Della's disoriented one.

But then, Della winked at me. It was exaggerated enough to make sure I noticed. Suddenly, she sagged against Lucas's arm, letting him catch her. If Della had a plan, I wasn't in on it, but I could give her some time to carry it out.

"I can't choose," I said. "Why don't you kill me instead?"

Libby stirred, digging her nails into John's arm. "No! Don't be an idiot."

"That isn't an option," John said. "If you refuse to pick one, we'll kill both. Lucas is dying to taste Della."

Lucas shoved Della's head to one side, taking a long sniff of her neck. Fangs came down over his teeth.

That was when she moved. Della lowered her chin and smashed her head back into Lucas's nose. It turned out a vampire's nose broke like anyone's.

Howling, Lucas held his nose. Della rolled over to Jared's body and whipped the stake out.

While Lucas nursed his wound, Della drove the stake deep into his chest. His face crumpled, revealing the boy he was. He fell, and I wasn't sad that he died. I was sad that he did this to us.

"You little bitch!" John snarled. His grip on Libby loosened and she took her chance to slip free, standing by Della to face him.

Della yanked the stake out of Lucas and pointed the tip towards John's heart.

"We already killed two vampires with this," she said.

"*All three of you stand still.*" There was that power again. It tore through me, and my body froze. "*Don't speak, and certainly don't move. You may breathe, but that is all.*"

I tried to move my feet, but my legs were locked together. My arms were glued to my sides. Wrongness weighed down my whole body. Even my lungs were restricted, allowing only the shallowest breath.

"That's better," John said. "If we're done playing games, there's really very little use for you. *She* didn't come to rescue you, so what does it matter?" He turned the gun on each of us in turn. He thought doing this to us would draw Mum out, and we were going to die because of it.

Blood sprayed us. Droplets of it trickled down my face, and I couldn't move to see who it belonged to.

John's face went blank. I strained to move, but his power held me. A crossbow bolt was lodged in his left temple. He swayed on the spot and I sensed the connection between us more keenly, the twisted evil of his control. Inky blackness flooded my head as he fell. The bond snapped, and I was free to move again.

That allowed me to see Armand lowering the crossbow. I swiped a hand over my sticky face, disgusted and so grateful to him, though I was clueless about why he came to help us.

The crossbow dangled loosely in his hand, and he stared down at John's body with his mouth downturned and shoulders slumped.

"You saved our lives," Libby said shakily.

"I should've killed my brother long ago," he said quietly.

Chapter 40

"You're Wayne Carter," I said, wrestling with disbelief. He had the same bright eyes and olive skin as John, but I couldn't see Armand writing Wayne's diary entries and living under his brother's control. Apparently he wasn't intimidated by John anymore.

"Afraid so," he said, "and I am deeply sorry for letting my brother go so far." His accent was more Southern gentleman than Dracula now, like John's.

Della put her arm around Libby, glowering at him. "Yeah, you should be."

"I am." Armand's clear eyes bored into me. "And there's more I have to tell you. The boy isn't dead."

Della, Libby and I dropped to the grimy floor. Jared was motionless and grey. From this close,

I could see the bloody hole in his chest through his T-shirt. If Armand was tormenting us like John . . .

Jared's eyelashes flickered, a simple movement that brought such happiness. Colour slowly leached into his face, and he groaned. "Please be OK," Libby said, her tone ragged. "I'm so sorry . . . He made me do that."

"I guessed," Jared croaked. I wasn't sure Libby deserved his forgiveness. She almost staked him, even if she did stop herself.

Jared sat, wincing. He poked a finger through the hole in his T-shirt. "How am I not dead?"

"She must have missed your heart," Armand said. "When Della pulled out the stake, you were revived. It was a close call, so it'll take time to fully recover. You'll need blood."

"So you're . . . a vampire slayer? Should I be worried?"

"Not about me. I'm Wayne Carter."

Jared choked out a surprised laugh and then locked on me. Everyone else fell away, and it was just the two of us. He looked drained and God only knew how hungry he was, but right then, I didn't care. His arms opened and wrapped around me. He felt cooler and harder than before, but it was still him.

I was the one to pull back, and he looked disappointed. I think he misinterpreted the motion. I was trying to protect him, not scared of getting bitten.

"What's happening to them?" Libby's nostrils flared, and she gagged.

It'd been only been minutes, but Lucas and John were already decaying. There was a rotten meat stench, and the skin of their faces was saggy dough. "Our bodies decompose quickly after death," Armand said.

"We should get out of here," Della said, covering her mouth with one hand. The other still held the bloody stake.

Armand hurried up the stairs with us. We moved fast until we reached the empty bar. "Thank you . . . so much," I said. "I'm sorry you had to kill your brother."

"I'm not," Armand said. "If I'd done it long ago, none of this would've taken place. You should go. It'll be better if the police don't know you were here. I'll tell them I discovered the bodies of my brother's victims down here, and when I went to confront him he'd taken his things and skipped town. By the time the police come, the bodies will be unrecognisable. John's DNA won't be in the system, so they'll hit a dead end."

"What about Veronica?" Della asked.

"When she hears about John, she'll leave town. She doesn't care enough to exact revenge on John's behalf."

Running off didn't sound like her style, but considering all the ways she could murder us wasn't a very healthy use of my time.

While I fretted, Armand went on. "Here – I'll take that." He offered a hand to Della and accepted the stake.

"Thanks," Della said.

"It's the least I can do."

No one had a response to that, and we left together in silence.

As soon as we got outside, Libby spoke up. "Do you think we can trust him?"

"Do we have a choice?" Jared shot back.

We stopped by Della's car. "My dad'll be freaking," she said. "I was meant to head straight home from work. Do you guys want a ride first?"

"No, you should get home," Libby said.

Della kissed Libby, then caught me up in a hug. "Love you, girl," she said into my ear. Ignoring Jared, Della climbed into her car and drove away.

Jared and Libby stayed where they were. Libby opened and shut her mouth while Jared stared down at his trainers.

"You guys need to talk," I said. "I'll be walking ahead, not listening."

I set off a few steps ahead of them and tried to keep my word. There wasn't much to hear aside from occasional angry whispers. I joined them when the arguing stopped. Jared had his arm around Libby, but I doubted they'd really patched things up so easily.

Before long, we were home. Jared dipped into the bathroom and soon returned with the blood and dirt washed from his hands and face.

"I'm going to wash the gore off. Don't bite her," Libby said.

"She's joking," Jared said. They were playing their usual parts, but he had to know how close she came to killing him.

"I get it. Are you guys OK?" I asked.

"Getting there," he sighed. "She did impale me, so there are some issues to work out." He took my bandaged hand, releasing it immediately. "I'm more worried whether you'll forgive me."

Pain pulsed through my wrist. "I already did. You're not the worst vampire I've met today."

"Can't argue with that. I don't believe what Lucas did . . . We got him back and now . . . He's gone for real."

"I'm so sorry."

"We've all lost people. Libby told me about Thandie." He still felt things because his face was a mask of grief, the lines around his mouth deepening and the corners of his lips turning downwards. "Did I lose you?"

"No," I said. The word flew out fast, but I meant it. It wasn't over between us, but what we were was harder to define. "I think we have to slow down though."

"Slow I can handle," he said, taking a step towards me.

He was close enough to touch. I wanted to kiss him and fall asleep snuggled against him again. The first time couldn't have also been the last.

"How's your chest?" I asked.

With one finger, Jared stretched out the hole in his top. The wound was black and thick with congealed blood. "So much for healing fast."

"You need blood, like Armand said." The advice came out easily, drilled into me by vampire books and movies. Reality was more complicated. Who would he take that blood from?

"I guess so," he agreed uneasily. "Mina . . . I want . . ."

He stopped, kissing my forehead with a cool brush of his lips and retreating fast. "That's progress," Jared said. "I only thought about biting you."

"And that's only slightly terrifying."

He chuckled darkly, though I wasn't joking. "You take the next shower. Libby might stake me again if she sees us together."

His tone was light, but his shoulders were low as he walked away. He'd lost his old life and most of his friends. That wouldn't be easy to bounce back from.

He paused in the doorway of his bedroom. "Do you mind if I stay here tonight? The mansion . . ."

"I don't mind."

Libby came out of the bathroom with a cloud of steam, her hair dripping onto the wooden floor. She tipped her head upside down, wrapping a towel round it. "You want to go next? I'll tell the cops what happened . . . Well, a version of it." She picked up the phone, and I closed the door on whatever fantastical story she was spinning. We'd have to match them up at some point, but my priority was showering.

I only caught a glimpse of myself in the mirror, with eyeliner stitches smeared over my face and John's blood in my hair. Anywhere else, we'd have been arrested on sight, but during Fang Fest, we'd just been more people in costumes. I peeled off my filthy, blood-caked outfit and climbed into the shower.

The hot water beat down on the knots in my neck and washed the blood and dirt down the drain. I was soon clean but I let more water run over my head, failing to wash away the day.

Libby was waiting cross-legged on my bed. "Is it OK if I sleep in here?" she asked, holding up a tiny key. "I found this in one of the kitchen drawers, so we can lock ourselves in."

That would've been useful before. "Sure," I said, taking the key from her and locking the door. It hurt that I was locking Jared out, but it had to be done. "How are you doing?"

"Not great. Thandie and Lucas . . . I can't talk about them. Can we . . .? I want to talk about us."

"Sure." I mirrored her cross-legged pose.

"I shouldn't have left you with Aunt Sandra. I was just . . . I didn't want to talk to you about trying to find Mum, so I hardly spoke to you at all. It was stupid."

"Yeah, it was," I said. "But I understand, sort of."

"Does it help if I promise never to leave you again?"

"As long as you mean it."

Libby nodded fast. Her eyes were bloodshot but steady. "You turn eighteen in a couple of months."

"Right," I said, waiting to see where she was going with that.

"You're staying until just before your birthday, so I was thinking you might want to finish school here."

"You want me to live in New Orleans?"

"You'll legally be an adult so you can do what the hell you want. We can get you a student visa like mine, but it's up to you." Libby hugged her knees against her and bit inside her cheek.

The past week had been the worst of my life, but John Carter was to blame for that and he was dead. I should have taken time to think about it, but I knew my decision. Home was with my sister. "So, looks like I'm moving here." I wasn't sure how Aunt Sandra would react to the news. She'd acted like getting rid of me was everything she ever wanted. To be honest, I didn't care what she thought.

Libby squealed and squashed me in a hug. She rocked me from side to side, and I let her. Releasing me, she flopped back on the bed. "I'm so happy!" Her smile faltered. "Even after everything that happened. Can we just . . . go to sleep?"

"Sure. Want to borrow some pyjamas?"

We lay back-to-back in bed like when we were kids. Also like when we were kids, Libby's head hit the pillow and her breathing slowed right down. I'd never been able to relax so fast and not after a day like that. I couldn't stop thinking about Lucas. Even though I hadn't known him long, I'd grieved for him. It must have been so hard for Jared and Libby to have seen him and lost him all over again. There was also Thandie to think about. She spent most of her life being scared of John Carter, and he ended it.

Chapter 41

I must have fallen asleep because I woke up next to Libby. She was wrapped up in my quilt, like always, and I was almost falling off the edge of the bed.

On the way back from the bathroom, there was a hard, insistent knock at the front door. I opened it to find Detective Cafferty.

"I can't stay long," he said. "I got Libby's message, and I wanted to update you that the perpetrator who was doing this has fled New Orleans."

"Oh," I said, hoping my surprised face was working out. "Thanks . . . for telling me."

"You'll have to give statements at the station later," Cafferty said, "but there's strong evidence that the man masquerading as John Carter is long gone and unlikely to return. You guys don't have anything to worry about. We can reassess the situation if anything changes."

It only occurred to me then that as far as everyone else knew, John Carter had become another city's problem, and we had to go along with that story. "That's great news. Thank you. I know you did a lot to help us."

"Any time," Cafferty said, "although honestly, I'd rather not see y'all again in a professional capacity."

"Fine with me."

Since Jared had become nocturnal and had healing to do, he didn't surface that day. Libby and I moved to her bed with every snack from the kitchen and we spent hours watching a string of romantic comedies, from *My Father the Hero* to *Sleepless in Seattle*.

The phone rang around three in the afternoon. Libby jumped up to answer it, so I followed her into the hallway. If I was going to eavesdrop, why hide it?

"Yes, speaking." Libby had a great telephone voice that made adults think she was responsible. "Yes, I . . . Thank you." She listened, twining the spiralling wire around her finger. The phone slipped, and she had to juggle it back into the spot by her shoulder. "Are you sure? I understand. I . . . Yes, I can come later today. Thank you, I'll see you then."

She let the phone clatter onto the hook, staring down at it.

"What happened?" I asked.

"That was Thandie's lawyer. She left the mansion to me."

"You're going to be my boss?" Jared asked. I didn't hear him come into the hallway. We needed to put a bell on him.

"I'm going to be everybody's boss." Libby spoke with disbelief, like she needed time for it to sink in.

We'd gone through so much, including Thandie's death. A good thing had come out of the tragedy, and I was going to be there to see Libby enjoy it.

After a last trip to the police station, Libby went to the mansion to straighten everything out. She told me later through hiccupping sobs that Thandie's body had been removed, though her lawyer said the police had struggled to comprehend the level of decomposition. They finally put it down to humidity. How convenient for every vampire that lived in New Orleans.

While Libby was out, there was one more place I had to go.

I wasn't sure Armand would even be there. He could've been off in quiet mourning or halfway across the country, trying to outrun his remorse.

I pushed open the door to Empire of the Dead, ignoring the 'Closed' sign. It was the first time I'd been in here alone and the place was spooky, with the lights out and the animal skeletons overhead. At least there were no police swarming the place. It would've been tricky to explain why I was here.

Armand stepped out of the storeroom and crossed the bar. He followed my gaze to the cages of bones. "I was planning to remove them but I think they have to stay – the dead watching over their empire. Now, I assume you came here for a reason."

"I wanted to say thank you . . . for saving us and handling the police." And killing his brother. The thought came through as clearly as if I'd said it, though he'd possibly plucked it from my head anyway. "Why did you help us?"

"I'd been doing John's bidding for too long – you witnessed his power of compulsion. I'm glad he's gone. Too many people have died over the years because I didn't stand up to him."

I could've questioned why he helped us and not them, but there were other things I wanted to ask. "So, John could compel people. Is your ability real too?"

His lips pinched together, like I hurt his feelings. "Of course."

Thandie told us vampires often had abilities, which meant Jared could have one. That was too troubling to dwell on. "And I'm guessing you sent me the diary."

Armand's eyes were hard, but he answered readily enough. "I thought you'd want to know what happened to your mother."

"We did . . . thank you." The truth hurt like mad but it was better than not knowing. "Why did John think she was going to save us?"

"It wasn't that he thought she would . . . more that he was desperate for it. He'd felt the bond with Emma slipping. I've felt it myself."

Armand took a moment and then continued. "That bond normally lasts up to a year, but John was losing his connection with Emma. He took great pleasure in tormenting the two of you and killing girls, but he genuinely believed it would make her come – that she'd rescue you. The festival was almost over, and he decided that night was his last chance."

So he really thought she was going to rush in to save us and make out with him. He didn't know her at all. "He got a lot of things wrong," I said. Armand was the one who did the right thing, eventually.

After that, we said our awkward goodbyes. As I walked out of there, I guessed it wasn't for the last time.

For the first couple of days, journalists were busy with the 'Fang Fest Fiend' who went on a last killing spree and then fled New Orleans for good. We watched the news and scoured newspapers, but there was no mention of fanged, decomposing bodies or teenage witnesses.

Once that died down, Libby's picture was printed with an article about the mansion and Thandie's funeral. They were holding a traditional jazz funeral for her, to celebrate her life. Libby was keeping busy at the mansion, but I had no idea how she'd deal with that. She'd decided to set up a memorial exhibit to remember Thandie, though probably only a handful of people knew the truth about her.

When the mansion reopened, Jared spent most of his time there, and I felt his absence keenly. I wanted to be there for him, but there was no manual for this situation. Where did he get the blood that made his manner and complexion so even? Should I be jealous?

All of that was bothering me when Jared walked us home from the mansion. I was still afraid of things that went bite in the night. Even though John Carter was gone, New Orleans wasn't vampire free. Jared was with us right now.

I was right to be worried. Another vampire was waiting by our door.

Chapter 42

Mum had hardly changed. Her hair curled over her shoulders like ours, and her eyes were a deceptively warm brown. The main differences were the unmarked skin on her neck and the lack of her usual confidence.

My loud, angry emotions had to be as obvious as her nerves.

Jared stepped up, bristling. "Want me to get rid of her?" So introductions were unnecessary.

"We're fine," Libby said. "We'll see you inside."

Jared frowned but did what Libby said.

John's plan worked after all, and Mum came. Just a week after he died.

Mum spoke as soon as the door closed. "I saw you in the paper." Her voice was the same. As much as I wanted to hate her, the musical quality of it brought all kinds of soothing sensations.

"I'm so sorry I left. I'd forgotten how beautiful you both were."

Because beauty was all that mattered. "You can forget a lot of things in a year," I said.

"I made a mistake." She twisted and flexed her hands in front of her. There were hollows under her eyes, and the whites were threaded with red capillaries. How long was it since she had blood? "I'm here now, and I want to make it right."

"Do you know John Carter almost killed us because of you?" Libby asked.

"I only just found out what happened. I would've . . ." At least she left the lie unfinished. She wouldn't have come to save us.

"Why did you leave us? And not turn up until now?" I had to get my questions out before she left again.

"Can we go inside?" she asked. "This isn't a short story."

"You can summarise," Libby said, folding her arms. There were two good reasons not to invite her inside – what she did and what she was.

"I was bitten by a human, back home in Whitby." I remembered the compress on her neck when she left. How many times did she let herself get bitten before she got her wish?

"I knew what I wanted then, and I didn't want to drag you girls into it, so I left. I came here because it was the only place where I'd met a vampire . . . the one who bit me before you girls were born."

Unconsciously, she touched the blank skin on her neck, which once carried the scar that revealed her true nature. I think we always knew why she left, even if we believed at the time that she was chasing a fictional creature.

"So becoming a vampire was more important than us?" Libby asked, sharp enough to draw blood.

"I . . . There are no excuses." Mum lowered her head and I knew that look. It was the one that said she'd never leave us again and we could rely on her. Except that neither of those things was true. "Can we try again?"

"We'll think about it," Libby said, glancing at me. I nodded in agreement. "This isn't a no, but you have to know you hurt us, and our relationship was never all that great."

"Things would have to change." I picked up where Libby faltered. "For now, I think you should go."

I expected that fire she passed on to Libby to come out in a flaming argument. She gave a quick, shaky nod. "Take all the time you need. Goodbye, girls. I hope . . . we can put this right." John was dead, which meant she could leave New Orleans if she wanted. She was here, so that was progress. There was no way of knowing how long her interest in us would last.

Libby grabbed my hand, and we watched as our mum walked away. We were stronger than ever and didn't need anybody else. For now, it was enough to know she was out there. We'd decide what to do about it together.

Acknowledgements

I've wanted to write this book since I visited New Orleans in 2012, but my love of vampires and ambition to get published have been with me a lot longer. I'm thankful to so many people for helping me to get here.

To my agent Sandra Sawicka for believing in this book from that first pitch at YALC.

To the amazing people at UCLan for giving me this opportunity and encouraging me at every step, especially Hazel Holmes, Chris Moore, Charlotte Rothwell and Graeme Williams.

To Becky Chilcott for creating such a stunning, Point Horror inspired design.

To everyone who helped me make this book as realistic as possible: David Quinn for advising on US police procedure; Lis Hoyles for answering medical questions and Rose Sinister and A.J. Gnuse for advising on my New Orleans details.

To Rachel Faturoti for your incredibly thorough sensitivity read and for our DM chats.

To Laura Poole for sharing your grammatical wisdom and reading everything I write.

To Mia Kuzniar for your constant encouragement, enthusiasm and friendship.

To the Write Mentor family, especially Stuart White, Marisa Noelle, Hannah Kates and Clare Harlow, for giving me the push I needed. Special thanks to Hannah for being an invaluable critique partner and an amazing friend. Who else would traipse around New Orleans taking extra photos for me?

To Lauren James for doing the early editorial critique that helped to shape this book.

To Laura Wood for your editorial advice and enthusiasm for my story.

To my early readers and supporters: Kim Curran, Gabriel Dylan, Louie Stowell, Aisha Bushby, Katharine Corr, Jamie-Lee Turner, Katie Webber Tsang, Chelley Toy, Jim Dean, Mariam Khan, Robin Stevens, Alison Whipp, Lucy Powrie, Kat Ellis, Cynthia Murphy, Alex Bell, Harriet Muncaster, Ava Eldred, Andreina Cordani, Georgia Bowers and Dawn Kurtagich.

To my Twitter DM groups, for your friendship, encouragement and entertaining chat.

To my readers and the book-reviewing community for choosing this book and supporting me. Special thanks to Team Mina for your photos, reviews and engagement!

To my family Jan, Trev and Ash. Your belief in me has set me up for life, and those notebooks you bought me for Christmas held my first stories.

To my son Nathan, who was born while I edited this book and will hopefully read these words one day.

To my husband Kev, for your endless patience, love and support. I couldn't have written this without you.

HAVE YOU EVER WONDERED HOW BOOKS ARE MADE?

UCLan Publishing are based in the North of England and involve BA Publishing and MA Publishing students from the University of Central Lancashire at every stage of the publishing process.

BA Publishing and MA Publishing students work closely alongside our company and work on producing books as part of their course – some of which are selected to be published and printed by UCLan Publishing. Students also gain first-hand experience conceiving and running innovative high-level events to leverage sales, as well as running content creation business enterprises.

Our approach to business and teaching has been recognized academically and within the publishing industry. We have been awarded Best Newcomer at the Independent Publishing Guild Awards (2019) and a *Times* Higher Education Award for Excellence and Innovation in the Arts (2018).

As our business continues to grow, so too does the experience our students have upon entering UCLan Publishing.

To find out more, please visit
www.uclanpublishing.com/courses/